Also by Rebecca Campbell

Slave to Fashion

Slave to Love

The
Marriage
Diaries

It was that first look of grimly malevolent humour, the look you might expect from a barbarian chieftain watching his favourite fool juggle with the heads of his vanquished foes, that made me stop thinking about the child as a thing, a consumerist nightmare of inconvenience and pain, and to start to understand him as a person, albeit one with mild psychopathic tendencies and a diaper full of dark matter stinking as though Death itself had come to nestle between the boy's coy and dimpled little bottom.

We were in the elevator, cranking and grinding up the four floors to our new wondrously huge, but ramshackle apartment. I'd spent half an hour walking around side streets, the stroller cocked at a lulling angle, monitoring his drooping eyelids with the rapt attention of a junkie boiling up his fix. The secret was to avoid the joy-bringers: the yellow bulldozer, scraping at concrete; the self-satisfied fire engine blowing it's own trumpet; the man dressed up like a Chernobyl rescue worker to trim the hedges. Any of these and Harry would ping awake, all chance of sleep blown away by the buzzing, the nee-nawing, the judder and scrape.

Well, today we'd done it, and sleep was approaching on little feet.

We're in the elevator: a tight squeeze, with a bag of shopping noosed around each of Harry's eyes, bluer than mine, paler even than Celeste's, are closed now. I carefully drag the stroller backwards up the steps to our block, feeling like a bomb-disposal expert handling a delicate fuse. There's 4p2It was that first look of grimly malevolent humour, the look you might expect from a barbarian chieftain watching his favourite fool juggle with the heads of his vanquished foes, that made me stop thinking about the child as a thing, a consumerist nightmare of inconvenience and pain, and to start to understand him as a person, albeit one with mild psychopathic tendencies and a diaper full of dark matter stinking as though Death itself had come to nestle between the boy's coy and dimpled little bottom.

We were in the elevator, cranking and grinding up the four floors to our new wondrously huge, but ramshackle apartment. I'd spent half an hour walking around side streets, the stroller cocked at a lulling angle, monitoring his drooping eyelids

The **Marriage** Diaries

A Novel

Rebecca Campbell

Ballantine Books
New York

A Ballantine Books Trade Paperback Original

Published in the United States by Ballantine Books, an imprint of The Random House Publishing Group, a division of Random House, Inc., New York.

ISBN 0-345-48588-2

Printed in the United States of America

www.ballantinebooks.com

2 4 6 8 9 7 5 3 1

Book design by Mercedes Everett

She no longer loves the person whom she loved ten years ago. I quite believe it. He is no longer the same, nor is she. She was young, and he also; he is quite different. She would perhaps love him yet, if he were what he was then.

— Blaise Pascal, *Pensées*

The
Marriage
Diaries

PRADAPRADAPRADAPRADAGUCCI 1

It was eight o'clock when I came in. The weather was filthy, and I was shaking with cold. My third-favorite Manolo Blahniks were ruined with the rain. It had been a day of such grinding awfulness that I just wanted wine and sympathy. My nerves were plinking manically like an avant-garde Bulgarian jazz trio. Usually Sean comes to meet me at the door to the apartment when he hears the jangle of my keys, but tonight there was nothing but the dark hall echoing to the clicking of my destroyed heels. Then I heard the TV murmuring and went into the living room.

At the sight of my two boys, I felt the horrors of the day depart like a shaggy old crow taking off from a tree. They were sleeping. Harry was wrapped up in his Spider-Man duvet, nothing showing except his white face and his flop of blond hair. He was lying on Sean's lap. Sean was half slumped on the sofa, his head at a crazy angle that gave me a neckache just to look at it. It's hard not to love someone when you see them asleep. I went over to them and picked up Harry—soon he'd be too heavy for me. He nuzzled into me and made that noise like an old man eating porridge. Sean stirred.

"I wasn't sleeping," he said sleepily. "Just resting my eyes."

It's one of Sean's things that he hates to be caught napping. He probably thought I'd use it against him—you know, totting up all his little sleeps and using them as an excuse for me to have a sleep in while he did the first diaper change of the morning.

"Harry wanted to watch this program about man-eating sharks."

"Man-eating . . . ?"

"Yeah, I don't know why it is, but there're only two types of documentary on these days. It's always either the Second World War or sharks. I should be grateful that Hitler never trained his own elite squadron of great whites or there'd be only the one documentary, 'Nazi Killer Sharks.' I suppose there might also be the porn channel version, 'Nazi Killer Sharks' Anal Adventures.' "

That was Sean all over. I mean, the way he could go straight from sleep to articulate rant.

"He shouldn't really be watching that sort of thing," I said, without edge. "It'll give him nightmares."

"No, it was one of those where they try to show the tender, nurturing side of the great white. Anyway, he fell asleep after the first attack. Seen one leg bitten off, seen 'em all."

I took Harry to his bedroom and went back to sit next to Sean.

"Good day?" he asked, half an eye on the sharks.

"Stinker."

"Sorry. Why?"

"Didn't you see the news? The papers?"

"Not really. Too busy looking after our child."

I let that one go.

"Erica Svebo."

"Who?"

"The seventh most famous model in the world. The one who's fronting up our new campaign."

"Oh, her," he said, clearly utterly baffled. I might as well have been talking about quantum mechanics to a pigeon. "What about her?"

"She was all over the tabloids this morning. They had a picture of her with a syringe sticking out of her groin."

Yes, there she was, blurry but all too recognizable, her Marc Jacobs skirt pulled up to her waist, injecting herself in the upper thigh, like any other self-respecting long-term junkie. It was a disaster. Erica was all set to be the face (and, more important, the body) of our spring/summer campaign. Of course, PR isn't my speciality, but I'm usually asked to sit in to give the buyers' take on things, plus I'm friends with Milo, who is to fashion PR what Afghanistan is to high-grade raw opium. Erica was his idea, which made her my idea, which was why the grief poured upon *me* from on high.

I'd called Milo. I had the papers fanned on my desk. Some of the pictures took in the whole scene: Erica against a grimy background, her head hanging low, hair cascading like a dark auburn water-fall. Some focused more narrowly on the honey-colored thigh, the hand, the syringe.

"You've seen the photographs?" No point beating about the bush.

"Yes. Shame she wasn't wearing one of your outfits. It's not as if Marc Jacobs needed any more fucking exposure."

"Milo, this is serious. Heroin chic is so 1990s."

"Hey, listen, the classics never go out of fashion."

"It's not funny."

"Who's laughing? Look, there *is* a problem here, but not the one you think."

"It's pretty obvious what the problem is. Our new face is suddenly in the gutter, and boy is she *not* looking at the stars. And then, well, the poor girl—"

"It's insulin, sweetheart."

"Insulin? You can't get stoned on . . . Oh."

"She's diabetic."

Pause.

"I guess that's . . . something. She kept it well hidden."

"Oh, there were telltale signs. There always are."

Diabetes. About as cool as colon cancer. I mean, there's not even a ribbon for it.

"What should we do?"

"You mean dump her or keep her?"

"We couldn't dump her just for being diabetic. We'd look terrible. And the campaign's ready to roll. And the money. Oh God."

"Okay, here's what I'd do." Milo was suddenly all silky profession-

alism. "Let's keep a lid on the diabetes. Just put out a press release saying that Erica knows she's got a problem, and she's receiving treatment for it. Which, you know, is true enough. And so you're sticking
by her till she gets well. You'll come across as caring and edgy at the
same time. It's a win-win."

"Milo, you're a genius."

I managed to sell the concept internally, but we wouldn't know if
the fashion world would buy it until tomorrow.

But I couldn't tell all that to Sean. It would reinforce everything
he thinks about fashion. He'd sneer. Or scoff. Probably some combination of both. And I didn't want sneers or scoffs, I wanted some love.

"That doesn't sound too good," he said, Sean, I mean, his eyes still
drifting past me to the gnashing teeth and roiling water on the TV.

"I'm having a bath," I said. "Need to relax. Any wine?"

That was a sort of hint. A glass of wine in the evening usually
meant that I had something more in mind. And it had been a while. A
month. Perhaps a little longer.

"Yeah, there's a bottle open."

"Bring me a glass in the bath, will you?"

Pause. More shark action. Or the hint that maybe he's thinking
something.

"Sure thing, babe."

And he did, after I'd shouted a reminder from the bubbles.

"I'm off to do a bit of work," he said, as he put the glass down
carefully on the side of the bath.

"Okay."

So then I decided to go all out, preparing myself like a courtesan. I
drizzled some scented oil in the bath, and when I emerged, I plucked
my eyebrows into a design of wry insolence and even dusted my
lashes, which is pretty impressive for postbath, late-night intimacy. I
slipped into my most alluring night attire—nothing tacky—think
1890s decadence, not Texas whorehouse desperation. Okay, then, if
you must know, it was a creamy silk chiffon slip from La Perla that
cost almost exactly one week's salary, but worth it, as you'd never

guess that a child-ravaged figure was concealed beneath its subtle folds.

When I was ready, I lit some candles. Not that Sean cares about candles. He'll look at a room glimmering with little flames and say "So who died?" or, shaking his head slowly, "Thomas Edison, you labored in vain."

I found him in his study (Sean I mean, not Edison), tapping away at the keyboard. He was wearing the deep green velvet dressing gown I'd bought him for Christmas back in the distant pre-Harry past, when we'd spent hours lying in bed with our fingers touching, watching the light come into the morning. He wears it now whenever he thinks he's going to be creative. The ivory silk lining is stained with coffee, and the velvet's worn and flattened, but it still has a certain faded panache.

"I'm going to bed," I said unambiguously.

"Okay."

"Coming?"

I mean, just how obvious was I supposed to be?

"Be through here in a minute," he said, without looking around at me.

I sighed. I tutted. I may even have groaned. He didn't notice, so I went to wait for him in bed. I arranged myself artfully and then changed my pose three or four times, revealing now more shoulder, now more leg. Then I got up and reapplied my lipstick, shifting hues from cassis to plum. After yet more carefully posed languorous lounging, I began to flick through *Vogue*, but I soon came across Erica Svebo looking beautifully debauched in a Calvin Klein ad, and I really didn't want to see any more of her, so I threw the magazine down and thought about Harry and how much I loved him—and Sean as well, of course—and how happy we all were, and how lucky.

I know that some people think I'm cold, and perhaps I can be. But that's because someone has to be in this relationship. We couldn't both carry on like college kids, dreaming and loafing our way through life. Someone had to earn the money. Someone had to put in the hours.

I suppose I must have known what I was getting with Sean. I was getting someone kind and funny, with a face that appeared quite handsome until he smiled, and then, once that smile was uncoiled, completely irresistible. Hair sometimes curly, sometimes just messy. Blue eyes, and again, you didn't realize how blue and how lovely they were until he took his glasses off, and it was a real showstopper when he did: people would lose track of what they were saying and fall silent and stare at him. I knew that he'd explain the world to me and make me read books I wouldn't otherwise have picked up. I knew he'd make a wonderful father, full of stories and games. And I knew he'd never earn enough for us to be able to forget about money.

What a very strange thing love is. *He*, of course, would leap like a wolf—and I mean a brainy wolf with glasses and messy hair—on my terminology, saying that love isn't a *thing* at all and that turning a *thing* that isn't a *thing* into a *thing* is the root of all our problems. He'd probably call it—I mean love—a "process" or dismiss it completely as a figment, a phantasmagoria, a myth, a tool used by someone, almost certainly the bourgeoisie, to control someone else, most likely his beloved toilers of the field and laborers underground. But all that doesn't mean that, whatever *it* is, *it* isn't strange.

By love, I don't really mean the feelings that burn away inside you with a desire you can never quench, or the other kind of love feelings, the ones that come in glorious engulfing waves like the epidural kicking in on top of the shot of really good stuff you've managed to plead out of the soft anesthetist. Or, for that matter, the love that comes over as fear when you look at your child asleep with his one-legged G.I. Joe, and you think of all the terrible things that might happen to him (the child, not the G.I. Joe, about whose fate I find myself curiously unmoved)—the falling out of high windows, the swallowing bleach, the cascade of boiling oil from the pulled-down pan, moving on to the stammering loneliness of school, the killing rejections from hard-faced girls (it takes one to know one), the growing depression and isolation, the bottle of pills and the stomach pump. No, I don't mean the *feelings* at all. I mean the *everything*, the situations you find yourself in, the things you do and don't do, the things you say and don't say. Without love, there'd be none of those, and life would come in a much simpler shape.

I woke up without realizing I'd fallen asleep. The room was dark, the candles burned down or blown out. I felt Sean beside me, breathing in a long, slow rhythm. I looked at the bedside clock. It was one thirty. I'd had nothing to eat, and I felt hunger kick inside, like a quickening baby. I weighed up the pros and cons of getting out of this nice, warm bed. But I was too hungry to sleep, and then there was all that futile makeup to remove.

I had to walk past the study. The door was ajar, and I could see the cold light from the monitor. Sean had forgotten to switch it off. There was a screen saver playing, the one that creates a perfect aquarium, with tropical fish turning slowly in the water. It was rather lovely, and so lifelike I didn't want to turn it off—it would have felt like draining the water from a tank of real fish. But as I turned to leave, I accidentally nudged the keyboard. The fish disappeared, replaced by words. At the top, it said "SEANJOURNALONE.DOC." And then it said "POOH." I smiled.

The whole journal thing had been my idea in the first place. Sean was very proud of his new video camera, which connected to his computer in all kinds of clever ways and allowed him to make and edit films, and start talking about Visconti and Tarkovsky and the "spirit of the beehive," whatever that was. The plan was to have a complete record of Harry's development, showing his first steps, his first words, his first successful circumnavigation of his potty, that sort of thing. He bought it in time for Harry's first birthday party. I'd invited a few friends round—Milo, Galatea, Katie, Ludo—and told them to bring champagne for us rather than presents for the boy, and we all got fairly sloshed. Sean took a couple of minutes of film and then gave the camera to Harry, who was strapped into his high chair, drunk on cake and apple juice. Being a baby rather than Steven Spielberg, he first tried to lick the camera and then threw it on the floor, where, upon impact, it made a sound like a pensioner's hip breaking. Sean found it funny until he realized that the thing was, in his words, "utterly and completely fucked."

Sean wanted to go out and spend £1,000 on a new one, but I thought that I'd already forgone enough pairs of new shoes in the lost cause of the original and forbade it.

"You're supposed to be good at writing," I said. "So why don't you capture it all in words?"

So was planted the seed. And now here it was. The first shoot.

We didn't have secrets, so I read on.

SEANJOURNALONE.DOC

POOH

It was that first look of grimly malevolent humor, the look you might expect from a barbarian chieftain watching his favorite fool juggle with the heads of his vanquished foes, that made me stop thinking about the child as a thing, a consumerist nightmare of inconvenience and pain, and to start to understand him as a person, albeit one with mild psychopathic tendencies and a diaper full of dark matter stinking as though Death itself had come to nestle in the boy's coy and dimpled little bottom.

We were in the elevator, cranking and grinding up the four floors to our new, wondrously huge but ramshackle apartment. I'd spent half an hour walking around side streets, the stroller cocked at a lulling angle, monitoring his drooping eyelids with the rapt attention of a junkie boiling up his fix. The secret was to avoid the joy-bringers: the yellow bulldozer scraping at concrete; the self-satisfied fire engine blowing its own trumpet; the man dressed up like a Chernobyl rescue worker to trim the hedges. Any of these and Harry would ping awake, all chance of sleep blown away by the buzzing, the nee-nawing, the judder and scrape.

Well, today we'd done it, and sleep was approaching on little feet.

Harry's eyes, bluer than mine, paler even than Celeste's, are closed now. I carefully drag the stroller backward up the steps to our block, feeling like a bomb-disposal expert handling a delicate fuse.

There's the usual performance with the key and the awkward, heavy door, and then another three steps. I press the button to call the old elevator. It can't be as old as our block. Did they have elevators in the 1880s? Must check. Probably won't check. Feels more like the 1930s: like something out of Raymond Chandler. But I'm no Marlowe, no elegantly cool, sardonic hero, in a sharp suit and sharper hat. Instead, I'm a sweating, grumbling lardass, dressed in the kind of cheap casual clothes designed by—how was it you put it, Celeste, in that way of yours?—"by a blind madman with no taste and a hatred of humanity and a toothache."

Yeah, well, thanks for that.

We're in the elevator: a tight squeeze, with a bag of shopping noosed around each of the stroller's handles. One of the thin, membranous bags has a rip and threatens to spill its guts, hara-kiri style over the floor. But, no, that won't happen. It won't happen because the bag only splits when I'm out on the street and when it has the chance to spew tubes of Anusol and verruca cream and extralarge bottles of the stuff for my flaking, itching scalp at the feet of pretty girls.

Girls like Uma Thursday.

The door cranks shut behind me, and I hit the 4 button. There's the usual mulish reluctance to move, and then we begin to soar, like a rocket fueled by damp peat and old tea bags. It's going to be okay. I'm going to be able to wheel him into his bedroom, unclip his straps ("Yes, Harry, you have to have them on. See, they're Buzz Lightyear space straps; it's part of your ejector seat; it's what firemen wear. Look, here's some chocolate") and lift him into his cot. Or maybe just leave him slumped in the stroller, looking, with his jowls bulging on either side of the dimpled chin, like a retired colonel, dozing after a rant against the Bolsheviks.

And once he's parked, well, then I could begin my time of ease: tea, made scrotum-puckeringly strong; the newspaper, read back to front the way my dad used to; the television on in the corner, just in case; trousers unbuttoned and unbelted to allow a little room for midriff settlement.

This is the only free time I have all day. The mornings are pure Harry. For the first hour, we usually get along. There's the park or a toddler group or chocolate to keep us happy. But then things grow tense as the jockeying for power begins over the nap, my willed "yes" coming up sharply against his equally adamant "never." The postnap afternoons mean more Harry, then work, then more Harry. The last bit of Harry is the worst. He's angry, he's bored: bored with me, bored with the world. It's the time when things get destroyed: things like wallpaper, like my new digital video camera, like my will to go on. The work bit is permitted by the intervention, for two hours, of either play school or childminder. Funny how work has turned into a sort of vacation. It's one thing the old me, the free me, would never have guessed. But only a *sort* of vacation. Work, having to do things for other people so that they give you money, still sucks like a leech in the blood bank.

When my wife, Celeste, the second of the two imperious deities ruling my universe, finally gets home, she "takes over." Harry, of course, is a joy for that hour before bed. The plan, it seems, is to make me look like a whining, chiding, grumbling ne'er-do-well—a grudger and a shirk. Who, after all, could complain about this angel, happily toddling about, naked from the waist down to encourage, futilely, the use of the potty, smiling and chatting to his yellow plastic bulldozer and the toy soldiers I really shouldn't have bought him? Here, with those blue eyes and the long blond hair, he looks like a child invented by a Victorian propagandist for the virtues of home and family.

So, you see, the lunchtime hour—two if I'm lucky—when Harry sleeps is a special time. It's not long enough to write an article or do anything useful, so I'm at liberty to vegetate or even to indulge in a little mulling over all the things in my life that haven't gone quite to plan. I begin, still in the elevator, to relax into the moment, mentally already in the armchair, mentally, in fact, already shifting uncomfortably in that armchair trying to avoid the broken spring that presents such a regular challenge to my anal integrity.

And then, just as the elevator door begins to rattle open, I catch the glint.

He's looking at me. Not straight at me, but bouncing his malevolence off the mirror that takes up most of the back wall of the elevator. And he has to work hard at getting his message through: after all, his gaze has to squeeze between the pressing mass of chin and cheeks and pudgy nose below his eyes and the tugged-down peak of his baseball cap above.

That baseball cap, by the way, was my masterstroke, the Pearl Harbor in the warfare Celeste and I fought over Harry. For this to make sense, I'm going to have to tell you something about Celeste.

Celeste works in fashion. There, I've said it. She's tried to explain to me what exactly it is that she does, but it won't seem to compute. Wait, let's try:

She works for a big French designer that even I've heard of. They have shops in which the clothes they make are sold as well as "concessions" in other shops. And then there are yet other shops in which there is not a special concession but that also sell these clothes. With me so far? Well, Celeste is something called The Buyer (I don't know if she really gets initial caps for that, but in my head, she does), which means that she *buys* clothes from the designer's *collections* (see, I know some of the words) on behalf of the label's shops and concessions. So she decides which bits of the current collection work best in the various locations.

Actually, I think I might have cracked it. So *that's* what she does.

The clothes in which she deals don't seem, on the whole, to be the birdcage-on-the-head kind. They don't incorporate or otherwise use in their designs chain mail, the dung of ungulates, spent nuclear fuel rods, objets trouvés, or live lizards. You're never going to get laughed at behind your back for wearing one of Celeste's suits or dresses. Well, when I say you, I mean you if you're a woman. *I'd* get laughed at. But then I get laughed at whatever I wear, black tie at a funeral, trunks in the sauna. But it's still the sort of stuff that would have my mum, back in Leeds, shaking her head in disbelief.

And being *in fashion*, it's part of Celeste's job to look fabulous. She looks beautiful professionally the way bartenders looked pissed professionally. When she enters a room, you can feel the tension. Most of the men instantly dislike her because they know they'll never get her; and you can almost hear the shriveling, mean contraction in the souls of the women.

Ugliness comes to us in a million different forms—limping, hunched, ill-knit, diseased, mutilated, poor. Ugliness is democratic: most of us partake of it in some aspect of our being, and this chiming with something in ourselves makes for the most human of responses—our hatred and our pity.

Beauty comes in fewer guises: as yielding feminine comeliness; in fatal, dark-eyed elegance; in stretched and sinewy Giacometti forms. Celeste's beauty is of another kind. It has a cold, flawless, crystalline perfection about it, like an electron micrograph of a mosquito's compound eye. It is the beauty of a stiletto, of a panther, of an impossible equation, of the silence at the end of everything.

And what is a woman like that, a woman for whom the world is all reflective surface, the eye's delight the *only* delight, going to *do* with a baby? I don't want to suggest that Celeste saw the child as a fashion accessory. She never fluffed his hair and draped him around her neck like one of those removable fur collars that were all the rage a year or so ago. She hasn't had him skinned, tanned, and turned into a handbag or even taken the Gucci branding iron to him. But nor was she going to dress him in any old rag, the stuff from Next or Woollies or the Gap, the stuff that I bought him or *my* mom bought him or *my* friends bought him. No, for Celeste, it had to be some unfathomable knickerbocker-like thing with a matching top part and some complex system of cantilevers joining the two,

purchased from a shop with, to the untrained eye, *nothing in it at all*
in Paris or New York or Tokyo, from a designer with quite possibly
pedophiliac tendencies, and at the very least an unhealthy disre-
gard for the practicalities of diaper changing and bum wiping. Don't
expect me to remember the names. Remembering names is not one
of the things that I do. But the prices I remember ("You spent £205
for *that*? What, even with the yen as weak as it is?") and the chill-
ing fact that, in the first year, Harry's wardrobe cost more than I've
spent on clothes *in my entire life*.

I'd get Harry dressed in the morning, in, you know, just normal
stuff: a pair of baggy pants and a sweatshirt. Like mine, but smaller,
and usually with more dribble down the front. And, okay, I'm not
saying that the top and the pants always loved each other, and the
chances of his little socks being the same color or size were fleeting,
but what the hell did he care? Well, Celeste cared, and if she had
time before going off to her studio, she'd raise an eyebrow, take
Harry firmly by the hand, and lead him back to his room for a
makeover, from whence he'd emerge like something the catwalk
dragged in.

Which was why the hat was so inspired. I'd seen it in Woolworths, where we went to ride the Thomas the Tank Engine machine. Thomas ate pound coins but was otherwise ideal: he moved
in monotonous gyrations like a three-toed sloth with Parkinson's
disease, giving just enough of a thrill to Harry to keep him interested but providing me with a fear-free five minutes in which I
could sit on a step and watch the thirteen-year-old girls in micro-
skirts busily shoplifting, while I contemplated what I should do
about Uma Thursday and her unexpected proposition. It was there
that I saw the hat, perched proudly on its very own floor-mounted,
revolving display.

Even a fashion refusenik like me could see that it was truly
hideous. The bits that weren't Pooh Bear–colored were a gruesome,
labial pink, like an embarrassed flamingo caught interfering with
himself in a public park. And it had ears. Two yellow Pooh ears,

standing proud on the dome. Magisterial. Best of all, as a special, Woolworths was throwing in a pair of matching sunglasses (normal price ninety-nine pence) for the four ninety-nine you had to stump up for the hat. Now that was a lot of hat-and-sunglasses action you were picking up for under a fiver.

Harry, of course, loved it. How could he not when it had ears and looked like a flamingo's fanny? That evening, Celeste, after staring at me and it as if we were something that Harry had vomited, expectorated, or shat, hurried him away, but the operation to remove the growth was entirely unsuccessful. Celeste came to know the wrath of Harry, and he did smite her, and the hat remaineth.

It took her a long time to get over the hat. The usual sanctions—withdrawal of affection, restriction of access to her side of the marital bed—were already in place, backed up, where she deemed necessary, by the forceful and often innovative use of hairbrushes and nail scissors. I think she may have briefly contemplated killing me, but the problems with disposing of my body, and the hassle of having to find another childminder for Harry, put her off. In the end, she settled for simply using the hat as a mobile and permanent demonstration of my mental cruelty, garnering what sympathy she could.

So that was the hat. And now he, my little baby boy, was looking up at me in the elevator mirror from beneath the pink brim. And below the eyes, that exquisite mouth of his was smiling: not his usual "Ah, here come the chocolates" smile, or the "Ha, I hit Daddy on the head with the potty" smile, but a smile that said, "Yes, I know exactly what you wanted me to do—you wanted me to go to sleep so you could loosen your trousers and sit in your chair and drink your tea—but I'm not going to, am I? Instead, you're going to spend the next hour singing me songs and telling me stories about monsters and giving me chocolates in the vain hope that I eventually drop off. Isn't that so, eh? Eh?"

And he was right, that's what I'd be doing. But I didn't mind. I didn't mind because Harry had shown that he wasn't just an eating, belching, shitting machine but a little man, a mini-me, with a brain and a will as well as a mouth and a bum. And most of all, I didn't mind because of the voice, born somewhere deep in our genes or our culture, that said, Go on, love him, love him, even if he's ruined your life and stopped you from doing all the things you like to do and made you do loads of other things you don't like doing at all.

You've got no choice; love him, love him.

PRADAPRADAPRADAPRADAGUCCI 2

Well, where to begin? Uma Thursday, I think. She seems the obvious place.

Oh yes, I know I'm supposed to rise to the bait of this mysterious Thursday woman and her unexpected proposition. A likely name I *don't* think. The Uma bit is obviously there to make me think of Uma Thurman, but if she exists at all, she probably looks like a gnu and lives in a council apartment in Kilburn with the five kids by four different fathers and has a septic hole in her navel where she botched a DIY piercing.

Or maybe I'm supposed to think of Robinson Crusoe and his Man Friday. The companion come to save the hero from a life of terrible loneliness. The poor lamb.

No, darling, you'll have to do better than Uma Thursday if you want to make *me* jealous.

Jealous or not, when I first read it, I huffed off to the spare bedroom, but it was cold and damp and had things in it that shouldn't have been there, like bits of bicycle and old shoes that Sean wouldn't throw away and inexplicable lengths of wire. So I went back in beside Sean and pulled the duvet off him round myself so that he couldn't get anywhere near me, knowing that he'd wake up cold in the morning, which was just what I wanted.

It was as I was lying in bed that the rest of it began to irritate me. For all his droning on about being a dead-tough, hard-as-nails, call-a-spade-a-spade man of the people, he's just a huge—and I mean *colossal*—ponce.

The huge-ponce thing comes out with all his drama-queening it, the way everything takes on an epic scale, every little problem becoming a tragedy. You'd hardly guess from his oh-so-moving description of the life of the practically single-parent family that he claims to lead, that we have in place, at the moment, three cleaning ladies, two additional childminders, a whole kindergarten, and my father, who does much of the collecting, driving, and depositing, as dear, dear Sean hasn't got a car and couldn't drive it even if he had and wouldn't drive it even if he could on account of the weight his conscience would have to bear for destroying the planet.

And on the subject of Sean's hidden seam of campness, I suppose that one does have to remember that he once bought a Kylie Minogue CD.

"It's from her rock period," he claimed lamely, when I found it, hidden in between Radiohead and Neil Young.

"She hasn't got a rock period. It's gay music, and that's all there is to it. She's a friend of Milo, you know."

"It's not *gay* music. Well, not this album. She worked with some proper musicians. There are guitars. It's really hard to dance to. It flopped."

"Stop making excuses. It's gay and you know it. There's nothing wrong with it, just stop wriggling."

"I don't want to listen to it while a man in tight trousers puts his arm up to the elbow in my ass. I just want to f— I mean, I fancy her, that's all. That can't be gay, can it?"

"And that's supposed to be better, is it? You bought it because you fancy her?"

"Not like a real person. I didn't know Milo knew Kylie. He couldn't . . . ? Only kidding."

As for being a "lardass," that's another example of his self-dramatizing. And probably a subtle attack on me. True, he's a bit doughy around the middle, but as long as he keeps his clothes on and minds how he sits, you'd hardly notice. And you see, by making himself seem ridiculous, he makes me ridiculous as well—he is, after all, *my* choice.

The boy's a genius at black propaganda. Take the beauty bit. Looks, at first glance, like a compliment, doesn't it? And then comes that creepy compound eye and the stuff about everybody's hating me. It's a verbal version of his most evil invention, the deafening kiss. Exquisite in its way. Up he'll sidle, in full view of the dinner guests or the party crowd, put an arm around my shoulders, and kiss me on the ear. Looks like the sweetest gesture, but what he's really doing is making a horrid vacuum, accompanied by a great loud smacking noise. It actually *physically* hurts, as well as being a bit of a shock. And so, of course, I reel away, usually crying out something like "Stop it" or "Fuck off" or "Drop dead," and so the whole world thinks that I've responded to a gentle endearment or soft nuzzle with a piece of naked aggression. It's all designed to make me look like a bitch and him the poor lost innocent.

Don't, by the way, fall into the trap of imagining that the vanity in our relationship is distributed purely on the female side. True, it's my job to care how I look, but Sean is as much the mirror's slave as I am. More so. I go to the mirror for help. It's a tool. Five minutes max of hair and makeup, and we part, without a backward glance, job done, mission accomplished.

But *Sean.*

Picture the scene. He's standing in front of the big hall mirror, groaning.

"Oh, good God in heaven," he moans. "What the *fuck* do I look like?"

"You look fine," I say, not really thinking or caring, but just, you know, being nice.

"I look like something shat out by a vulture."

"You don't look like you've had anything to do with a vulture. You just look like you always do, normal."

"Look at these clothes. Why don't I have any nice clothes? I look like the tramp the other tramps hit with sticks and throw bricks at. I look like—"

"Well, go and buy yourself some new things, then."

"What's the point? I'd look just as bad. Like a tramp in a new suit. And anyway, nothing ever fits, and you know how shopping always makes me sweat and stammer and the store detectives follow me like dogs after a bitch in heat."

And by that stage, you can forgive me for losing it.

"Well, perhaps it'd help if you *washed* your clothes occasionally. Look, you've got stains all over your trousers. And you keep taking things out of the washing basket and wearing them again."

"That's because you keep putting things in there that aren't dirty."

"The stains," I say, pointing.

"Yes, but in between the stains, these trousers are *completely* clean."

And then back to the mirror for more groaning.

So, you see, if anyone's vain, it's him. It's just that he has negative vanity, and it brings him only suffering.

I never quite twigged that the grotesque baseball cap was part of his deviousness. I had simply, and understandably, assumed bad taste. Perhaps I've underestimated him. I did try weaning Harry off it by being less affectionate to the child whenever he wore it, but either the hat meant more to him than my love or he still hasn't got the mental facility to make the connection. He'll learn.

Oddly prescient, by the way, that thing about killing him. One does sometimes, in idle moments (not that I have any), speculate on . . . things. I remember sixth-form debates about whether it would have been okay to kill Hitler before he came to power. And Tolstoy drones on about it at tedious length in *War and Peace* or *Anna Karenina* or somewhere, doesn't he? (Ha! See, I can do it, too!)

But I suppose it would be pretty tough to make a case for killing your husband on the grounds that he's frequently annoying. Must have a look in Sean's philosophy books (there are, dismayingly, shelves of them), just in case someone has tried.

Now that would be pleasingly ironic, wouldn't it?

Leaving aside the issue of killing people (and I *was* kidding, by the way), there are a couple of other moral dilemmas in the air, one being the whole thing about reading other people's intimate thoughts without their knowing about it. I considered telling Sean that I'd found his journal, just to see him squirm. But then he'd either have stopped writing it or done a better job of hiding it. And the truth is, I want to carry on reading what he has to say. I don't suppose there will be any revelations about affairs with Uma Thursday or whomever—I do actually trust him. And anyway, none of my friends has ever suggested that he might be affair material—you know, the kind of man who gives out the aura, who has the look, the smell . . . He has something else altogether, a kind of innocence. It's one of the reasons I fell in love with him. That and the smile and the eyes and the gush of words. So it's not that I want to trick him into betraying himself; it's more that, well, I really want to see what he says about things. And yes, by things, I include me. And Harry, of course.

Although discovering Sean's journal was due to simple good fortune, continued access relies on a little more cunning. Sean has two computers—the "big" one, on which he does all his "work," and a cute baby laptop, which seems mainly to be decorative. He devised some cunning way of making them talk to each other without any obvious external connection and proudly announced that he had made a "wireless network," without explaining why this was good or necessary. His next mistake was to let me use the laptop when I needed to work at home. It took very little clicking to find that the wireless network thingy gave me access to the hard disk on his main machine. It asked me for a password. "Celeste"? No, the swine! "Harry"? Bingo. How like children men are.

Of course, most of the stuff on there was of somewhat specialist interest. Worryingly, I found no pictures of naked girls but much information about submarine warfare, Jacobean tragedy, and batting averages, which is all downright kinky.

I also found the artfully disguised SEANJOURNALONE.DOC, in a folder labeled "Sean's Journal." No doubt SEANJOURNALTWO.DOC would follow.

But I don't want you to think that this was all quite as easy as I've made it sound. I am aware of the moral dilemma. Is it right to read someone's diary? No, it probably isn't right. So it was lucky this isn't a diary, just his silly scribbles, and no dates. And anyway, if he didn't want me to read it, why did he put it where I was bound to find it? The first time, I mean, it was just there on the screen, practically pleading with me to read it. I thought that rather left me, if not exactly in the clear morality-wise, then at least in the middle of an exploitable gray area. Another *anyway* was that Sean was always the great advocate of the "Totally Integrated Relationship"—which, on his part, mainly seemed to take the form of using the lavatory while I was having a bath, back in the bad old days when both functions had to take place in the same room. Yuck. And what is the point of a Totally Integrated Relationship if there are secrets?

But still, as I said, it was a gray area. And what was the point of Raymond if not to help me with my gray areas? Raymond de Calvery doesn't like to call himself an analyst. When I told Sean about him, he said he sounded like Counselor Troi from *Star Trek: The Next Generation.* I'm not sure if that was meant to be illuminating or an amusing piece of self-parody. Either way, it didn't help much.

I began going to Raymond because of the sex thing. The not wanting to, hardly ever. It's been six months now, since our first talk, and it hasn't worked so far, but it's quite nice having someone there to talk at, and besides, it annoys Sean, who thinks it's all "unfalsifiable pseudo-scientific bullshit."

When I told Raymond about the journal at our last session, he seemed very interested. He thought it was okay to read it, and to carry on reading it as long as I discussed its contents with him, because then it could come under the heading of "therapy," and therapy made *everything* okay. There was something else to do with asserting my personhood, but I wasn't really listening, which is silly given how much he costs.

But there it was. Reading Sean's journal was all part of my treatment, and given that *Sean* would be the main beneficiary should the treatment succeed, then reading it became entirely *the right thing to do.*

It was Raymond's bright idea that I keep what he called a counter-journal, recording my responses to what Sean had written as well as setting out my own more general impressions and ideas. Raymond was particularly keen that I put down sexual fantasies and erotic dreams. Chance would be a fine thing.

My own password is "pradapradapradapradagucci." Let him crack that one!

SEANJOURNALTWO.DOC

THE GHOST OF A FLEA

It all goes back to Max, and whoever it was who dropped out of his lunch party, leaving a gap for someone who could be guaranteed to have nothing better to do and not mind the fact that the lunch was *today*, in half an hour's time. A gap shaped exactly like me.

"Look, Sean, old chap"—and, yes, he really did, and does, say things like "old chap" and "jolly good" and "pull yourself together, man," but for some reason, you don't want to spit in his face or pelt him with rocks for it—"there's going to be a surfeit of girls, and there's the best part of an ox on the fire."

"Ox, eh? You know I'm technically a vegetarian? But I suppose, as the beast is already slaughtered, there can't be any harm . . ."

Max didn't have to do the spiel. My alternative was to sit on the corroded foam of the couch in Carol's living room, eating cornflakes out of the packet and watching the fleas jump on and off my bare legs. The fleas, and therefore the bare legs, were Carol's fault. Aided by Clare and Cathy (the other girls in the house), and chided but not actively resisted by me, Carol had lured in some stray cat with choice tidbits, and it had brought, in the way of strays, a cargo of arthropodic freebooters. It had also brought along its bad gums and scattergun digestive tract, but they have less direct bearing on my story. The girls called it Tracy, which had a certain plangent inaptness.

Over the years, I'd made passes, generally unsuccessful, at all of the girls. Except Tracy. Not with those gums.

The bare-legs thing was part of my campaign to keep at least my bedroom and clothes flea-free: the little fuckers, horribly exposed on the white killing fields of my thigh and calf, could be picked off and popped with comparative ease. It wasn't my first brush with ectoparasitism. The subject of what was then my only published work had actually been a solitary pubic louse I found cramponed forlornly to my undercarriage. The poem had appeared on the number 19 bus, running from Euston to Stoke Newington, as part of an ill-starred attempt by London Transport to widen the Poems on the Underground concept. Part of the deal was that I had my e-mail address printed underneath the text, to "facilitate the breaking down of barriers between the artist and the audience." Dialogues were envisaged, in which the writer would explain the use of imagery and rhythm, passing on tips about caesuras and metonymy. But my only missive was from a woman called Mandy, a close friend of Jesus, who recommended a toxic scrub for the genital region and close study of the Bible for the rest of me.

Max was living in a little house farther up the Bakerloo line. I hadn't spoken to him for about a year. We'd known each other since our Manchester University days, when he lived in the same house as my then girlfriend. He stood out even more back then. It was in the mid-eighties, and the student body were engaged in a life-and-death struggle to bring down Margaret Thatcher—and with her, capitalism, apartheid, and the price of beer. I was briefly lured into the Militant Tendency group, by Sarah Benn, who never washed but just put on a new layer of makeup and perfume every morning, and who had tiny ears and enormous breasts, and who let me sleep with her on our first date, making me think that I had entered a glorious new world full of adventure and sexual fulfillment, before dumping me on the grounds that I "wasn't really a *political* person" and "had crap clothes."

There was one Tory, a heavy-metal fan, who was more the object of wonder than violence. In the three years he was around, I
never once saw him speak to another person.

Max was far from being the *only* Liberal, but he may well have
been the only heterosexual one. He polished his shoes, his hair was
neatly trimmed, and he sometimes wore ties. He spoke clearly
rather than in the surly mumble that most of the rest of us adopted,
and he told anecdotes about his dad, probably the finest orchestra
conductor in the country. And he laughed at your jokes with a
huge, braying bellow, which made you think that perhaps you were,
after all, quite funny. But for all that, he wasn't like me, and so our
friendship was never intimate, and the year or so in between our
post-university carouses suited us both fine.

So, a surfeit of girls.

I had to make some important decisions. I hadn't washed my
hair for a couple of days, so it looked a bit greasy, but at least that
meant it would stay roughly in the right place. If I washed it, it
might stage a revolution and overturn the established order (my
hair had never abandoned the political commitment of my youth).
It could go bouffant or cubist or choose some new way of making
me look like an idiot. No, best stick with slick. Then, what to wear?
Do you put on a suit to a posh Sunday lunch? I only had one, a
light summer affair made from asbestos and llama, in a fetching
shade of gravy. It had been rained on a month previously and had
shrunk and stretched in random directions, and to wear it, I had to
hunch and twist, and raise one leg off the ground at all times. So
maybe not the suit. Jeans and a shirt then. Inspiration! I'd bought a
white silk shirt at a sale a year before and never worn it. Surely that
was the thing, both sedate (it was white!) and flamboyant (it was
silk!).

No time to get to the liquor store, but I had half a bottle of
whiskey, saved for emergencies. Might look quite bohemian, that, I
thought. Or like a drunken stumblebum, it occurred to me as Max

welcomed me in and all eyes in the dining room moved first to the half-empty bottle and then to my face and then back to the bottle again.

I can't remember much about what followed immediately, as I was temporarily blinded by a supernova of blond hair and white teeth. The room seemed to be full of light, and nothing would come clearly into focus. The next thing I knew, we were at the table. There were three very pretty girls, Max, me, and a slab of meat, which looked as though Phil Spector's famous wall of sound had taken on bovine form and fallen dead before us. The conversation— which was about City things, business, PR, stocks, and shares— seemed to have been chosen with particular care to avoid those areas in which I could operate comfortably. But soon the wine did what wine does, and everyone was happy.

I studied the Three Graces more carefully. Two were not, in fact, that beautiful. Just tall and blond and posh. One had slightly coarse skin; the other, a sharp nose with a curious tip that vibrated as she spoke. And both had that faint edge of hysteria, a leaning-too-far-forward-as-they-spoke, laughing-too-loudly-at-the-wrong-places feeling about them. Not that they weren't good company or, for all their minor failings, easy on the eye.

But then there was Celeste. She was different in those days: less sculptured than she is now, less poised, less polished, less scary, less elegant, less cynical. And, as I'll discuss anon, with larger breasts. So, *so* beautiful. It was not her beauty, however, that captured me: it was her intellectual dazzle, the way she could engage each of us at the same time on a different point, like a chess master playing several simultaneous games, and never lose her thread, never miss a point.

Max was his usual agreeable self, fussing over the condiments, ensuring glasses were kept full. He brought up the fact that I was doing a Ph.D., and I think I managed to make my work sound interesting and comprehensible, which always involved some ingenuity.

There was only one moment when things looked as though they might take a wrong turn. I'd made a joke about the Young Hegelians' not being a song by David Bowie but a proto-Marxist philosophical movement. No? You had to be there. Except that that obviously didn't help either, because I was trying to explain, "No, you see, 'Young Americans' is the song by Bowie, but that sounds a bit like Young Hegelians, which isn't—" when a flea jumped from out of my hair onto the table, making a tiny, but distinctly audible, "tock" as it landed on the polished wood. Everything stopped.

"What the hell was that?" said Max. He seemed to reach around behind him, as if searching for an elephant gun.

I thought fast. "Bloody fly in my hair," I said accusingly, as if there'd been a failure of hospitality on his part. "Damn nuisance!"

I put my finger on the little black scab, which looked like it was about to make a play for one of the girls. There was an open window behind me, and I flicked it out, saying cheerfully, "Out you go, little fellow, back from whence ye came." I looked at Celeste, and she looked back at me and smiled.

It was all over far too soon. Of course, I was too scared to make any kind of move. Max gave me back the bottle of whiskey as I left.

It was months before another chance encounter brought us together again. In the meantime, Max, whose motives were highly dishonorable, had warned her off me, as a "dangerous character, famous lady-killer. Avoid like the plague."

It was the best PR I'd ever had. Who could resist it? Although I hadn't called, and we hadn't spoken at all, when she turned up with Max for a party at our house, sometime in the dead zone between Christmas and New Year's, I think we both knew that everything in our lives from now on was going to be different.

Why had she come? Was it just a chance or some whim? Or something more considered and calculating? I could ask her, but she'd never remember. Women are too sensible to waste energy on nostalgia. She'd say something like "Party? And you did what? And I *let* you? Didn't I have any Mace?"

We didn't even talk much during the evening, but I knew where she was every second. In the early hours, the party had dwindled to half a dozen half slumbering in my bare room. One by one, they drifted off, until just Celeste and I remained. She was lying back across the foot of the bed, her eyes closed, her hair arrayed around her, like dead Ophelia floating.

For the first time, I touched her, reaching down to stroke her hair. She didn't smile or move, but I sensed that her flesh, her nerves, the tendons snaking through her body, her veins and arteries, the electrical and chemical dance of neurons, all spoke a silent yes, and I felt like leaping naked through the sleeping house yelling my delight.

We didn't even kiss that night. The first took place sometime during the following week, and it was that that sealed my fate. It's all to do with what industrial confectioners call mouthfeel. What the scrofulous consumers of Snickers candy bars and the other quasi-toxic products that the English eat instead of vegetables most like, according to market research, is an initial resistance from a firm outer coating, followed by a melting interior. What they don't like is a sticky outside leading on to a tough core. Or sticky giving way to more sticky. Or hard followed by more hard. No, it has to be firm, then soft. The engineers and industrial chemists manufacture this with hydrogenated palm oil, glucose syrup, malt extract, and xanthar gum. (No coincidence, surely, that "xanthar" is an anagram of "anthrax"?)

But I was talking about kissing. Kissing Celeste. I've had girl-friends who got things the wrong way round—sloppy, drooly lips first, then all clashing teeth, as well as one or two all drool or all teeth. But Celeste got her mouthfeel exactly right. Hard and then soft, hard and then soft. My God but she was a wonderful kisser. After the first kiss, I knew that I didn't want to kiss anyone else ever again and that I still wanted to be kissing this mouth in forty years' time.

Seven years ago, that kiss. Or eight. She was twenty-two years old, and I was twenty-six.

But that was in another country, and besides . . .

But that was in another country, and besides, the *wench is dead.* Ha bloody ha. If I thought it meant anything beyond a vague determination to let us all know he's read his T. S. Eliot, I'd make him regret that. I was hoping that this diary-reading business was going to be funny and cute. I now rather fear that annoyance will predominate. Still, the allure of SEANJOURNALTWO.DOC has proved too much for me.

Of course, I remember the party in his grubby old house in Finsbury Park. I remember the batty, hopeless girls, and Tracy, with her gums. I also remember rather more about Max's lunch than Sean seems to. I remember his arrival with that determinedly bohemian bottle of whiskey. I remember his white shirt, a nasty thing of cheap lining silk, thin enough to show the dark circles of his nipples.

And I remember well the little flutter that ran through the girls.

But then two of us were single and one unhappily engaged, and so a reasonably well endowed Mormon missionary would have had us perspiring with lust.

He was on form that day. I was used to two sorts of company: fashion people, who tend to know about how to look nice but little else, and my old friends, most of whom I'd known since school days, cozy as an old cardigan, reassuring, lovable, but not exciting, challenging, inspiring. If I craved novelty, then here it was. Sean, it seemed, knew everything. Or perhaps one should say that he had an opinion about everything, which, given enough self-confidence, is often indistinguishable from the real thing. He could switch from high to low culture and back again in a sentence, dangling Derrida and doughnuts, Foucault and fish cum, before us, and always moving too quickly for anyone to scrutinize the sense, or senselessness. He carved glittering ice sculptures, which dazzled the eye, and then seduced us on to new delights before we noticed how quickly they melted.

I really ought to explain the fish cum.

"What do you think taramosalata's actually made of?" he said, as we were dunking our strips of pita.

"Fish roe, I thought?"

"Fish eggs, isn't it?"

"Oh no. No no no no no." He was smiling broadly, using that lovely roller coaster smile of his. "Roe yes, eggs no. You see, there are two different types of fish roe: hard roe, which is the fish eggs, the female gametes, and soft roe . . ."

It was about then that I realized what was, well, coming.

". . . soft roe is the male gametes," he continued.

"You mean . . . ?"

There was the little pocking sound of pitas being dropped.

"That's it: spunk."

Needless to say, the taramosalata stayed mainly in the dish that lunchtime. And yet before our nausea had the chance to settle in, Sean had whisked us away to the realms of Greek myth and the story of Aphrodite, born of the foaming semen spilling from the severed testicles of poor old Uranus or Saturn or whoever it was (this is a long time ago, and a lot of fish spunk has passed under the bridge). From there, we found ourselves in a discussion of the differences between ancient Greek and modern forms of homosexuality, which *would* have involved a simulation of the preferred method of intercourse among the Greeks (face-to-face, standing up, between the thighs, apparently) had Max not, very sensibly, declined, and then we were back to Foucault, who'd written a book all about it.

After lunch (I couldn't eat a thing, but I didn't want to come across as having, you know, *issues* about it, so I endlessly forked food halfway toward my mouth or moved it around the plate in geometric patterns), we settled into the living room. I made sure I sat next to Sean, and every time our thighs touched, I felt a surge of energy like nettle rash. His hair was long then, and the overall impression was definitely Byronic, although with a kind of edge that said, "I know that you think I'm trying to look Byronic, but I'm actually just playing with the image, so this is in fact *ironic* Byronic." He wore little round John Lennon glasses, too, in those days, which added to the general air of doomed Romanticism.

He didn't flirt, didn't flatter, and although I had the impression that his performance was aimed slightly more in my direction than elsewhere, I couldn't be sure.

And then we were all leaving. I was desperate for some sign that he'd noticed me. And just as I was beginning to despair, he said, "Would you like to do something sometime?" and I can't remember what I said to that, but I doubt if it was clever, and then he said, "I'll get your number off Max."

I went away dizzy with excitement and puzzlement and hope. It seemed that I had finally found someone who really did live the life of the mind (sorry, I can't say that without thinking about the scene in the Coen brothers' film *Barton Fink*, in which a manic John Goodman runs down a burning corridor screaming "I'll show you the life of the mind, I'll show you the life of the mind" at a cowering screenwriter). Someone who felt ideas the way other people feel hunger. And the best part was that, what with that whole Byronic thing, he was actually quite good-looking and even, under certain special conditions, given the right preparation and lighting, gorgeous.

So when he didn't call me, I sulked. Well, to be honest, the sulking followed something a bit more dramatic, involving a fair amount of crying and the sort of "What's wrong with me?" questions that I don't normally hold with. But that couldn't go on for long: I was too busy. I'd just made the move into fashion from my wilderness period as the world's worst banker, and I was desperate to make it happen. But whenever I thought about it, about him, I felt a little pang of loss and a huge desire to hit him with a blunt instrument for being so stupid.

I couldn't say exactly what the proportions were of hope, desire for revenge, curiosity, and boredom that came together in my decision to go to the party with Max, but as soon as I saw him again, through a room full of smoke and people and laughter, I felt only the happy knowledge that it was going to be all right.

He was wearing a blue velvet suit and a pair of black Chelsea boots, and he looked good. And I completely understand what he means when he says that he knew where I was every second, because I felt it, too, and whenever I couldn't see him, I felt the light go out of the world, just a little. I remember his flustered apologies for not calling me, and I sensed it was shyness and not arrogance that had stood in his way. And I remember the agony and the embarrassment of waiting for the waifs and strays to leave his room, and the sudden quiet in the darkness once we were alone. And he's wrong, because we *did* kiss that night. He lay behind me, and his lips brushed my neck and then my ear, and then the corners of our mouths touched, and that is how we kissed, chastely, and still in our clothes.

For the next couple of years, there followed what we saw as an innovative hybrid of intellectual debate and love affair, but which, to most of my friends, looked a lot like one long, tedious bicker. Yes, that's it: the long great bicker of humanity.

He proposed without much ceremony in a dark pub, where everything that wasn't already brown was stained umber with nicotine. But the ring was beautiful—a copy of a Roman original—and I didn't mind much at all that the stone was a red garnet and not the huge, vulgar diamond so many of my friends seemed to be getting or that the metal was silver and not white gold or platinum.

We married in a pretty church in the countryside, and it was fun, although I was a little jealous of those of my circle who had hugely glamorous London weddings, with receptions at The Dorchester and a double-page spread in the *Tatler.* Sean wore contact lenses, but he lost one halfway through and so has a strange squinting look in all of the photographs, as if he's slyly winking at the photographer.

After a year, and without trying either way, I found that I was pregnant. And once I'd worked out exactly how we would manage, I was happy. Sean looked delighted, then dismayed, and then delighted again, as he ran through what it would mean to our lives, or perhaps just to his. I suspect the sequence of alternating dismay and delight continued for some time. I guess it continues still.

That flea, by the way, was almost certainly made up.

INFANT SORROW

I should never have gone down to the business end. Up top was fine. There was a sort of green canopy thing that shut everything out and made it feel as though we were having a campout in the garden. Just occasionally, you could see elbows working furiously above the canopy, as though someone were pumping up a tire or punching a rabbit to death. There was a hairy moment when Celeste started to feel things. She'd been warned that it would be like someone reaching down into your handbag: you'd be aware that something was happening but not be in any pain.

Well, this was pain.

"Will you tell them," she muttered into my face.

"It'll probably pass. Just hold on."

"Fucking tell them."

"Um, . . . excuse me, I think it hurts."

So they put some specially strong stuff into the tube, and then she seemed fine.

"You've got a baby boy," said the doctor, the one who looked like a doctor. He leaned over the green partition and beckoned me. Without thinking, I walked around. I saw them holding the baby, wrapping it in towels, weighing it. It looked like something that had just been torn out of a living body, like one of the less fashion-able organs, the spleen or pancreas or large intestine, all coiled and knotted and slithery. On impulse, I looked back at Celeste, not at her face, which was hidden now by the green canopy, but at her torso. If you're the kind of person who has nightmares or sits up in bed at noises in the night or watches scary films from behind the sofa, don't ever do what I did, don't look back, don't look down, don't look *in*. My first thought was to wonder how anyone could survive what they had done to her. It looked like they'd gone in with a sharpened spade, with an ax. I thought of the thing bursting out of John Hurt's stomach in *Alien;* I thought about the blood eagle, the terrifying rite performed by Vikings on their living captives, involving ripping back ribs and pulling out lungs. I thought of my poor girl having these things done to her by strange men who did not love her. I didn't think anymore about the spleen-boy in the blanket, beginning now to cry like an old man caught up in the ongoing tragedy of his phlegm.

I ran back to Celeste. She was hurting again and stared at me pleadingly. Someone brought the baby round, and Celeste tried to look as though she were pleased, but there was too much pain. Then I was holding the baby, but I still just wanted to take care of Celeste. Somehow I found Bella, Celeste's mother, who hated me, and gave her the baby. I don't think she expected it and looked at me as if I'd just proposed a quick blow job in the lavatory.

They were still pulling things out of Celeste—big, heavy clots of stuff, dense as manure. She was white with shock now. You could see how time had slowed for her, and she lived in her pain like a hermit. I don't know if I was useful or just another object there, like the instrument stand or the epidural line.

I've no idea how we got out of the place, but my next memory takes us upstairs to the room with its flowers and her parents and at least one of her eccentric sisters. A titanic black midwife is holding the baby at Celeste's breast, shoving its face into the flesh like a naughty puppy having its nose rubbed in its muck. But it works, and now I can see the child—who must by now have been given his names—working his jaw like a seasoned tabaccy chewer, and Celeste pulling a getting-into-a-hot-bath face. I deduce it hurts.

•••

I still hadn't had time to work out what I felt about the whole thing.
I'd been thrilled when I saw the urine-washed blue line, and I may
even have offered then and there to stay at home and look after the
baby. I'd always thought of myself as the kind of man who would be
good with children. I couldn't imagine a more interesting or fulfilling job, and it certainly compared well to sitting at my desk at the
Department for Culture, Media, and Sport straightening out paper
clips and trying to smuggle double entendres into the Minster's
speeches.

(There'd been a report about how conventional games such as
netball and hockey were putting teenage girls off exercise altogether. It suggested that if they had the choice of other vigorous ac-
tivities, aerobics or dancing, they might establish the good habits
that would keep them healthy for life, avoiding the obesity, diabetes, halitosis, piles, thromboses, rickets, Ebola, split ends, drug addiction, and so forth that went with a sedentary lifestyle. For a week
or so, I'd been working out how to phrase it for our man's address to
the annual conference of the Association of Physical Education
Schoolteachers [APES]. "It's time," I wrote, "that schoolgirls were
released from the tyranny of their gymslips and allowed more freedom in choosing which bed to lie in."

I thought the grammar error might help: there's nothing a civil
servant enjoys more than finding a split infinitive or a sentence
ending in a preposition; and the various layers through which the
thing had to pass might content themselves with underlining and
rescoring the error, thereby perhaps missing the now-naked schoolgirls' bedswapping. But no: no matter how hard I worked at it—and
whatever my reports said, I could be a hardworking and dedicated
civil servant—it just wouldn't come out *funny*.

Perhaps, instead, I could develop my idea for the Fast Action
Response Team [or FART], which would deal with arts-based emer-

gencies, or continue the in-depth research I'd done on the Annual Network-User Statistics [ANUS]. But I'd come to accept that the Western and Northern Knowledge Evaluation Register [WANKER] was never going to get off the ground.)

So, no, there wasn't any kind of counterbalancing weight on the side of Work to match the gross, massy tug of Paternity. And with children, surely, I thought, there'd be the downtime. You'd play with them for half an hour, then you'd put them in one of those baby jails with their rattles, and squeaky whatsits, and cuttle-fish and millet, where they'd gurgle happily while you read or watched TV for a couple of hours. And then, if necessary, you'd play with them a bit more.

That's how it was, wasn't it?

And soon you'd be able to teach them things like cricket and the names for the successive periods of the Paleozoic era ("Okay, listen"—*dummy down, now*—"first comes Cambrian, then Ordovi-cian, Silurian, Devonian, Carboniferous, and Permian. Got that? Have you soiled yourself?"). That would be fun. And fulfilling. And *admirable*.

The fury and flurry of the operating room had come between me and the massive love surge I confidently expected to feel on first set-ting sight on my baby boy. That and the spleen-pancreas thing. There'd been no flash of light, no trumpet blast, no instant bond. I was too scared and too tired. But now here they were, safe and well: my wife and my child.

Together.

Locked in an embrace I couldn't share.

The two of them with me on the outside. I felt dull and numb. I hadn't slept for forty-eight hours. On the way home, some feeling did seep back into my nerves: depression, disappointment, the longing for a chicken kebab, with onions, chili, and garlic sauce. If only I'd known what was coming, I'd have thanked my lucky stars

about the exclusion business and got in as much carousing and loafing as I could: "Oh yes, look at them," I should have yelled, "united,
contented. They don't need me. I'm spare! I'm free!"

Things got better as the week went on. More friends and flowers
came to the room. Because it was classed as an emergency cesarean, we were covered by Celeste's health insurance. If everything
had gone smoothly, not only would I have betrayed my socialist
principles, but it would also have cost me some thousands of
pounds. God bless you, lazy cervix! Well done, Harry of the huge
head!

The private-health-care-birth thing was an argument I knew I
couldn't win. Over the years, most of our disagreements ended up at
the place where Celeste would say something like "well, you do
it then!" And I would trump her with the martyr's "I will, I will!"
But that pattern just didn't fit here. It was her burden, her pain,
her enormous belly, and I couldn't get my way by offering to share.
All I could do was hope to wear her down by a drip drip drip of
whines and complaints, which I knew was both unattractive and futile. Way to go!

And then it seemed that nature and history were conspiring
against me, as all of those friends of Celeste's who'd beaten us to the
tape reported terrible experiences in National Health Service hos-
pitals. Surgical gloves, probes, and hacksaws were "left behind"; babies were thrown away and afterbirths smacked on the bottom;
midwives boiled up cauldrons of ready-mix eye of newt and toe of
frog. It was a miracle anyone came out alive.

So the Lindo Wing it was, with its wooden paneling and the
knowledge, heavy in the air like camphor, that princesses had bled
here and princes been born.

After a week, they came home and took it in turns to cry. But I felt
quite good, because I had an obvious purpose again—i.e., doing
everything. There had always been certain things that I had done.

Cooking. Rearranging books. Cleaning the lavatory bowl by peeing around it in a truly methodical way. And there were things that Celeste did. Making the rooms look spruce. Shouting at me to pick up my clothes. Picking up my clothes properly when I'd picked them up in the wrong way. But now Celeste was too sore to do any of her usual things, and so I had to do them all.

I don't understand tidying. I spend half an hour in a room moving things about, and at the end, it looks more or less the same as it did at the beginning. But Celeste goes in there for five minutes and suddenly everything's different *and* better. I don't really hold with evolutionary explanations for particular bits of human behavior. I don't believe there's a gene that makes people like Celeste (i.e., girls) better at tidying. For that to be true, we'd have to posit a profoundly unconvincing just-so story. You'd have to invent a little drama enacted among the early hominids—let's say, homo erectus (because I like saying "homo erectus"; it's a funny name!)—in which the alpha erectus (sorry, still chuckling) male is confronted with a choice of sexual partners, some of whom are slovenly and keep a bad cave, with bits of mammoth bone all over the shop and a serious buildup of lime scale around the stalactites, and others, obsessively cave-proud, spending all their time straightening the cave paintings, beating the bear rugs, and generally making things look nice. And then the alpha male has to pick the one in the hairy-rhino pinafore, dusting the shelves and tutting to herself. It's just not gonna happen. We all know he's going to choose Raquel in her fur bikini over the shrew with the dustpan every day of the week. And without that selection, and the reproductive advantage it imparts, then the tidy-cave gene just can't get going.

But none of that helps me to explain why, after a week without Celeste-love, and *despite* the world-class peeing around the lavatory bowl, the apartment looked as if a family of refugees had moved in and then moved on again, complaining of the poor facilities. Things that shouldn't be sticky were sticky. A pair of my underpants (*not* sticky) were draped over a lamp. I knew I had to move them. I *would* move them. The very next time I was in that corner. No, *really* I would move them. And the cubist pagoda of CDs two feet in front of the stereo. I'd do something about that. Maybe shift it about six inches to the left so it was out of my peripheral vision as I watched the TV. The laundry basket had taken a nasty wound to the leg and been forced to shed some of its burden in the hallway, partially blocking access to the kitchen and exposing for the first time in eons some of the stuff at the bottom that never quite made it into a wash. Tights and panties, of course, but also a purple shirt neither of us has ever owned or worn and some unidentifiable matter, molded into lifelike forms by the extreme temperature and pressure conditions prevailing down there. But once you'd stepped over all that ("For God's sake, be careful, there's broken glass there and some concentrated nitric acid I've been meaning to . . .") and made it to the kitchen, you couldn't help but be impressed by how neatly the four bin liners full of trash were lined up behind the door.

And all this was before Harry, that maestro of mess, the king of clutter, the lord of misrule, had extended his powers beyond the reach of his own bum.

There was another message on my answerphone today. Uma still wants to meet me somewhere *without* the children. The walk back from the playgroup isn't enough for her anymore. She has to stop calling like this. It's only a matter of time before Celeste picks up the phone or gets back before me and plays the messages. I've asked her to e-mail me instead, if she must, on a Hotmail account Celeste doesn't know about. At least, that way, I can contain the situation. I know nothing's happened, and nothing is going to happen, but, well, I don't understand how she can be so controlled and cool in the group and yet so *abandoned* outside.

PRADAPRADAPRADAPRADAGUCCI 4

Okay, relax now. Deep breaths. Control that urge to break something, to kill someone. *Abandoned!* What the hell does that mean?

Make some coffee, then start again.

Nothing happened. Of course, nothing happened. Am I mad? Am I jealous? Maybe I should be, but I'm not. Not now. No, I'm cool about it. Really. I still don't know what he means by "abandoned," but deranged women are always falling for Sean—he has some sort of affinity with them. There was one crazy Welshwoman (whoops, tautology!) who wrote him a letter after he tutored her at an Open University summer school. She wanted him to come and join her commune, where they could bring in the harvest together, mow sheep, pluck trout from the clear, ice-cold brooks, make love under the stars etc., etc. He showed me the letter (which was written on childish notepaper with flowers and things), no doubt in an attempt to prove to me how much in demand he was and yet at the same time so honest and trustworthy. I ate it, but purely for comic effect, as we had friends around at the time.

As the Sean Lovell journal is clearly going to be a bit light on facts and rather stronger on fantasy, I ought, perhaps, to set some facts down. Or one big one, at least. Harry was born on January 15, exactly two years, three months, and six days ago, which makes him twenty-eight months, or according to Sean, two and a bit. For Sean, there are two units of measurement when it comes to children's ages. There is the year. And there is the bit.

That also makes him, like his father, a Capricorn. Sean told me that, according to an ex-girlfriend of his (there are lots of them, and he has a very bad habit of beginning a sentence by saying "My ex-girlfriend . . .") who used to work as an astrologer for a Sunday tabloid newspaper, 50 percent of prison wardens are Capricorn. Reliable, steady, ambitious, rule-obsessed, boring. If only Sean had been truer to the type.

I can't remember anything about the cesarean, so I'm afraid we're stuck with the recollections of our unreliable narrator. But if I'd known how bad he thought it was for me, I'd have made more capital out of it. Such a missed opportunity.

The week in the Lindo Wing of St. Mary's hospital, Paddington, was one of the loveliest of my life. Showered with flowers (except by Sean—he brought me a supermarket pot of basil, which he thought "more practical"), brought food on a tray, nothing to do but lie with my beautiful baby. "Beautiful" I should have said, stressing the quotes. I'd always assumed that I was above the foolish delusions of motherhood, but looking now at the photographs of Harry, I can see that he wasn't remotely beautiful; no angel then, but an imp, red and blotchy and oozing. But he sucked and slept, in an easy rhythm, and I showed him to all my friends with a "Beat that, then" look on my face.

Sean bicycled backward and foreward, and my main concern that week was that he'd be knocked down by a bus before he'd had the chance to keep his promise about being a househusband. And though, of course, that wasn't the main reason I married him, it was, you know, part of the package. I loved my job too much to want to give it up, but I never liked the idea of depositing my child with strangers. A partner who actually seemed to want to stay at home sounded like the ideal solution. I'd be lying if I said that a worm of guilt didn't wiggle and dig at the back of my mind. Guilt about leaving my boys to fend for themselves. But the world is the way it is, and wishing can't change it.

The first week back at home was more traumatic. I still spent most of my time in bed, but I knew that the apartment was slowly decaying around me.

It was then that I started to interview cleaning ladies. Someone recommended Janice, and she seemed quite capable. Sean gave a sort of grumbling approval, swayed by the fact that Janice was, for a cleaner, quite pretty. Certainly a notch up from the old Irish and Polish women with varicose veins and head scarves, their mops at the ready, who passed for the competition. After a few days, it was safe for me and the baby to come out.

Sean's general hopelessness around the house used to bother me more than it does now. Even more than the messiness, I mind his inability to find anything. Almost every morning begins with a list of "wheresmys": "Where's my socks? Where's my trousers? Where's my wallet? Where's my keys?" When I berate him, he just says, "I'm not very good at finding things; I'm not very good at looking." Now, as far as I can see, not being good at "____" works where "____" equals tennis or tightrope walking or algebra, but not for things such as ordinary walking, not on a tightrope, or breathing or finding things. Oh, unless, of course, you're one of the people who are *supposed* to find those sorts of things difficult, if you haven't got enough legs or whatever. It's all because he just can't really be bothered with it and nothing to do with not having the right genes or, his usual excuse, having his mind fixed on "higher matters."

Harry slept a lot, and we had peaceful mornings reading the newspapers in Starbucks, only slightly spoiled by Sean complaining about globalization and saying that with every sip another child died in slavery or poverty or impoverished slavery, and it was all my fault. It didn't seem to stop his eating two muffins with his grande latte.

It must have been a black, cold time, but my memories are drenched in warmth. My abiding memory is of the two of us walking through the streets soaking up the admiration of the world for our baby. Think new mothers must get tired of strangers cooing? Think again. You're perhaps confusing it with the heavily pregnant woman's hatred of having her bump patted by anyone other than her gynecologist or her husband. On second thought, strike "husband." And particularly by the sort of weirdo perverts who just come up to you in the street and have a feel, as if the bulge belongs to the world. "Fancy a squeeze of my tits as well, eh?" I often wanted to yell at the postman or the old bag downstairs with her lipstick and her claws. "What about my fanny? Go on, have a feel." But once the thing was out of me, I bitterly resented anyone who didn't stop to ogle the contents of my stroller.

I seriously thought about fashioning a giant pointing finger to suspend above the stroller, with the words "I MADE THIS" painted on it. But that was the time of hormonal flux, and I thought lots of crazy things. The maddest of all, the one that should have been enough on its own to get me institutionalized, medicated, possibly even lobotomized, was "Oh, wouldn't it be fun to have another."

Raymond is disappointed about the continuing poverty of my sexual fantasies. I told him about Uma Thursday, and he suggested that I might secretly want a threesome, and couldn't I open myself up to that in imagination as a way of transcending it?

"No," I said.

On a whim, I looked up "xanthar gum" from the previous journal entry. I thought it was too good to be true. It should be "xanthan gum," an anagram of "thannax" and "naxthan," but not "anthrax." I wish I hadn't looked it up, because the actual substance turns out to be even more disgusting than the name sounds. "A powdery polysaccharide composed of glucose, mannose, and glucuronic acid, produced"—and this is the yucky bit—"by the bacteria *Xanthomonas campestris* and used in drilling muds and the food industry."

And they put it in baby food! Such are the pitfalls on the quest for knowledge.

SEANJOURNALFOUR.DOC

NYMPHO WOMAN FROM PLANET IDIOT

With my accumulated vacation and paternity leave, I had, if I needed it, three months off work. Celeste had arranged the same amount of maternity leave. Bliss predominated. Celeste was proving to be a surprisingly competent mother. I'd secretly had her down as the kind who would eat her own young when stressed, but as the breast-feeding took hold, the eating was all the other way round.

Although I'd promised to look after Harry, we still weren't sure exactly what that meant—whether I'd go part-time or take a longer break or pack the whole thing in forever. But as those three months progressed, the knowledge grew between us that I wouldn't be going back to work at all. We *did* discuss other possibilities: muddling through, with both of us working part-time, her parents helping out, and some kind of childminder taking up any slack. But fitting all those elements together was an intellectual task beyond either of our sleep-deprived brains. Celeste earned a lot more than I did, or could, and so she was never going to take the permanent-full-time-mother route. Logic, circumstance, and Celeste demanded that it be me.

So I went back to the Culture Department for a day and handed in my notice. The resignation letter wasn't hard. I'd been writing them ever since I first became a civil servant, and I'd saved them all on my hard disk, numbered joy1.doc and so on, right up to joy9. Joy4 was the shortest ("I find that I am unable to go on"), and joy7, the most baroque, beginning as it did with a detailed description of the glorious death of the last Byzantine emperor, Constantine XI, before the walls of Constantinople in 1453 and going on to mention the battle for Stalingrad, the extinction of steller's sea cow (a close relation of the manatee and dugong), the breakup of the Beatles, and England's exit from the 1996 European Championship finals after a penalty shoot-out.

My manager looked relieved rather than actively pleased, as though she'd finally found a cigarette machine prepared to believe that her stash of Polish zlotys were really pound coins. At least she didn't whoop. Leaving necessarily involved a leaving party and some sort of presentation. I made it clear that, instead of the usual parting gift, any collection should be given to charity. In honor of my new status, I suggested either Save the Children or Children in Need. From the puzzled looks around me, I deduced that there had, in fact, been no thought of a collection. But after my hint, the hat was passed around pretty quickly, and upon my departure, the children of the world were better off by nearly seven pounds, or one and a half measles vaccinations, a new bucket for the well in Somalia, or a two months' supply of condoms for an overstretched family in Peru.

There was also an embarrassingly large leaving card signed by lots of people whom I didn't know and who were unlikely to have known me. Trying to write something original and witty on a leaving card is one of the great trials of civil service life. I had some success, in my time, with anagrams, my best achievement being, on the retirement of a senior official: "Did you know that *Stuart Kingaby* is *a big nasty turk?*" But nobody had bothered much with mine. There were several "cheers," endless "best wishes," and one "love" from somebody called Humbert, which, unless it was the little man with whole-body dandruff who hung around by the water cooler, was likely to be a nom de plume. Lucinda, the office fox, hadn't signed it at all, despite the fact that we had a seven-minute snog in a cupboard followed by a nine-second shag in the service elevator at the

Christmas party the year before I got married. Perhaps she'd just never recovered from the blow of losing me or was still irritated about the dry cleaning bill ("It won't come off—they'll all see." "Try spit." "I've tried it. Have you got a hanky?").

Then, as I was finally leaving the civil service altogether rather than just skipping departments, some of my old colleagues from years gone by turned up, in a *Night of the Living Dead* kind of way. I'd managed to forge myself a reasonably cool persona at Culture, but the sudden appearance of the bandaged and bedraggled crew from Customs, the Department of Health, and the Overseas Development Agency hauling themselves through the pub door did nothing for my credibility. At least two old flames materialized, both looking much, much worse than I remembered. Shirley Essen had run to fat, and Miriam Restorick now appeared to be sixty-two years old. The worst thing was that they actually looked quite disappointed at how *I'd* weathered.

The drift away began as soon as the fifty quid I'd put behind the bar ran out, and I was left almost on my own, chatting with the One Who Might Have Been Humbert. He was telling me about his skin condition. Already, twice that evening, he had disappeared into the gents to reapply his WD-40 cream (or whatever it was), but within ten minutes of the ritual smearing, his skin would lose the fatty glisten it had temporarily acquired and again take on the look of scorched puff pastry. Many of his words began with a peculiar nasal sound, as if he were trying to swallow a buildup of snot from the back of his face.

"Nnngthbegan when nnngthI was nnngthseven," he was saying.

I tried not listening and just saying "Really" and "Oh" in a prime-number sequence of my own devising.

And then there came a tiny shimmer from the line of optics behind the bar and a sound of sighing, and a light without source filled the pub, and Celeste stood by me. I'd forgotten she was coming. Her parents were babysitting. It was the first time she'd been out since the birth. It was about eight o'clock.

"Hi," she said. "Your crowd not here yet? I've brought Milo and Galatea along."

Fantastic. Just what I needed. Celeste's two most fashionably sneering friends to witness my shame. Milo was the head of some sort of PR company and combined a camp effervescence with a streak of cartoon villainy. I'd first met him at a party years before, and his barely understandable opening words to me were, I'm fairly sure, "Sorry, can't kiss now, mouth full of cum." I'd heard he'd recently arrived back from "updating" the Dalai Lama's image. ("Think we need a harder edge, you know, more street punk, more leather, more spacey, yeah?") Galatea was the world's trendiest designer. Celeste would soon ask her to work on our new apartment, but she replied that she didn't "do domestic" with all the haughty grandeur of a high-class prostitute saying that she didn't *do* anal.

I knew that my job had always been a bit of a joke to Celeste and her friends. Apart from me, she didn't know anyone who wasn't either doing something glamorous in fashion or the media or at least earning enough in the City to buy into those worlds, taking on the glamour by association. There'd be a look of mixed puzzlement and boredom when I told her friends what I did. "Why?" they'd ask with their eyes, "why do *that?*" as if I'd just told them I was a professional fish wanker. But they managed to make me feel embarrassed, despite myself, and then I'd feel ashamed of being embarrassed.

"Here yet?" I said. "Well, some have gone already, you know . . . top civil servants, early starts . . . and we began drinking, . . . but there's still a few around. This is, um, Humbert."

"Nnngthello," said Humbert.

Before he had the chance to show them his embrocation, I hurriedly waved behind me, saying, as I turned, "And here's . . ." But all I could see was Shirley, sitting with her chubby legs and mouth open, looking, in her white vinyl microskirt, like an extra from the 1950s cult classic *Nympho Woman from Planet Idiot*. Obviously the succession of Tia Marias had softened her disappointment in my appearance, and she was hanging on in the hope of a knee-trembler round by the garbage cans.

"Such a long time since I've been to an *actual* pub," said Milo. "All this *jouissance* I've been missing out on. And, look, they have etched glass, and here's a man with authentic BO and a *real* stain down his trousers serving people drinks."

Galatea sniggered.

I'd always fancied Galatea—she had the kind of dark naughtiness that I prized—but now I hated her for being there. I had no word for my feelings about Milo, more just a series of images: a mushroom cloud with the word *Why?* emblazoned across it, a swarm of locusts, a skull and crossbones. He represented everything I despised about the modern world: he was shallow, cynical, rich, good-looking, successful, popular.

Celeste, Milo, and Galatea were whispering together.

"We thought we'd go on to the Met Bar," said Celeste cheerily. "Why don't you come along? It'll be fun. Most of the gang'll be there—Katie, Veronica, *everyone*."

"No, you go on. I'll stay here. Not the done thing to flee your own leaving do while there's still a man left standing. Anyway, me and Humbert were just about to get to the bottom of his skin complaint."

They left. After half an hour—no, it wasn't psoriasis or eczema, but a rare and deep-seated fungal condition (and sadly he was allergic to most of the antifungal agents)—Shirley came over, and she and Humbert soon went around the back, his love for me proving as fickle as hers.

And so I departed the civil service, with no regrets and an index-linked pension already worth £42 per calendar month, payable from August 2025.

No e-mails or calls for six days now. I feel *something* about this, but I genuinely don't know if it is relief or disappointment. She makes things difficult and complicated, but in a way I seem to like, seem to want. Funny. What she doesn't do is make me feel good about myself. She has a way of maneuvering me into situations in which none of the things that I say—I mean, none of the things that I usually say, my little evasions, jokes, routines—work. So I'm left like a big, dumb idiot, with no choice but to act. And this vexes me because my whole life has been based around saying and not doing.

PRADAPRADAPRADAPRADAGUCCI 5

What now, after SEANJOURNALFOUR.DOC, should I make of Uma Thursday? After reading Sean's last paragraph, I seriously thought about bringing her up. But that would have given away the fact that I've been reading what he writes, and then I'd lose my advantage. I assumed that he'd have dropped her into the conversation before now. I mean, it's what you do, isn't it? You talk about people you've seen during the day, funny things that happened. So why hasn't he?

She obviously goes to his playgroup, and so I tried asking about the other mothers, what they were like. He just said, "God, I couldn't even begin to describe them. They're from all over the place, and most of them are insane or disturbed. There's someone called Brenda. She doesn't like being called Brenda."

"Are any of them pretty?"

"Pretty? Jesus, no. Well, there's a beautiful Somali woman. Can't remember what she's called."

What could I then do? Ask if there was anyone there named after a day of the week? No, as long as I'm confident nothing has happened, and as long as I have the journal to keep me up to date, I think I should keep my powder dry.

Anyway, I feel relatively benign after finding out that at least *I* wasn't the *Nympho Woman from Planet Idiot*. And so, Uma aside, I'm prepared to let go the gratuitous dragging in of ex-girlfriends and the frankly disgusting tales of office-party fornication, assuming it really *was* before we were married.

But of course, whatever he believes, we'd thoroughly discussed the arrangements for Harry, and of course, Sean had insisted that he would leap at the chance to give up his boring work to look after him. Too, too naughty to suggest that he was somehow bamboozled into the whole thing.

As for his paranoid fantasies about none of my friends liking him, well, it may be true that some of them were a *little* surprised about my choice of life partner, but, on the whole, they were fully supportive of my right to make my own mistakes. And if he was (and is) looked upon as something of an oddity, I don't believe that there has been anything that could be called a discourteous or malicious snubbing. All of the rudeness has, in fact, been directed the other way, with Sean playing his man-of-the-people part or setting himself up as a hammer of the London Elite. *Most* unconvincing now that he's become part of it.

The root cause of the incompatibility was, I think, Sean's need for "mastery" (the terminology is Raymond's). It's not that he strives to dominate in company—that would require too much effort—it's just that whenever he doesn't dominate effortlessly, by *right*, then he simply retires from the fray. He won't bother to charm or amuse, or even look interested—and he's perfectly capable of all those, because I've seen him do it—and instead, it's all dark rages and uncomfortable silences and a general ruining it for everyone else.

I always found *his* civil service friends perfectly acceptable. I wouldn't want to be trapped in an elevator with any of them, but they were usually amiable enough to make five minutes of chitchat bearable, on those rare occasions when I was permitted to meet them. (Okay, not *quite* rare enough for my taste, but I never showed it.) The leaving drink wasn't anywhere near as horrendous as he paints it. There were still half a dozen stalwarts in cheap suits and polyester ties when we arrived, none of whom bore any relation to the description of "Humbert." We stayed for a good half hour, which I think was duty fulfilled. It was, as Sean says, my very first night out after weeks of nurturing, and can he blame me if I wanted to leave that nasty smoky pub to go to a lovely smoky bar?

We drank sea breezes till two in the morning, and I even agreed to share a couple of lines with Galatea, just to be companionable, and anyway, it was business of a sort, as she's helping with some of the detailing on the new shop in Bond Street. Luckily I'd expressed and frozen enough milk to keep Harry going till it was out of my system, so I didn't have to worry on that score.

Everyone *was* there—it was still when people went to the Met, because that's where everyone went; a month later, and nobody went to the Met anymore, because that was where everyone went. People thought—or at least said, which is as good or better—that I looked incredible, and for once, I knew I did. I was wearing a pair of Bella's antique emerald earrings and a cleavage-maximizing jade green wrap dress in silk jersey that I'd reclaimed from my earlier, slightly rounder self, and I don't believe that anyone would have guessed that it was only two months previously that I'd been relieved of ten pounds of baby boy. Bliss was it in that dawn to be alive, but to be young and free (for a while) and stoned and smashed and flirted with by the gay and the straight was very heaven.

And screw Sean if he didn't think I'd earned it.

HOME ALONE

So we had our time together, the three of us. Days filled with cold sunshine and hot coffee. We spent whole hours just gazing at the little man, breathing him in like nicotine, humming and thrumming with the sheer joy of having made a thing so beautiful.

I think the best bits were the mornings after his six thirty feed. He'd usually go back to sleep again, and we'd chat and snooze, and then he'd wake between us and turn his head from one to the other as we spoke, his huge eyes watching so intently, as if his life depended on catching every movement of our lips.

But then, bud by bud, winter began to open into spring, and Celeste went back to work.

Her first job was to go to Paris at the start of the buying season. I've never worked out how fashion seasons mesh with the real ones, but it meant three days and nights alone with Harry.

"Will you be okay?" Celeste asked, trying her best to look concerned. The taxi was waiting downstairs, which inhibited any desires I might have for a long discussion. She was wearing a hat with a wide brim and had on a beige leather coat, made from dolphins.

"It'll be fine," I replied, hoping to get the message across as succinctly as possible that we probably wouldn't be fine, no *not* fine at all, and she'd better not even think about having a good time in Paris because we wouldn't be having one here in London, no sirree.

True, we'd survive, but the emotional scars would run bone-deep, and any future irresponsibility on my part along the lines of excessive drink, football, and loud music would be justifiable, perhaps even necessary. Got that?

"Oh good," she said. "I knew it would. Bye."

And of course, it was. Or at least, the things that might have been difficult weren't really very difficult. Harry took to the bottle like a dipso. I blame Celeste's breasts. You see, the girl I had first courted had been whittled down by diet and exercise to the bare essence of a woman. And if she had lost some unnecessary (though, in my eyes, *nothing* was superfluous) baggage—a little something above her hip bone, a parabolic smidge beneath her chin—gone also were those glorious orbs of yore. Yes, I'm afraid the new slimline Celeste had nothing like the firepower up top she once possessed. There was, *is*, nothing to be ashamed of in the new models: they don't droop forlornly or flap like leathery bat wings, but nor are they the staggering, genuinely life-changing breasts that I'd first fondled, leaping like salmon, springy, vibrant, B-I-I-I-I-I-G. When I first saw them, I swear to God I heard music, and not just any music but the miraculous fanfare from Monteverdi's *Vespers*: a fanfare so good he had to use it again in his opera *Orfeo*. And I'm sorry if that makes me sound like a big ponce, but you'd only think that if you've never heard the music and, more particularly, if you haven't heard the fanfare and also seen Celeste's breasts, back in their glory days, boundless in their joy.

True, there was a temporary renaissance, a late flowering of breastly magnificence, during and just after the pregnancy; but the necessary transience of the phenomenon gave the breasts a poignancy that somehow forbade lasciviousness. There was something in them of the overripeness that tells of the decay to follow, the engorgement of Hellenistic art after the unassailable *rightness* of the classical, the trying-too-hard-to-please of Bollywood, that melancholy we find in all fading civilizations facing the barbarism that will engulf them.

Not to mention the issue of seepage. No, call me old-fashioned, but I like my breast, as it were, *black*. Yup, hold the milk. Nope, not frothed or foamed or creamed, not full-fat, semiskimmed, or even skimmed. I don't care what anyone says, it's pervy.

Milk's where I came in, wasn't it? Yeah, you see, the slimmed-down tit, howsoever bulked by maternal processes, didn't seem to have the storage capacity to sate the boy. Like a good performer but a bad mother, she always left him wanting more. So the transition to the bottle, so endlessly replenishable, so free from all that annoy-ing, style-cramping breastly matter, was painless, although it did mean that I had to start getting up for night feeds rather than just hunkering down and waking Celeste with a hip thrust at the first growl from Harry at two in the morning.

Celeste's departure did not, therefore, mean starvation. Nor did it mean, for Harry, a deterioration in personal hygiene, as I'd always taken charge of matters excretory; yes, I got the bum deal.

Do you mind if we discuss poo for a while? You see, poo was one of the things that I was worried about. I mean, in everyday life, *it*—other people's poo—is not something you have to deal with or even think about. But suddenly there it is, often quite literally *in your face*. One of my earliest diaper-changing experiences featured a spectacular vertical spurt from a faceup position (one of the tricki-est of all defacatory maneuvers to pull off), which showered my spectacles, hair, and mouth with liquid shit the consistency of a good, thick milk shake from Ed's Easy Diner.

But this is where my point comes in. Changing a baby's diaper—proviso to follow—changing a baby's diaper is not *anywhere near* as disgusting as you'd think. And my proviso is not that it has to be *your* baby, although that may well add a smear of Vaseline to the lens, but that the baby be milk-fed and, even better, *breast*-fed. A breast-fed baby's poo smells of almost nothing: just the merest hint of butterscotch or perhaps a whiff of the sugar jar stashed with a se-cret vanilla pod. Would I go so far as to say it's nice? No, not quite that far. *Agreeable* hits it on the head. It's agreeable.

Freshness, as with all dairy and dairy-based products is, naturally, the key. If it's not fresh, the situation changes. One of my grimmest discoveries was the encrusting of dried matter I found that had seeped its way between the cracks at the end of the useless IKEA flatpack changing table with handy drawers I had insisted upon rather than the antique mahogany (or was it Bauhaus-influenced chrome and plate glass?) piece that Celeste would have preferred. Occasionally she'd let me have these little victories to create the illusion that the contest was equal. Anyway, after four hours of bitter struggle, I'd erected something with enough gaps, holes, fissures, and crevasses to very nearly count as netting rather than a piece of furniture, and Harry, over the next few months, managed to fill most of them with well-aimed fecal squirts and sprays. It was a friend who first noticed the smell—I supposed we must have grown too used to it. Perhaps even become part of it. I pulled away the loosely attached piece of laminate at the foot end of the table to find, well, several months' worth of caked-on shit. Yum-yum. Cleaned it off with an old toothbrush. Can't remember which one, but I'm pretty sure I threw it away afterward.

But my point wasn't to disgust, it was to say that we survived without Celeste quite well, thank you. Toward the end, I may have begun to jabber, and I didn't change my clothes while she was away, or wash, and my red-rimmed eyes told of sleepless panic, but Harry was clean and full and happy. He enjoyed sleeping beside me (Celeste had banished him to his own room as soon as it was established that he didn't need us to help him breathe), and he particularly relished forcing me into remote corners in his quest for *lebensraum*. He didn't miss Celeste at all. I'm told it's because babies have only a thirty-second memory, and so the past simply does not exist for them, and, as I can't think of a more amusing alternative, we'll have to stick with that.

I only realized fully how exhausted I was when Celeste came back. I handed her the baby like an ultimatum before she'd taken her coat off and went to lie down. She spent the next hour unwrapping the presents she'd bought him: mainly unwearably delicate garments and the sort of handcrafted wooden toys that bore children but make parents feel like they're doing a good job.

I didn't get anything, needless to say.

I have a problem: how must I deal with Sean's standard technique of comingling compliment and insult? I'm really not sure where my boobs stand at the end of all that. And it isn't just my body that comes in for the treatment. So often he'll begin a sentence with "I do love you, but . . . ," and what follows is a list of things that make me, one would have thought, entirely unlovable. It's all shorthand for: I do love you, but you have thoughts that aren't exactly the same as my thoughts and that must therefore be wrong or irrelevant.

For the first time, I feel genuinely hurt, as opposed to annoyed or frustrated, about something he's written. He implies that I had no sadness at leaving Harry, that I scurried from the apartment like a burglar stealing her own freedom. Now I know I'm not the most gushing of women, and that my emotions are not usually for public consumption, but only a fool, or someone trying to squeeze both the maximum amusement and maximum pity out of the situation, could fail to see that my reticence, my haste, was born of anguish. I can't pretend that Paris wasn't a joy, but it was also work, and I longed for my boy, longed for both of my boys.

The reason Sean didn't get anything was because he'd always complained if it cost too much and put whatever it was away "for best," never to retrieve it again, or at least not until it had gone completely out of fashion. Or he'd moan about my not making enough of an effort. "Oh, how nice. Another T-shirt from Office [a very nice

Parisian shop, by the way, like the Gap but good]. I'll put it with the other nine."

So I'm sure you understand.

As for all that verbiage about poo, all I have to say is, yuck! But at least, he didn't drone on about the frightful Uma Thursday this time.

Oh yes: must must must get a new toothbrush.

Yesterday I went to see Raymond at his office in Wardour Street. It wasn't really just to annoy Sean or simply about the sex thing that I went. Besides the sex, I had been having some "symptoms" that my general practitioner thought I might need help with. Sometimes I couldn't swallow. Sometimes I forgot who I was. Twice I was on the tube on the way in to work and I just couldn't figure out what I was supposed to be doing. It only lasted a couple of stops—say, from St. John's Wood to Bond Street. But still.

Raymond isn't a dream analyzer or a tell-me-about-your-childhood merchant. We sit opposite each other, me in a comfortable lounger, him in an office chair. He's a long, thin man, with lots of carefully combed wiry hair. He has an academic look about him, right down to the leather patches, and the spectacles on the end of his nose. The friend who recommended him to me said he was gorgeous, but I couldn't see that. I did get a vague feeling of sexual interest from him, the idea that he would love to flirt but was too professional to do so.

"What shall we talk about today?" he began, as he'd always begun.

"How about why I come here?"

"That's good. Why do you come here?"

"Because I'm ashamed to admit anything's wrong to anyone else."

"Why are you ashamed?"

"Because I hate whiners, and now I'm one of them."

"You're not a whiner. How about we lose that vocabulary?"

"I'm afraid of failure."

"You're not a failure."

"But I'm afraid of it."

So it went on. As well as trying to steer me round to talk more about sex, I suppose what he was trying to do was to uncover my insecurities and then gently reassure me. I kept saying what I thought he wanted to hear, that I was under pressure to succeed and that I had trouble balancing work and home, all that stuff. But it was just noise. Nothing I said got anywhere close to what I was feeling. None of the clichés I came out with quite fitted my anxieties or whatever it was that I had. Sometimes I thought that that meant that I didn't have anything at all.

And then I said something to try to shock him. We'd got on, at last, to why I didn't want to sleep with Sean. It wasn't that I was repelled or hated the thought of it or him. It just didn't tempt me. It felt like when you go shopping and you forget something really trivial, some polish or stamps or some standby for the food cupboard, and you'd have reached out for it if you'd remembered, but nothing so important that you'd bother going back out for it again.

"I think I want more sex."

He sat up, and I think his eyes swung for a second down to my breasts. I'd noticed that he did that whenever we mentioned sex. It might have been an embarrassed avoidance of my eyes, but then again, it may just have been an involuntary male response.

"But you've said that you feel sexually . . . uninterested in Sean."

"I want more sex with someone else."

"Why do you think that is?"

"Can't you tell me?"

"You love Sean?"

"Yes, of course I do."

"You've said before that he annoys, irritates, you in the same way your father does."

"So?"

"Only an observation. Is there someone you have in mind, the someone else you mentioned?"

"Not really."

But perhaps I did. I'd only said what I said to lift the boredom, but now, once it was out there, staring at me, I thought it might be true. I wanted more sex with someone who wasn't Sean. Yes, with someone who was . . .

The hat was a Philip Treacy trilby. The coat was camel, not beige. It wasn't made from dolphins. It can't have been made from dolphins. Is anything made from dolphins, apart from other dolphins?

THE MECHANICS OF IT

We did it last night. First time in two months. And I don't mean to carp, but, well, it was terrible. I remember when we first discovered our thing. I read about it in a *Marie Claire* at the dentist, trying to take my mind off the impending two fillings and descale. It absolutely *promised* an orgasm every time. Not very likely, but worth a shot. Celeste said she'd heard about it, too, but was never sure about the mechanics of it. So we tried. It was fun footling about trying to find the right place, fun in a fun way, not fun in a sex way. And then . . . *click*. She stopped smiling, opened her eyes in astonishment, and said "yes." It was as if she'd suddenly seen the point of the whole thing. The point of sex.

The key to it was immobility. I had to stay completely still but for a kind of hydraulic pumping or throbbing action with the mighty tool itself. (That's meant to be ironically self-deprecating, by the way.) All the movement was down to her, below me, and even that was a matter of millimeters, like polishing a diamond.

And fuck me if it didn't work. There had been nothing especially wrong with our lovemaking before we discovered our thing, but nothing like this. Historically, for a woman to come while I was still actively about my business was a happy accident. But now science had been introduced, and results could be guaranteed. It was the industrial revolution, the invention of the microchip, the bagless vacuum cleaner all rolled into one.

It took about six months for the novelty to wear off. Six months during which Harry was well and truly conceived. The wearing-off process began when I realized that the discomfort of our thing almost exactly equaled the pleasure of it. The process involved Celeste's grinding against . . . against, well, I don't really know the name of it. Pubic bone? Can that be right? Do men have a pubic bone? Am I thinking of public phone? Well, anyway, *that* bit, a bit that didn't particularly enjoy being ground against. Certainly not one of my pitifully few erogenous zones. I've always envied people with multiple erogenous zones. Ears, feet, napes of the neck, some small section of the back, bottoms. I only have one, and it's my knob. Not, as I say, my pubic bone.

But it was more than the discomfort, which hovered somewhere a notch above a nuisance and a smidge below a pain. It was more that I felt—get those hankies ready—*used*. I was a mere device, an object, a—yes, let's say it—a dildo. I stopped being a person to whom Celeste was making love and became a shape. To return to Kant—and how can we ever fail to return to Kant? (see my earlier comments re: self-deprecation)—I was a means to an end and not an end in myself. There's a sexual pun in there that a less serious person would have wasted valuable time trying to extract.

And that's what I was last night. It was joyless and uncomfortable. Once she'd stopped, I started, and I could see that that part was as uninteresting to her as the preceding had been to me.

Afterward I felt as though I'd been sacked and then got a letter through the post telling me I wasn't entitled to any redundancy money.

"Night," I said. But she was already sleeping.

PRADAPRADAPRADAPRADAGUCCI 7

Not sleeping. And if I didn't reply to his good-night, then I certainly stretched a toe back and nudged his foot with it, in a consoling way.

Oh yes, I meant to say,

BASTARD

BASTARD

BASTARD.

SEANJOURNALSEVEN.DOC

TEMPTATION

She did it. She e-mailed me. I wasn't expecting it. I thought I'd been rude enough to dis-
courage her. I thought it was over. Now I'm sunk.

I see I may have to fill in a bit of backstory. I've been trying to
remember, trying to tell the story of Harry from the beginning, but
I find I'm going to have to leap over a year and a half of his life—a
year of some joy, a little misery, a lot of work. It means missing out
on his first words (*mutt*, meaning "milk," and *no*, meaning "no"),
his first tottering steps, his first authentic tantrums. It means passing over without comment the growing chill between Celeste and
me—intermingled with plenty of thaws and one bout of global
warming but tending in the same direction: nuclear winter.

The problem was that my involvement in the relationship was
like the Augustinian view of the relationship between God and the
world. For St. Augustine, God had to act constantly to keep crea-
tion ticking over. Without the gentle pressure of his hand, a
dropped stone would cease to fall and would hover, perplexed, in
midair; the planets would cease to revolve around the earth; the
very matter of our bodies would disintegrate into its constituents—
yellow bile, black bile, blood, phlegm—and in time, they would return to their essence in fire, water, or earth. In the same way,
without my unfailing attention, our relationship stopped working.
The little endearments were left unuttered, the cement that kept us

together crumbled, and we separated like oil and vinegar in a neglected French dressing.

But, as I said, all of that must be omitted, and we speed ahead to
Harry's initiation into the strange world of the Freudian playgroup.
I'd heard about this organization through a mother I met in the
scruffy park in Kilburn. We were chatting about the usual mother
things—walking, talking, sickness, sadness, fish sticks, eggy bread—
while pushing our charges in the swings. It was important not to
synchronize the pushes with each other, as that might be taken for
flirting. I was complaining about the need for new things to do with
Harry. She began to enthuse about the Freudian playgroup her son
had just, at the age of three, grown out of.

"It's not what you'd think," she said. "They don't do your head
in with mumbo jumbo. It's just a normal playgroup, but with students watching behind one-way glass. And it's free."

"Free!" I almost certainly exclaimed. Possibly in a comical Scots
accent. "And you're sure they don't go in for all that fancying-your-
mom stuff?"

"Not at the playgroup. Really, it's just a big room with toys and
a supervisor. The students have to observe how the parents and
children interact. There's no therapy or anything."

"Oh. And you're sure it's . . . free?"

I phoned up the next day. They had a place. They seemed quite interested in having a "male carer," which should perhaps have set a
smoke alarm off somewhere. But I was getting desperate. We spent
most of our afternoons in the children's library at Swiss Cottage.
There were a few dirty toys, and lots of books and videos for Harry to
throw on the floor, but it wasn't much of a place, really. Nannies—
it was mainly nannies: Australian, Filipina, Czech, Welsh, mostly
thickset and swarthy, sometimes actively misshapen—sat around a
central arena while their charges fought and bit one another. I
could see why the nannies liked it. The kids were more or less safe,
and they could all meet up to bitch about their employers and com-

pare notes about how vigorously you could shake a child without killing it. But for me, it didn't feel like good parenting. Not day after day. Not hour after hour. It was time for new delights.

And then I craved company. It's different for real mothers, mothers with wombs and so forth. They, *you*, have networks. You can get together and talk about the things you talk about. You can roll your eyes about how stupid and untidy men are. There are makeup tips and amusing sanitary napkin stories to exchange, i.e., things that *aren't just to do with baby*.

But with me, a *male* mother, there was always going to be a gulf. True, there's baby stuff. We can talk about poo. And then I can try to widen the subject by comparing the types of poo-squirt Harry is capable of to the different shapes of spout produced by the various species of toothed and baleen whale—the aggressively forward angle of the sperm whale, the bifurcated V of the right whale, the pear-shaped plume of the rorqual. And then I could try to impress further with a smattering of high culture. "And talking of sperm whales, you know, of course, how in chapter twenty-eight of *Moby-Dick*— What? You haven't? Oh, well, you see, the harpoonist who killed the whale is put in charge of cutting it up, and the first thing he does is to make a kind of temporary mackintosh for himself out of the whale's *foreskin*. Yes, yes, it's true. Cuts holes for his arms and puts it over his head. I believe it may be the only time a character dresses up in a whale's foreskin in a major novel in the Western tradition. No, wait. Please come back. I promise to stop talking about whales' genitals."

Except I never get that far. It would all have been different for Celeste. At least three of her friends had babies around the same time. She could have gone round for coffee mornings or just generally hung out. But they don't want a big, smelly man hanging around, a big, smelly man who might, just might, start talking about whales' foreskins in front of their kosher kids.

So I was lonely, and the Freudian playgroup seemed the ideal opportunity to talk to people who wouldn't be allowed to run away.

Monday morning came around. Celeste dressed Harry in his fussiest clothes and made me promise not to change him back.

"Please, can he not be in gangsta mode today?" she implored. "I want him to look nice for his group. They probably have contacts with social services."

"No, you're right. We don't want Harry taken into care because he looks too comfortable."

But I gave in. It was before the Pooh hat.

The Freud people seemed to have taken over a whole street's worth of prime North London real estate, but the Freudian playgroup lived in a portacabin around the back of one of the main buildings. Harry's initial reaction to the place was to say "no" decisively, nine times, as I unstrapped him from the stroller.

Stacey, the ringmaster, came out to meet us. She was a small, severe American woman in her fifties, I'd guess. I mean guess that she was in her fifties; I knew she was small and severe and American.

"Hello, you must be Sean, and this is Harry," she said, getting it the wrong way round. I had a feeling a secretary somewhere would suffer later on for the mistake.

I tried asking her about the methodology behind the group as I unhooked Harry from the Jean Paul Gautier bustier affair into which Celeste had bolted him.

"I have nothing to do with methodology. I just make sure the children have a good time without burning the place down."

I made a joke about how, yes, that would be terrible and might cause several pounds' worth of damage. She gave me a resigned look and introduced me to the other mothers.

I was maybe a little disingenuous when I went through, earlier on, my reasons for wanting to meet more people in a mother-and-baby-style context. I left out sex. I'd read somewhere about the exciting new concept of the "yummy mummy": foxy twenty-somethings who wouldn't let child raising get in the way of being beautiful. Technically Celeste was a yummy mummy, but she didn't count, as she was also my lifey wifey. I didn't want to *do* anything with the yummies; I certainly did not, back in those days, want an affair. There was no room for an affair. I had as much spare time as I had spare energy, and I had enough spare energy to uncork the evening bottle of New Zealand sauvignon, and that was it. If it weren't for the remote control, I wouldn't even put the TV on. So affairs weren't on the menu, but maybe a little innocent lechery, followed up by harmless flirting, might not be out of the question.

It didn't take long to establish just how low the yummy quotient was. I'd been fooled by the "Freud" bit of the playgroup into thinking that it would be full of middle-class mums, the sort who had peopled the tedious National Childbirth Trust classes Celeste had made us attend. Perhaps prone to tie-dye and sandals and alternative therapies, but basically *nice* and quite possibly pretty. What fun we'd have discussing interesting Freudian concepts, the universal incest taboo, the death wish, the relationship between pipe smoking and stool retention.

I should have been alerted to the truth when the lady I first spoke to on the phone asked me hopefully if Harry had any problems.

"Do you prefer them with problems?"

"Well, no, not necessarily *prefer*, but we—"

"He's fairly quiet. Is that enough of a problem?"

"I suppose it will do. You've nothing better?"

"He sometimes throws things."

"Ah, good, violent behavior. That's fine."

First to be introduced was Stanka, a squat Pole, along with her enormous daughter, Natasha, who looked about seven years old. Then came lank-haired Julie, who seemed to have crocheted her own poncho, which concealed, deep in its folds, a boy called Ricky. Over the next few months, he made three forays from the poncho to snatch food from the table at snack time. Both he and his mother needed not so much a good wash as a thorough pest eradication program. I wasn't too concerned until I saw the telltale red-rawness of scabies in the webbing between Julie's fingers. Next was Brenda, with her cute little girl, Maria. She looked normal enough and smiled pleasantly but then spent five minutes apologizing for being called Brenda and cursing her parents for inflicting such an awful name on her. I tried to assure her that there were several worse names than Brenda, including Galatea, Clytemnestra, and Nigella. Luck was on my side, and there weren't any Galateas, Clytemnestras, or Nigellas among the ones to come.

Next up, Stacey introduced me to a Bosnian refugee whose name seemed to be Aargh Ack Ack Aarghk. In the nick of time, a mere nanosecond before I proved my cosmopolitan savoir faire by a perfectly accented rendition of her name, Stacey apologized for the frog in her throat, and the Bosnian lady became Vesna. Her child, a bullet-headed boy whose name I didn't catch, was rampaging around like an enraged rhino, butting the furniture and other children. I was inclined toward sympathy—after all, who could know what horrors the family had endured?—but I still tried hard to keep Harry out of goring range for the time it took Stacey to find a game reserve prepared to take him. That just left an impossibly elegant Somali woman and her beautiful, willowy boy and, finally, an eighteen-year-old DJ and her daughter. These last two mothers were undeniably attractive, but the look of disdain the Somali woman (whose name sounded like, but could not have actually been, despite my speculations about Welsh missionaries reaching the hinterland in the 1870s, Myfanwy) threw my way, and the impossible youth of the DJ, Miranda, who was clearly fighting the urge to call me granddad, prevented either from fully entering the yummy zone.

Miranda was one of those people blessed with a name they themselves can't pronounce, like lispers called Sebastian or stammerers called Titus. Her problem was *r*'s, which became *w*'s, leaving her Miwander. In my head, this soon transformed itself, as these things will, into Rwanda, which is how I always think of her.

The odd thing is that I felt instantly comfortable—much more so than I usually felt when thrust among Celeste's successful and glamorous crowd. I suppose it could just be that as a *man*, as a stay-at-home dad, I was the weirdest of them all. Or perhaps it was the fact that Harry suddenly found himself in heaven. He took to the place like a vandal to a bus shelter. Here were new experiences: whole farmyards to explore, train sets, dolls in ministrollers, a trampoline, curious little mind-expanding puzzles involving mazes and wooden balls, Play-Doh still in separate colors rather than squidged into an amorphous brown, and two sinks full of water toys.

At that stage, he didn't bother much with other children, but he liked adults around to pass him things. As well as me and Stacey (who roamed around alternately saying softly "That's nice" and loudly "No!"), there was also Stacey's helper, Anita, to keep Harry occupied.

Now Anita *was* yummy but not mummy. She was also far too professional to flirt with me. And probably a lesbian.

No, I promised I wouldn't do that anymore. Say it fifty times: Not fancying me doesn't make a woman a lesbian. It makes her sighted.

I spotted the mirrored glass of the cubicle where the students lurked. Stacey hadn't mentioned them, no doubt to keep it "natural," but I made sure I did all my best parenting over in that corner. My God, I was good: we did the puzzles together, read through a Noddy book, assembled some several miles of railway track. I soothed his hurts and cleaned his nose. In short, the very model of a modern carer. And then Stacey made a general announcement about the students' term starting the next week and we'd all get to meet them then. So the booth was empty. I thought for a moment about comparing my ridiculous performance before the empty room to Wittgenstein's black box theory of language, but then I realized that I didn't know what Wittgenstein's black box theory of language was, and that besides, it would have been *insane*.

About halfway through the two-hour stretch, the door was flung open and a huge coat came in, carrying one small child under its arm, like a big log of firewood.

"Sorry I'm late, Stacey," said a voice from within the coat. "Complete cunt of a time. Couldn't find a parking space, so I had to drive home again and call a taxi."

What a crazily rational, strangely *Celeste*-like thing to do, I thought.

The coat came off, and a woman stepped out. I felt an instant prickle of unease. She wasn't a stunner. Her features were maybe 5 percent below what she'd need to be a stunner, and she was dressed carelessly, in a pink cardigan and a tweed skirt and thick tights, so that even I could see that she wasn't interested in style. But she was still mighty fine, and she had a laughing, immoral confidence about her, and the sort of crinkly eyes that could well spell trouble. In general, I could never decide if red hair was a good or a bad thing. You know, up top, good, down below, less so. But it was impossible not to be impressed by the way she threw her locks around like an actress "doing" a free spirit.

Yummy? Yes, I think you would have to call her yummy.

She came over and introduced herself.

"I'm Uma," she said, with another extravagant hair-flourish. "You must be the Token Man Stacey warned us about."

Before I had time to come out with anything witty (or, more likely, a sound like a man who has just put a whole pork pie in his mouth trying to yodel), she'd leaped across the room to save her child, who wore an intimidating and superior look, from the rampaging rhino.

For the next hour, she danced around the room, returning every few minutes to make some more or less offensive and more or less generally audible remark about the other mothers and children. It was top-class stuff. It turned out that she had a list of irrational prejudices almost as long as mine: she was against sportswear in a non-sporting context (Rwanda the target there); against overlarge children (sorry, Natasha); against small, severe American women in their fifties (a bit obvious, that one); and against people called Brenda (well, . . . Brenda, I suppose).

I found that I wanted more. It was home time. Coats and bobble hats were thrust onto unwilling children. There were a couple of major tantrums. Irresistible force met immovable object when rhino-boy ran into Natasha. I quite liked the idea of walking a little way down the road with Uma. I'd finally thought of something interesting to say that had nothing to do with fish or whales or Wittgenstein or potty training. And I got the impression that in the general jockeying for pole position in the stroller Grand Prix, she might have been maneuvering in my direction.

But then I found that I'd been cut off by Brenda, who said, "I think we're walking the same way, aren't we?" in a voice that brooked no disagreement. And true, she lived distressingly close, which meant that for the next twenty-five minutes, I was treated to a detailed analysis of exactly what was wrong with Brenda's parents.

"I wouldn't mind, but they were spaced-out hippies living in a fucking wigwam in a commune in Wales. All the other kids were called Starvoyager or Fern or Moonshadow. And what do I get? *Brenda.* And, you know, they never bothered to help out. *She* once said, 'Shall I come down and give you a hand?' and I said, 'No, stay in your fucking wigwam.' And do you know what? She never offered again, which just sums them up. *Brenda.* It's just not funny, not funny at all."

I listened for the first five minutes and then settled in for a good long think about Uma Thursday. But soon the prickle of fear at my neck and the iron grip of angst around my testicles drove me back to Brenda and the wigwam.

PRADAPRADAPRADAPRADAGUCCI 8

Okay, okay, just what the fuck is going on here? Suddenly I can see her. So, she's a stunner? He thought it was over. She e-mailed. He's sunk. Say *that* again. I had to bite my tongue when he came to bed tonight, after I'd finished reading this. He obviously likes the bitch. But has he done anything? Not based on what he has written. Can I trust that? Well, if he was going to write as much as he did, then why would he stop short of *that*? No, I don't think he's slept with her. But I think he might. Should I talk to him about it? The same problem. I'd have to admit having read his journal. The only way I'll know the truth is to keep reading. If he sleeps with her, I'll leave him. I might leave him anyway. I don't think I love him anymore.

But Harry I love. He woke for a moment when I went in to kiss him good-night. He gripped my shirt and said, "Stay." I lay with him till he went back to sleep. Oh God. This is terrible.

I tell myself that nothing will come of this. Such a drama queen. So much sound and fury signifying nothing. It will pass. But how can I love him anymore?

A BAGEL WITH HEGEL

After the group today, Uma said, "Let's take them for a bagel."

"Okay."

I sometimes took Harry up to the new McDonald's in Hampstead, the one that nobody wanted. I knew it was bad, but he liked it, and the toys that came with the Happy Meal kept him busy while I read the paper. But, as I said, I knew it was wrong, and I was glad for an alternative. And I thought it might be fun. With Uma.

The bagel café was on one of the cute little historical alleyways that's hardly changed since 1998. And yes, there were bagels. Harry liked bagels. He liked them plain, with nothing on them except more bagel. Uma gave her boy one piled high with broccoli and alfalfa sprouts and other good things.

"Funny," I said, "how many philosophers have names rhyming with bagel."

"Yeah, funny," she said, rather than a helpful "Really, I hadn't thought. You mean like . . . ?"

"Oh yes, many, er, many." Now I'd gone and fucking forgotten them. Uma was looking out the big window at people passing by, many of them with dogs.

"Tell me, if you must."

"Well, Hegel, of course. And Ernst Nagel. And the brothers F. W. and S. F. Schlegel."

"You made the last two up."

"I didn't. Well, the initials. I can't remember what they were, but they were definitely called Schlegel. They invented Romanticism. And there are more, but I can't remember them now."

Uma had by now entirely disengaged from the discussion. When I didn't say anything for a few seconds, she looked at me and said, "Have we finished with the bagel talk yet? Because, you know, really it wasn't very interesting."

I was embarrassed and annoyed.

"Look, Uma," I said, making sure that Harry and Uma's child were out of earshot—yes, they were playing on a squidgy sofa upstairs—"first, and I've noticed this about you, you never try to say anything interesting yourself, and then when anyone else makes a bit of an effort, all you do is slag them off. And second, if you find my company so distasteful, then why do you send me what can only be described as flirty e-mails, full of explicit stuff? Christ, I mean I didn't start flirting with *you*. If truth be told, I don't even want to flirt with you—I was just doing it to be polite."

"Flirty e-mails? My God but you're prim. I send about a million e-mails a day. The ones I send to you I send to almost everyone I know. It's what e-mail is for. It's not flirting, it's communicating."

"So that stuff about needing a fuck and using the doorknob if you didn't get one wasn't . . . aimed at me?"

"Did you look at the address list?"

"My program doesn't show it unless I tell it to."

She laughed her throaty, dirty laugh and then set her face in a mask of mocking piety.

"I'm really sorry if I gave you the wrong idea or caused any offense. I won't send you any more."

"Doesn't your partner mind? I mean about the mucky e-mails?"

Uma had never mentioned the father of her child. I presumed he was something boring, and, as we've established, she didn't like to talk about boring things.

"Don't ever use that word again. If you mean boyfriend, say *boyfriend*. If you mean husband, say *husband*."

"Jesus, I said *partner*, not *pimp*. What's wrong with *partner?*"

"I don't like it."

"Doesn't your *husband* mind?"

"I'm not married."

"Doesn't your *boyfriend* mind?"

"I haven't got one. I'm a single parent."

"Oh. Sorry."

"Don't be. I'm not."

I don't know why, but after that, we started to have a good time. The tension between us disappeared, and I gave her an amusing account of Hegel's philosophy, and she told me her favorite sexual positions, but in a very nonflirty way. I realized that I'd made a bad mistake. She was just a larger-than-life character, full of sauce and vim. And now it looks like we might manage to be friends.

Ah. Just when I'd managed to work myself up to the point where I might be able to have some fun with revenge, it transpires that they are nothing but good friends. But it doesn't get him entirely off the hook. The fact is, he's been flirting with this bizarre woman, this fiend with her "positions" and no *partner*, and who sexually assaults doorknobs and God knows what else. I mean, how the hell does she do that? I tried—I don't mean tried doing it, I mean tried seeing how it might be done, if one wanted to, which I certainly don't. It's impossible, and I've had four years of yoga. Unless you stand on a pile of books—say, four inches high—and bend down facing away from the door, and let it take you from behind, praying all the time your mother doesn't pop round or your toddler wake up. No, you'd have to be mad.

And though he's off the hook in terms of immediate retribution, reading about his *involvement* made me feel that something had changed, that the complicated balance of dissatisfaction, inertia, virtue, had swung or dipped or whatever complicated balances do. Or perhaps more like a tooth cracking, and though it may hold out for a while, you know that eventually it means the dentist; it means the drill.

I'm trying to make light of it, but I do feel hurt by all this. Not just Sean's flirtation with the Uma woman; more that sense that I'm not at the center of his world anymore. For so long, I was. Each morning

I knew that he would wake up thinking about me and go to sleep thinking about me and then think about me for a lot of the time in between. And it worked the other way round, of course. He was at my center, too. Even at work, when I was supposed to be Little Miss Focused, I'd come across something, a picture, a word, and think, Sean would laugh at that, or I'd pull off some minor triumph, and it would only count for anything once I'd told Sean about it. When Harry came, things changed, and the love and attention got spread around a little more, but there was still plenty of it, or there seemed to be. But now it feels as though the spreading's gone too far, and there's not enough left to cover us all.

Is this the way a marriage ends, like the bathwater going slowly cold? Or does something dramatic have to happen, a big bang, some shock and awe, a 9/11? I don't want it to. End, I mean. But I miss the being-at-the-center feeling. I miss the love piled thick and heavy.

And then, talking of something dramatic, Sean arranged a night at the theater with Katie and Ludo. Not exactly my idea of fun—something improving at the National. More Sean's kind of thing than mine, really, but for Sean to arrange anything at all is a rarity, so I was happy to make the most of it. And I hadn't seen Katie for a while, and she always has something vicious to say to help the intermission drinks go down.

Shame, in a way, that Ludo was going to be there. Easy on the eye, of course, if you go for that grim and chiseled look, but you'd hardly call him amusing company. If it were just me and Katie, we could cut the play and spend the evening being funny about our husbands. Our husbands. How strange and grown-up that sounds.

But then, half an hour before blastoff, the babysitter, Astrid—a sallow German girl somehow related to the people who live below us, and here to study medicine—called to say she had jaundice and couldn't make it.

We looked at each other. I didn't want to go on my own, but he got in first with a typical "You go. Anyway, I've got work to do. I need to finish my piece for the radio tomorrow. It's about the time I left Harry on a Jubilee line tube and had to collect him from lost property."

"Please tell me you didn't really do that. Did you?"

"No. But I nearly did. Poetic license. They expect it of me now."

So I went. At least it meant I could get a taxi and not wait for a bus, or until they built a methane gas–powered hydro-tram, which would have been Sean's preferred option. And then, the strangest thing. Ludo turned up on his own. I was in the lobby, exactly on time, as I always am, and he just strode in, wearing tweeds worn smooth with time, and said, "Sorry, Celeste, Katie can't come."

"Not ill, I hope?"

"No, not ill. A production crisis, she said. Had to stay late at work. Where's Sean?"

"Bloody babysitter. Needs a new liver or something, selfish cow."

"Drat. I'm sorry. If you'd rather just go home, that's fine."

I won't say my heart hadn't sunk. This was the nightmare scenario. Just Katie would be great, ideal—we had plenty to bitch about. Ludo with Katie was bearable. But Ludo *on his own*! And then I looked at his face. He so expected me not to want to be there with him. Humility is seldom an attractive quality. Too often it's a weird way of showing off, and when it's not that, then its just sickly. But there was nothing flashy or sickly about Ludo's humility. He just didn't expect me to want to spend the evening in a theater with him. It was sort of nice and unassuming. And the wholly appropriate humility exuded by a pimply jerk (sorry, but I have someone in mind) is not at all the same thing as humility in the form of six feet two of big bone and muscle and broad chest and handsome head and gray-brown eyes. And those hands of his. Broken but clean nails, fingers that looked like they could tie knots in razor wire. Strong, competent, mastering hands. Even thinking about them now makes me feel funny.

"Fuck it," I said, knowing the impact it always had on men when I swore, how they were shocked and yet liked it, liked it a lot. "I'm here now. And I've always wanted to see . . ."—I looked quickly at the poster . . . Shit, how do you pronounce that?—*"Philoctetes."*

Ludo looked for a second as though he were going to correct me but then said, "Yes, it never gets a run out. Sophocles' most neglected work. It's the subject matter, of course."

"Mmm," I said, as he guided me into the bit of the theater where the seats are. Because I'd assumed Katie would be there, I was wearing the sort of clothes that she would appreciate and, with any luck, be put out by—my Miu Miu sixties shift in jade silk. Too demure for a boy to understand, but at least I'd been waxed that week, and I had on my Emma Hope beaded gold T-strap heels. Very sexy.

Ludo was right about the subject matter. A man has a bow-and-arrow arrangement that can't miss. Some other men want him to help them fight a war. But he gets bitten by a snake, and the wound turns into a horrid, smelly, suppurating boil, and he moans a lot. So they dump him. Then things start to go badly in the war, and so they send someone to get the magic bow. Long arguments follow, but the upshot is that he goes back, and the Greeks beat the Trojans and Helen's restored to her rightful place and Troy gets burned to the ground. The play only had the middle bit, the bit with all the talking and none of the killing, but with lots of boil and lots of wailing.

Sean would have done several things with a night like that. He would first have royally slagged off everything about the translation, the performance, and the staging. He would then have launched out on some crazy interpretation of his own, gesticulating and shouting and making people on the underground stop and stare. All Ludo did was tell me the backstory, as we sipped our intermission gins, and nod when I, quite out of character, suggested that the "message" (how I cringe now) was that you can't have the good thing (the magic bow) without the bad thing (the smelly boil). I may even have said that marriage was a bit like that, although I'm sure I stopped short of pointing out what about Sean was bow and what was boil. He looked very earnest at that, furrowing his brow in a way I'd never seen anyone do before. When I told him how good he was at this sort of thing—encouraging and explaining—he said, "I should be. It was my job. I was a teacher."

"I had no idea," I said. "I thought you'd always worked at Penny Moss with Katie. Isn't Penny your mother?"

"Yes, but, well, I only started there when Penny . . . when Penny left. I had to help out. It meant . . . losing a lot of things that had been important to me. But, hey," he said—and I could see the effort he was putting into sounding cheerful—"there were big gains, too. Working with Katie. It's good having something in common we can talk about."

Well, that didn't sound too healthy. They'd reached the stage at which the only thing they had left to chat about was business. At least Sean and I still talked about, well, *things*. Didn't we?

After the intermission, I found that we were, mysteriously, sitting slightly closer together. There was a space under the armrest, and our hips touched in a way I hadn't noticed before. Perhaps, I thought, it's because we were both angling our upper bodies away and leaning on the opposed armrests, me on the left, him on the right. I tried shifting so that my right arm was on the rest. And a thrilling second later, he did the same and our arms were on abutting rests, touching from elbow to shoulder. It quite took my mind off the boil, which, all things considered, was good.

It must have been then, or around then, that I realized two things. The first was that Ludo was attracted to me. It wasn't a tough call. His movements, his voice, his eyes—they all said the same thing. But I also sensed the struggle within him, the battle between his desire and his conscience. And that struggle, the twists and contortions, gave his desire a rich and sinewy quality, and I liked it.

And that was the second thing I realized. Sometimes you stumble across a feeling you never expected to find, and it can either be a nasty shock, like the moth in the cupboard, or a moment of stunned pleasure. And there it was, lying inside me, tightly bound and coiled but impossible to ignore.

When the play ended, and the interminable clapping died away, I suggested that we go for a drink somewhere. I mentioned a little bar I knew, a fashiony hangout. It was a test. Ludo famously hates the fashion world, more even than Sean. If he agreed to come along, well, then, . . . well, then, who knew what he'd do?

It wasn't very full, and there was no one there I knew, which was lucky, but also a bit disappointing. I could tell that Ludo was uncomfortable in the blue neon, and he looked at the Philippe Stark bar stool as if it were a gay sex toy with designs on him. He bought me a green cocktail recommended by Vic, the Australian barman, who was the one person there who did know who I was. He gave me a smirk, which was sweet of him.

"So, apart from working all hours, how *is* Katie?" I asked, as soon as we were comfortable in a Barbarella booth.

"Well, you know how Katie is," he replied.

I did know just how she was. Katie had used Ludo as a ladder from the shop floor up to the production office. People sometimes said that we were alike. And perhaps we were, in some ways. In fact, if you set out our likes and dislikes side by side, you'd find a lot of things in common. Clothes, books, films, music: the things you pick up from the world around you. But I'd been luckier than her, and my path had been easier. Things had been given to me that she had had to fight for. And the fact that she'd had to scramble had left its mark on her. You could sometimes sense resentment in the set of her jaw, fear in the lines around her eyes, anxiety in the quick, nervous movement of her fingers.

Great shoes, though.

"And you, Ludo, how are you?"

He didn't answer but took a swig from his bottle of beer. I'd known Ludo, or rather known of him, for a long time. He was at school with several of my exes. I'd always thought of him as the dull one, and my boyfriends always laughed at him behind his back and almost as often to his face. He liked birds. I tried again.

"How do you like working in fashion? I never pictured you at Penny Moss."

"Not quite how I pictured myself, either. But I'm not really any-thing to do with the fashion. I help with the books. And delivering. I drive the van."

He was looking like a downed pilot interrogated by the Iraqi secret police.

"Are you happy?" Not a fair question, I know, but sometimes that's just the way things are.

He looked at me. "I enjoyed tonight. Did you?"

"Apart from the boil."

"How's little Harry?" he said after a moment, in an obvious at-tempt to steer the subject to safer waters.

"Sweet as anything."

"You're lucky that Sean's so . . . good with him."

"Ha! And doesn't he let the whole world know about it."

He laughed. "That's not fair. He never . . . criticizes . . . you. He does moan a bit, though. In a joking way."

Ludo and Sean weren't exactly friends, but they'd been out for a few drinks together, along with Sean's other weird "mates." During some football tournament or other, they used to go to a pub and watch the games on a big screen. Once the girls were invited. It wasn't a success. Not so much the game as the venue, and the ugly shouting men, their beer guts bursting out of replica England shirts. The experi-ment wasn't repeated.

"And you and Katie? Any thoughts . . . ?"

"We were both keen for a while. When I came back from Scotland—I'd been helping there with a conservation project. But nothing came of it, and now, well, she's very busy."

"And very slim."

He guffawed.

"Look who's talking."

I smiled back. I knew this was his way of making a compliment.

"Everyone's thin in fashion."

Although the booth we were in was very nice and cozy, there was none of the thigh touching we'd had in the theater. In fact, he seemed to be trying deliberately to distance himself and had slid around to the far side.

On an impulse, I asked him, "Has he ever mentioned someone called Uma Thursday? Stupid name."

He looked uneasily at the label on his beer bottle.

"That's the woman at his playgroup. The Freudian one. He's very funny about it."

So, she did exist. Or at least her invention wasn't confined to his silly journal.

"What did he say about her?"

Ludo was famous for being honest, and I knew that he wouldn't lie.

"Nothing much. He said she was a bit flirty, that's all. Made a joke about her being after him. Said she was mad."

"I have to get going," I said. Ludo winced. He was completely incapable of hiding his feelings. "But I had such a nice time tonight, we must do it again." It was all that I meant to say, but somehow I couldn't help adding "You could always try to think of something else, ah, *cultural* for us to do."

He looked startled. His features really were actors, playing out his thoughts to the gallery.

"Yes. You mean just the two . . . yeah, that'd be . . . good. I'll try to think of something. I'll call you."

So I enjoyed the taxi ride home—the first part, at least, feeling warm and excited and nervous. I didn't want to think about what might happen. And nothing would, probably. Just a harmless flirtation. Like Sean's with his Uma Thursday. But then thinking of him, of her, the pleasure of the evening leaked out of me, and by the time I reached home, I wanted nothing but bed and oblivion.

DADDY ON THE RADIO

"How would you like to chat about being a single parent on *Woman's Hour*?"

"What?"

There was a lot of screeching and clattering, low moans, a hideous twanging noise. A passerby might think a rehearsal for a Greek tragedy, put on by The West Hampstead Amateur Theatrical Society (or TWATS, as they would be called, if they existed), had reached its crisis point, with Oedipus about to put out his eyes, or Clytemnestra on the verge of stabbing someone, to the accompaniment of authentic ancient Greek flutes, drums, and lyres.

"I said," she shouted, "would you like to talk on *Woman's Hour* about being a single parent?"

Susan was a friend of Edwina. Edwina was a friend of Celeste. Edwina allowed her house to be used for "music" sessions on Thursday mornings. Celeste talked me into going, despite the two buses it took me to get there. Edwina herself was wise enough to shun the events, leaving the shepherding of her two sons to the nanny, while she had her talons clipped at a nail bar.

Ten children sat around a large woman wearing a guitar and a smock and a crazed smile. Parents formed an outer hull, restraining and encouraging, as best we could. The children banged arhythmically on a range of percussion instruments, including Nepalese temple gongs, African talking drums, Peruvian llama-skull tympana, and one another. The ones who were banged cried loudly. The ones who did the banging, principally Harry, also cried. After ten minutes of clanging, most of the children had wandered off to find things to break, leaving the parents and the music lady more or less alone, like the ribs of a picked carcass. For no very good reason, I found myself scraping at a serrated stick with another stick, not serrated.

"But I'm not a single parent," I said, unsure whether to be annoyed. Perhaps it was flattering to be thought capable of doing the whole job on my own. Or maybe I looked like the kind of sad bastard who just couldn't hold on to a "life" partner, probably because of erectile dysfunction (should stress here that I haven't, oh no, not at all, not me, not ever) or obsessive interest in spanking. Susan looked disappointed.

"Oh, I was led to believe . . . But you *are* the main carer, aren't you?"

"Yeah, I suppose so."

"And you *are* a man, aren't you?"

"Last time I looked."

I wished I hadn't said that. It was the sort of embarrassing banter that got you the reputation for being a boob.

"Well that's something. You see, we like to have new angles on *Woman's Hour*. It's one of the things I was brought in for. Making up new angles."

In the flurry of accusations, I'd failed to properly absorb what she was talking about. *Woman's Hour*. Radio show. About women's stuff. Occasional piece designed to appeal to humans *in general*. I used to listen to it in bed when I was a student, when it had the twelve-till-one slot, just before the news. Then it switched to 10:00 a.m., and several years passed before I caught it again. As a virtual woman, I did sometimes listen in, while pottering, until I'd be driven insane with boredom by someone complaining about how their Chronic Fatigue Syndrome made it difficult to get the soufflé to rise, or mildly enraged when the program reached the part (as it always did, usually about two-thirds of the way in) at which the panel laughed about how generally useless men are, as opposed to women, who were generally clever and nice. If I wanted to be patronized by harpies, I'd grumble to myself, not infrequently aloud, I have a wife quite prepared to do the job in-house.

"What would you want me to do?"

"Well," said Susan, keeping one eye on her little boy, who was trying to escape from Harry, who wanted to use him as a cymbal (and I do mean *cymbal*, as in gong, and not *symbol*, as in a symbol for all that's wrong in modern society), "I'm putting together a feature on . . . I'm not exactly sure yet, but it's on something. An aspect of something. Parenthood or life, one of those. And you could talk about it. From your perspective. As a man."

"And just remind me, what do you do again?"

"I'm the producer."

"Wheels on the bus!" screeched the music lady, in a final, desperate attempt to wrest the attention of the kids away from Edwina's knickknacks.

"Go round and round."

"And you're a journalist, is it? Or something to do with the Web? I can't remember what Edwina told me."

"Round and round."

"Sort of. I used to be a . . . yeah, journalist."

"Round and round."

It was very nearly true. I'll have to rewind a month. Harry is two. He's started nursery school, which will need a chapter to itself. Only three afternoons a week, to begin with. And I still have the mornings to cope with. Nursery just gives me a four-hour breathing space to get my head together. But to Celeste, it suddenly means that I'm not fully employed: a situation she endeavors to rectify with instructions, commands, suggestions, and notes. She seems to think that I've suddenly become a handyman and can do things like fix the light in the bathroom or put away the box of bits that have fallen off my bicycle, a box that has remained bravely at its post in the middle of the hallway since we moved into the new apartment. I don't want to move it because that means I'll never get round to putting the bits back, and for all I know, some of them (odd toothed, coglike things; a small section of chain; a piece of wire inside a rubber insulating sheath) might be important. I needed the box there as a reminder. And, I've tried arguing, it had, in its metallic, oily randomness, certain aesthetic qualities, on the same plane as Duchamp's urinal.

Anyway, Celeste was furious that I had some "free" time and seemed determined to ruin it for me. It was Carol, my old landlady, who came to the rescue. She phoned up one evening with a proposal. She'd just taken over the editing of a website. The previous team had been lured away entire by a rival, and she was desperate.

"You can write, can't you?"

"Physically, yes."

"Good. Well, you can be the content person."

"But I've only really done civil service stuff. Speeches for ministers, where I get them to say *wank* or *bum* without realizing it."

"Nonsense. What about all your poetry and odes and things? You used to leave them in the toilet, for emergencies."

"They weren't for emergencies. I just left them there by mistake. It was a good place to contemplate. What do you mean emergencies?"

"You know, when we ran out—"

"Carol, you're not telling me that you . . . with one of my *odes* . . ."

But I said yes, in the end.

I admit that starting a job was a pretty desperate way of avoiding being given jobs, but these were desperate times. And it had the advantage of being hugely flexible. I was based in a high-tech, swanky office in Camden Town, but the regime was fairly slack, which meant that I could spend some mornings working from home, have relaxed lunch hours, and generally piss around, as long as I churned out ten thousand more or less relevant words each week. The contract was for three months, initially. After which . . . ? Well, who could say what bright vistas might have opened up? The child care did take some finessing. Celeste's dad, Magnus, strode manfully into the breach, ably assisted by Natasha, who'd been helping me for a few months. It was a big wrench. Harry had been as close to me as a tumor for almost two years. He'd been the thing that was always there, like Mt. Fuji in Japanese prints—the presence that made everything else small and unimportant. Now suddenly I had to start thinking about other things, other people, again.

I wasn't at all sure that I could do that. Babies are great things to talk about when you can't think of anything to talk about. And I was good at baby small talk. I'd hardly ever offended anyone by pointing out how much her baby looked like a gibbon or what a shame it was that she'd never managed to get her figure back after the birth. I never failed to praise the delicacy of the girls or the robustness of the boys, except when the mother clearly signaled her abhorrence of gender stereotyping, in which case I smoothly slipped into the groove, pointing out how caring the boy seemed to be and what an excellent male nurse he'd make, or how feisty the little girl and how suitable for space exploration, coal mining, or football hooliganism.

But now I was going to be in a place where none of that would wash. I was going to have to find some new material. I thought back to the time before Harry, the time when I talked about other things. What were they? TV, of course. But two years ago, people were still saying that there was never anything good on, apart from the nature docs. Was that still the same? Had the conversation moved on? Perhaps now the thing was to say that TV was wonderful, a glorious cornucopia, a box of delights. Except, of course, for the nature programs, which now were rubbish. Or perhaps people didn't have TVs anymore and to mention them was as grotesque as belching loudly on a crowded train. Perhaps now people went on rambles in the countryside or fished for eels or practiced archery on the village common.

What else apart from TV? Two years ago, the new lad was all the rage. Boys were allowed to get pissed and play video games and be interested in football as long as they were also reasonably correct about sexism and racism. So should I burst into my new office on a skateboard wearing an Arsenal soccer kit, my eyes dilated from hours of slaying the bad guys in Unreal Tournament? But no, that surely had all passed. Perhaps we were *caring* again, or maybe militarism was in. Or Maoism. Or bestiality. There was just no way of knowing.

My friends—Leo, Andrew, and Ludo—were no use. The stuff we talked about was, well, marginal, to say the least. We were like a club the rules of which were so long and complex that only the four of us could ever get in. It was a miracle we ever found one another. No, when it came to the world, I was on my own.

What about preparing a few conversational gambits? "So, the assassination of the Archduke Ferdinand in Sarajevo—if Princip's bullet had missed . . ." "Oh yes, it's interesting that the origins of the unicorn myth should have come up, because, you see, my theory is that the Arabian oryx, a small, goatlike antelope, with remarkably long, straight horns, when viewed in profile . . ." "No, you're quite wrong there: the reason why pop music was better in the sixties is because almost every band then had a designated rhythm guitarist, and his job was to add melodic complexity, within the otherwise simple . . ."

Of course, I never needed them. The place was full of geeks and gimps, and what we talked about was ISDN lines and what a bunch of cunts the bosses were.

The website was called livelifetothefull.com and was all

about illness, death, and dying. I spent three weeks writing
articles about terminal cancer, how to help a colleague cope
with bereavement ("Alcohol can be a great friend in a period
of personal crisis"), woodland burials (very environmentally
friendly), cremation (nastily polluting, it turns out), and other
suchlike topics, hastily researched or completely made up, as
whim dictated. The work was easy and amazingly well paid. Then
the money ran out, and we closed down after receiving fourteen hits, only one of which generated any income by clicking
through to the site of our major partner, the Crickelwood Funeral
Parlor.

I was mildly annoyed when the stupid thing went belly-up. The job
made it look like I was making an effort. It also meant that I could
claim to be a journalist or working for a dot-com or in the high-
technology sector or in the death industry, as circumstances
dictated—the circumstances being: talking to pretty studenty girl
at party (journalist); pretty girl in black-rimmed square glasses (dot-
com); pretty girl with shoulder pads (high-tech); pretty girl with
pale skin, long black hair, blood-red lips, and fangs . . . You get the
picture.

"So," continued Susan (sorry, better explain that we're back in the
music class now, and the *Woman's Hour* producer is talking at me),
a slight smile playing across her face as she saw a child not her own
gouge a groove in the parquet flooring (also not her own) with the
surprisingly sharp toe of an action figure, "if you're a journalist,
you'll know all about it."

"About what?" I tried again. But the dogs of war had been un-
leashed. Two kids were fighting over a bongo drum; the maracas
were being hurled backward and forward like those German stick
hand grenades; and one child was lying motionless on the floor as
his mother ululated in grief. Death by triangle? No, he's up and

laughing; mother looks like she's going to do the job properly later on.

"I'll call you," said Susan, as I made for the door, pushing Harry before me like a lawn mower.

So that's how I came to find myself talking to a presenter over the phone, my words being recorded for use in that day's program.

"Do you feel at all emasculated?" There hadn't been much in the way of preliminaries, and so I was a little taken aback.

"No, why, should I?"

"Well, a lot of men would, wouldn't they, in our society, doing what you do."

Obviously I was supposed to launch into a stout defense of the masculinity of parenting, the hearty outdoorness of it all, the Iron John bonding side, whittling harpoons together, getting in touch with the inner yeti; or, failing that, to shun the gender stereotyping implicit in the underlying assumptions, deconstructing the binary division between male and female, blah blah blah. I could have done either of those. Have done both of those, in other situations. But I didn't feel like it that morning.

"You know, maybe you're right. Maybe I should feel emasculated, and maybe I do, a bit. But what I mainly feel is bored. I push a stroller around the streets for hours on end. Then I sit in Starbucks praying he won't wake up before I finish my muffin. Then I go to the supermarket, and old women coo at my child, while the line in front gets longer rather than shorter. Then I walk round some more. Usually it's raining. I go to the library and watch him fight with other toddlers for half an hour. Most days, I don't talk to anyone apart from the checkout cretin or the shelf stacker with learning difficulties who gets lost in a pattern in the lino when you ask him where the tinfoil is. Do you know how much conversation a two-year-old has? 'No,' 'more,' 'chokt candy,' 'mine,' 'ow ow ow.' They're boring, they're selfish, they're stupid, and they're not funny.

And they smell of poo." It went on like that for quite a while. I think—what am I saying? I know—I mentioned the look of grimly malevolent humor, the look you might expect from a minor barbarian chieftain watching his favorite fool juggle with the heads of vanquished foes. But I didn't swear, which took some fucking doing, I'll tell you.

My assumption was that they wouldn't use the piece. Susan said as much. They always recorded more than they needed in case things didn't work. She didn't seem to have much confidence in my working.

Nevertheless, I meant to listen, just in case. But Harry swallowed a wolverine and I had to take him to the ER. A wolverine (Latin *Gulo gulo*), should you be unfamiliar with the quadrupeds of northern Europe, is a large, brown badgerlike animal of famous ferocity, although Harry's was made of plastic in China and was about the size of his thumb. But still, swallowing it was an achievement, doublingly baffling when you considered how reluctant he was to put anything sustaining in that lovely mouth of his. Perhaps it was a message: Lay off the broccoli and spinach. What I want is roast fox, served on a bed of puréed squirrel, and garnished with weasel kidneys.

As it happened, the wolverine was passed with minimal discomfort during the two-hour wait in casualty, and we never even saw the doctor. But at least we avoided another black mark in Harry's medical notes. By the time I'd dropped Harry off at the nursery school, done the shopping, and stood with my head resting against the wall for an indeterminate amount of time, it was late afternoon. I checked the answering machine, which we keep in the Room That Nobody Ever Goes In, for maximum inconvenience. There were six messages, which was quite exiting. There were usually two. One from the morning, with Celeste telling me to do something, and then another one from the afternoon, with Celeste again telling me to do something—sometimes the same thing she told me to do in the morning message and sometimes something else altogether. The first and sixth messages conformed to this arrangement. The middle four were all from Susan.

"We're using your piece. About eleven fifteen. Bye."

"Just had a couple of calls in. Want to know if you were serious."

"Switchboard flooded. Love your stuff."

"Call me."

I called her.

"We've never had a response like it. Not since our male breast cancer feature."

I couldn't let *that* lie.

"Male breast cancer?"

"Yes. Reasonably rare but kills a few dozen men each year."

Great. A new one to worry about. What next? The male prolapsed womb?

"Oh."

"People seemed to find it very funny. What you said, I mean, not the cancer."

"That's nice."

"Yes, and, well, Jemima and I thought that you might like to do a piece in the studio. A sort of essay."

Christ.

"Okay," I said casually, as if I were used to this sort of request. "If I can work around my, er . . ." What? Tea drinking? The urgent need to arrange my shoes in alphabetical order? ". . . other commitments. But I don't quite follow. I mean, I just, you know, complained about stuff. I didn't even think you'd broadcast what I said."

"No, that's the funny thing. The reporter wasn't sure about you, but there was a problem with the trains from Taunton, so our lesbian jam feature couldn't go ahead."

"Pity. I'd have liked to have caught that."

"But it turned out to be a lucky break. You were exactly what we were looking for. You see, without wanting to be antiman (no, we're not antiman *at all*), we like to show how men should take on more of the work usually dumped on women—children and ironing and so on—but how they still aren't any good at it."

"Damned if you don't and damned if you do."

"What? No, I wouldn't say it was a religious thing. But we thought you summed that up very well. I mean, you're looking after . . . Horace?"

"Harry."

"Sorry, *Harry*, and Celeste is out working, and that's as it should be, but, well, it obviously isn't your forte, is it?"

I wasn't going to argue myself out of a job. And perhaps she was right. Maybe I was a shitty parent.

"Well, it's a pretty tough job. And I suppose there are often things I'd rather be doing than—"

"Precisely. So our vision is that you produce these weekly talks about how things have gone wrong, your failures, and general mess-ups. We like those."

So that was how I came to be spending my Wednesday after-noons in a cramped recording studio in one of the really out of the way bits of the BBC, a tea-stained script before me and a crazed technician with bloodshot eyes and the tang of cheap ganja clinging to his lank, yellowing hair staring at me through a glass panel.

The first week, I came on after a feature trailed as "Anal fistulas—curse or secret blessing?" Tough act to follow. I didn't understand how anyone could bear to listen to my whiny voice, replete with its half-lisp and the ever-present threat of a stam-mer breaking through. I was relieved when the postponed lesbian jam makers burst forth, and I certainly never listened to myself again.

But it seemed that Susan was right. My failures were exactly what the listeners to *Woman's Hour* wanted to hear, and I had me a job and, within a couple of weeks, a cultish following of mad-women. And now, at parties, I said I was a radio journalist, which, I thought, had a good old-fashioned ring to it, sounding interesting enough to be interesting but not interesting enough for anyone to want to know more about it. Perfect.

Sean's always been embarrassed about what he does. He was embarrassed about being a student for so long, he was embarrassed about being a civil servant, he was embarrassed about being a sad sackofshit (his phrase, naturally) stay-at-home dad. For a long time, when people asked him what he did, he'd say that he worked for the Laboratoire Garnier. If they ever asked him what he did there, then his answer would vary depending on whom he was talking to. If it was a respectable aunt of mine, for example, then he would tell her that he donated his unusual pH-neutral bodily fluids at £5 a shot, which were then used in face creams and hair conditioners. If it was anyone young or leftish-looking, he would claim to be developing animal-friendly forms of vivisection, by breeding rabbits with less sensitive eyes or monkeys that enjoyed having the tops of their skulls sawed off. So I can quite see why he snatched at the chance of pretending to be a journalist, whether of the Internet or radio variety.

The first I heard about the *Woman's Hour* thing was when Edwina called me.

"You should listen. It's quite funny," she said.

"Does he moan about everything and make a big deal about small problems like always being in the wrong supermarket queue and dropping pile ointment in front of pretty girls?"

"Yes. That's it exactly."

"I've heard it all before."

And so I had. It was only a matter of time before he told the story about staying the first night at some new girlfriend's flat and nipping out in the night stark naked and finding the floor of the loo flooded with some disgusting liquid and standing on top of the seat to keep his feet dry, while peeing down between his legs, and then the door opens behind him, and he thinks it's his girlfriend, and he shouts over his shoulder "Look, look, I'm a gymnast," and then he sees that it's not his girlfriend at all but some poor frightened flatmate of his girlfriend, who'll never be the same again. Well, I didn't really want to be there for that, not even listening to the radio.

After two days, it became perfectly clear that Ludo wasn't going to call me, which was a slap in the face.

So I called him.

Katie answered.

"Hi, Katie," I said, a little panicky. "Sorry you couldn't be there the other night. You work too hard. But then I suppose you have to, don't you?"

"God, Celeste, now that Penny's bowed out, I've begun to appreciate more what she did. All that being crappy to people to make them do things. And sacking people. And telling them they can't have any more money. Do you do all that yourself?"

"Course not, darling. I don't get involved in the mechanics; I just buy. I suppose it's one of the advantages of being . . . well, working for a different sort of company."

"I'm sorry I missed the play. Ludo said it was fun."

"Fun? Well, not quite the word I'd have used about the *play*. But Ludo was very gallant."

"Yes, he said you went for a drink afterward."

"That's what I'm calling about, actually. You see, I left my . . . thingy behind in the bar."

"Thingy?"

"Scarf. Yes, scarf. And I wondered if he picked it up."

"I don't think so—he would have said."

"Can I ask him about it? Perhaps he saw where I left it."

"Sure. Hang on."

"Celeste? Hello."

"Hi, Ludo. Thanks for calling."

"What do you . . . ? I don't follow. Did I say I would phone?"

"You didn't specifically *say*, no. But I thought you would. Is Katie right there?"

"No, she's in the other room."

"I thought that we had such a nice time, you might want to do it again."

"There's not much else on at the moment. Unless you fancy *'Tis Pity She's a Whore* at the Barbican."

" 'Tis *what?*" I laughed nervously. Ludo wasn't known for taking the piss, but you never knew. Perhaps Katie had rubbed off on him over the years. I suppose she owed him something: after all, she got his flat, his money, his business (well, if you assumed Penny Moss would go to him one day), and his rich-boy status.

"The John Ford play. It's a masterpiece. About incest. And revenge."

"Actually, the part I enjoyed was the drink."

That was as far as I was going to go. Too far, you might say. He was silent for three very painful seconds.

"Okay."

COMPLETELY NO PANTIES

"The chairs are really low, you know, *kids'* chairs, but that's all there are, and so when you sit in them, your knees are up around your ears. It's not a comfortable place. Harry was being a little fucker."

We were in the Black Lion—Leo Kurtz, Andrew Heathley, Ludo Moss, and me. I was telling them about the Monday group. Harry had been a beast all morning. He kept snatching stuff: bits of the train set, a naked black dolly, a crane, and the ear of the beautiful Somali boy, whose mother probably wasn't called Myfanwy. Stacey, who by now had decided that Harry was not a happy boy, kept following us around, waiting for the next episode. When Harry made his lunge, she'd dive in and take the thing away from him and give it back to the original owner, shouting out in her strident American voice *"It's hard; I know it's hard,"* which was supposed to be a way of acknowledging, while resisting, Harry's covetousness, but which sounded for all the world like the moaning of a porn star, midshoot. Brenda was trailing me as well, determined to talk about being called Brenda, but I left all that out because the boys didn't want to hear about it. But I did do my impersonation of Stacey saying *"It's hard, it's hard,"* like a porn star, because I knew they'd like that.

"And I looked up, and there it was, staring me in the face. Her fanny."

"The fanny of Myfanwy?" said Andrew, being funny.

"The fanny of Uma Thursday."

Uma had come into the group late, as always. She was wearing a short skirt, but I hadn't particularly noticed because legs don't do much for me. They're just the things that keep the rest of you off the ground. Pudgy or long, I don't care, honestly don't care. But then she'd laughed at nothing, and I'd looked, and there it was.

"And you're sure," said Andrew. "*Completely* no panties?"

Leo cuffed him. "What the fuck do you think he means? With panties, the law of the undivided middle applies: you can't be *partly* no panties, can you? Either you're panties, or you're no panties."

"I meant that . . . well, it could have been *small* panties. You know, the ones with the string, like bum floss, and the little tiny thing at the front, like a slingshot."

"Thong," said Ludo glumly.

"No, it was *completely* no panties," I said. "And from then on, it was like the eyes of a religious picture that follow you around the room. Wherever I looked, there she was, aiming it at me."

"What does it all mean?" asked Leo seriously. "Is she making a play for you?"

"Maybe she's got a condition," said Andrew. "Some kind of rash or fungal infection that needs air. I once had a thing like that, when I was fifteen. I played cricket without any underpants, because of the chafing, and then my trousers split when I was coming in to bowl, and my knob was suddenly just *there*, like a baby shrew. Fucking umpire no-balled me, you know, for comic effect, but it still went down in the score book."

He shook his head, upset by the memory.

"Definitely wasn't a rash. All looked very healthy to me. You know me, I never think that women fancy me . . ."—there was some general scoffing, but that's what you'd expect—"but I . . . I don't know. Maybe she is. After me. But it's a strange way of making a first move. She hasn't even really flirted with me up to now, unless you count talking as flirting."

"Which you do," cut in Andrew, although whether the *you* was accusatively singular or embracingly plural I don't know.

"Which I'm trying not to," said I. "And, I suppose, an e-mail in which she described trying to have sex with a doorknob and another where she asked me if I'd ever been rimmed."

"And have you?" asked Andrew. I gave a shuddering negative.

"What's she like?" asked Ludo, looking up from his Guinness. We were all drinking Guinness. It's what you do in Kilburn. "Apart from being the kind of girl who sends that sort of e-mail."

"You mean what does she look like? Gorgeous. No, that overstates it. Pretty, very pretty. You know, hair"—I did a head-tossing movement—"and all that."

"No," said Ludo, "but what is she *like*? Is she . . . nice?"

"Nice? Uma? She's the opposite of nice. That's part of her appeal. Talking to her is like taking a plunge in a cold mountain stream. Not that I've ever actually plunged into a cold mountain stream. Or any other kind of stream, come to think of it. Quite happy with a nice, warm bath, on the whole. But, well, you know what I mean about the stream. Very refreshing. In theory."

"You're not going to screw her, are you, Sean?" That was Andrew.

"No. Nooooo. No. Well, maybe. I mean, no."

It had to come down, publicly, to a "no." For a bunch of guys, they were a curiously puritan lot. Leo was blissfully married to a woman called Odette, to whom he had a slavish devotion. It may have had something to do with the fact that he was a funny-looking little fellow and she was rather pretty, albeit it in a gangly way that didn't do anything for me. But the point is, there's nothing like thinking you've pulled above your natural level for setting your mind in that slavish-devotion mode. Andrew's girlfriend was in Mauritius studying snails. Yes, I know. He went out to visit her whenever he could scrape the fare together, but distance is another of those things that can keep you slavishly devoted. Whatever it was she was doing there (studying snails, stupid!) was due to come to an end quite soon, and her return would, I guessed, be a bigger challenge to their love than her departure. So Leo and Andrew were both raised by love into a zone of moral purity that wasn't, perhaps, their natural homeland. Ludo was different. He had a kind of moral solidity about him, a conscious doing-the-right-thing weightiness, that would have been unbearable had he not . . . um, been our friend.

I'd known Leo and Andrew for a couple of years, Ludo for a bit longer. The common link was a guy called Tom, who was part of Celeste's fashion set. He knew Ludo and had been at school with Andrew in a hellhole town in the Midlands. For some reason, Tom dropped out of the gang, leaving the four of us as contented, grumbling drinkers. As I've said, Leo was a bit odd-looking, small and dark and long-faced. But he always wore pretty cool clothes in a black-polo-necky kind of way. Andrew was taller but often walked hunched over to be on the same level as Leo. He was a failed dandy in dress, never quite getting it right. Ludo always looked like he was about to go off on a grouse shoot, with his leather patches and country cords. All of them had the advantage over me of not being splattered in baby drool.

"Have you noticed," said Andrew, "that we always end up talking about sex in the Black Lion? It's like that book *Songlines*, you know, where the aborigines always recognize where they are by which bit of the song they've reached, so the song's a kind of map. We always talk about football in the Mitre, music in Power's Bar, and sex in the Black Lion. If I was blind, I'd know exactly where we were."

"If you were blind, you'd have an excuse for wearing that shirt," said Leo.

"What does Celeste think about this?" Ludo asked, filling the smiling silence that followed as Andrew tried and failed to think of a smart reply to the shirt jibe.

"Do I look like a shit-fer-brains? Why in the name of fuck would I tell Celeste about this? It doesn't matter that I haven't done anything; it doesn't matter that I'm not going to do anything; just the very fact that I've seen someone's fanny means that I'm dead."

"I think you should tell her," Ludo persisted. "Things like this can . . . fester." He was still looking down into his pint.

"There's an argument that too much openness is selfish," said Leo. "You talk about that kind of thing, which gets it off your chest, but then you deposit it right onto someone else's. Sometimes it's best just to carry the burden yourself. Especially if nothing's going to come of it."

"Of course, nothing's going to come of it. Why would anything come of it? I couldn't be happier with Celeste. She's astonishing."

"She's certainly a beauty," said Andrew. Leo agreed loudly. Ludo drank some of his beer, but in such a way as to indicate concurrence.

"It's amazing what you'll put up with for the sake of beauty," said Leo. "And it's hard, in a way, to work out why. I mean, in a relationship, you can see how kindness or generosity or being good at ironing might well be useful things, things that you'd really want to find in your partner, but why beauty? It doesn't do anything, does it? It's just *there*."

"Isn't beauty nothing but the promise of pleasure?" said Andrew, quoting Stendhal and so ostentatiously putting on his quoting-Stendhal face.

"I don't really get that," replied Leo. "It begs the question. Why should bedding a beautiful woman be any more pleasurable, from a sensation point of view, than an ugly one?"

"From my experience," I said, "sleeping with beautiful women can be highly unsatisfactory, sensationwise. And vice versa. There is a promise-of-pleasure kind of woman, but they're not the beautiful sort. More the ones who have that naughty look, the I'm-up-for-anything look."

I was at least half thinking about Ludo's girlfriend, Katie. She certainly had that naughty look. Was that why Ludo had never gotten round to marrying her?

"Yeah," said Andrew, smiling, "and they always seem to be the ones who smoke and have their roots showing. I like that. I've found the ones you need to steer clear of are the crazy ones."

"But haven't you ended up with one of the crazy ones?" I said. I'd heard some very strange stories about Alice, his snail-loving girlfriend.

"She stopped being crazy," he said seriously. Leo gave me a look that suggested I drop it, so I did.

Ludo looked me in the face and said quietly, "So what are you going to do?"

"I've told you, nothing. But she's, um, coming round tomorrow afternoon. For a playdate." They all, Ludo excepted, whooped and hollered. "Fuck off," I said, grinning. "It's a kiddie thing. She's bringing her weirdo child along. And we'll hardly be at it in the bedroom with the kids running riot next door. She does give spectacular blow jobs, though."

"*What*," all three shouted in unison, getting us a stare from the blunt-faced barman.

"Not what you think. We were walking along the street last week after the group, and she asked me what I was best at—I'd been telling her about all the stuff I'd failed at lately. And I said, *"Nothing,"* you know, what I always say about flattering to deceive, starting off well, and then wilting under pressure, and she said that everyone was the best at something and that she gave porn-star blow jobs, whatever they are—I mean, however they're different from the normal kind."

"I think it's how far they, ah, draw it in," suggested Andrew helpfully. "You know, all the way, not just mucking about with the terminal fifth."

"Isn't there supposed to be a funny bit in between your arse and your balls?" said Leo, a little too graphically for anyone's taste.

"Maybe it's something to do with that. Licking it or biting it or something."

"Deep throat," cut in Ludo, surprising and silencing us. "You have to train yourself not to gag. There was a boy," he explained, when we all looked at him in astonishment, "who used to do it for Mallomars in our dorm at school. Tomkin, his name was. I never partook. I wanted my own Mallomar. I offered him a penguin once, but it was Mallomars or nothing."

There was a pause, and then he smiled, and we all laughed, relieved.

"I always said you public schoolboys were a bunch of fucking bum-bandits," said Andrew. "But we're getting off the point. You sure you're not going to call her bluff on the blow job?"

"Sure. And it wasn't a bluff."

"You mean it was for real?" said Ludo.

"No. It wasn't for anything. It's just the sort of thing she says."

But still, on the walk home, I thought about those porn-star blow jobs, a pleasure intermittently interrupted by the appearance of Tomkin and his Mallomars.

I know that I'd decided to forgive and forget the Uma Thursday thing, but for Christ's sake, what kind of slut would go to a playgroup in a miniskirt without her panties? No kind of slut. He's lying, he's showing off. Weird how boys need that kind of fantasy to make them feel like men. Even that sad little crew. I don't mean Ludo, I mean the others. I've only met them a few times. Sean had a party for his thirtieth. Leo and Odette came, looking like a comedy double act—she all knees and elbows and pageboy haircut, and he small and dark with existentialist angst written all over him, like someone going as a Parisian philosopher to a fancy dress party. Andrew jabbered nervously when he came in, and I thought he was going to wet his pants, he looked so scared of me. He stammered something about the crazy woman in Mauritius, obviously trying to impress me with the fact that he'd found some girl to tolerate him as a suitor as long as he stayed more than seven thousand miles away from her.

What a horror that party was. Sean wouldn't let me get in any caterers, so he spent most of the time panicking and shouting in the kitchen while I had to do front-of-house duty. "I just want to make it a normal party," he'd whined, "not all people in bake-o-foil suits and zebra handbags." At least Katie and Veronica were there, and we spent some quality time making fun of the fashion retards. At about two in the morning, an ex-girlfriend of Sean's managed to get in and smashed a sausage roll into his face, breaking his glasses—though

I'm not sure if that's an indictment of the density of his puff pastry or the flimsiness of his eyewear. The last thing I heard as I went down the corridor to the bedroom was her high-pitched screech: "You said you were just going out to get some chips . . ."

I'm jealous. There: it's out now. I'm jealous of a woman I don't even believe in. Is that because jealousy is *always* a phantom that stalks your brain and never a real thing? Is it because jealousy only lives when you think, fear, suspect, dread, and then when you find him in bed with some lumpy creature, tits flopping like dead jellyfish, what you feel is either hatred or contempt but not jealousy? It's never happened to me before, so I don't know.

I met Ludo in a bar in Camden. A bit grungy for me, but at least there was no chance of seeing anyone I knew. It was funny walking through Camden. Of course, I spent some wild teenage years here, back in the late eighties when Camden felt like the beating heart of cool. Music blasted out of pubs and the place felt young, and I was blind to the drunks and junkies strewn lifelessly about the pavements like victims of a nerve gas attack. I was a victim of a different sort in my huge Doc Martens, my thick black tights, my miniskirt (straining at the seams), and a T-shirt—yes, a T-shirt—with, in the name of God, *shoulder pads.* I don't want to think what was happening with my hair back then. I sometimes have a scary dream in which my hair is like one of the new high-tech fabrics engineered with a "memory" so that it goes back into shape after it's been stretched or crushed. At some vital engagement—say, for example, meeting some guy . . . anyway, at some time when I least want it to happen, my hair suddenly zaps back into a feather cut or a shag or a bob, or whatever, or even reverts to a time—and yes, there was such a time—when I simply had hair on my head in no special style at all.

Well now at least I had my hair right. Subtle, wheat-field highlights, with a Bardot blow-dry. The slightly scary thing is that, as I was coming out of the salon, whom should I meet going in but—yes, you've guessed it—Katie. We kissed quickly—she wanted to hurry on to sort out those roots, and I wanted to get away from her because hypocrisy really isn't one of my vices. Which reminds me of something that Veronica once said. We were at a party and Katie had been making a joke about her cynicism and manipulativeness, and Veronica said, "You aren't really like this, Katie. You're just pretending to be a hypocrite," which I didn't properly absorb at the time but which later seemed both funny and true. It was then that I began to think that Veronica might be something more than just the slightly lumpy PR creature of first impressions. Of course, she and Katie went back some way to when they were both dowdy provincials in Slough or Berkhamsted or one of those places.

I was five minutes late. We'd arranged to meet early, at seven. I don't know, it seemed somehow more innocent that way. And easier to excuse our way out of. Ludo was standing at the bar, looking awkward. He was poking about at the top of a bottle of Mexican beer. He was smartly dressed in a dark suit with a deep blue open-necked shirt. I was wearing my Sunday-best jeans (dry-clean only), the ones with an appliquéd winking dog on the bum pocket, and then I'd let rip with a slither of midriff below my expensively distressed cashmere top. Hair down—obvious but effective.

He looked up as soon as I came through the door. It must have been coincidence, or perhaps he'd been checking every few seconds, but it felt like magic. He didn't really smile but went back to playing with his bottle.

"I thought they'd stopped doing this years ago," he said.

"Doing what?" I'd expected a kiss or something.

"Putting lime in the neck of the bottle. I tried to pull it out, but it just went in deeper."

"That can happen," I said, with a heavy dose of filthy innocence, and he blushed.

"Can I get you a drink?" he asked, still looking uncomfortable.

"A glass of white wine would be nice."

"I'll get a bottle." He looked quickly at the scribbles on a blackboard over the bar, and turning to the barman, a gaunt, weak-looking

Latin boy with a thin line of beard drawn carefully around his face, he said, "A bottle of . . . the New Zealand sauvignon, please. Thanks."

We found a table. The barman brought the wine over and, with what was either a smirk or a leer, lit the stubby candle between us.

We made some conversation. My work. His work. Christ, perhaps even how pleasant the weather was, for May.

Finally, after an embarrassing pause, I asked, "What did you say to Katie?"

"To Katie? Oh, you mean about tonight. I said I was meeting the boys. I said football. A TV in the pub. There's a European Cup game. Liverpool are playing Marseille."

"It's the new Barcelona, apparently."

Ludo looked strangely interested by this.

"Marseille the new Barcelona? No, they had a good spell back in the early nineties, but they've fallen away since then. Only scraped into the European Cup this year because of the general weakness of the French league. But Barcelona . . . Ah, that's not what you meant, was it?"

I giggled.

"No. I meant, according to all the magazines, it's the next new style capital. Trendy place to live. Stylish hotels. Good shops. *Wallpaper* very keen on it."

Now he laughed, too. "*Wallpaper*! God I hate that. The way it assumes that you simply don't count, don't count in *any way* unless you've got the right kind of chairs, unless you live solely for labels and names and New York and Milan, unless your idea of heaven is lying languidly on a Mies van der Rohe lounger with two male models draped across you."

It was the longest speech I'd ever heard him make.

"Sounds okay to me. And you're forgetting, I've seen your apartment."

"That's Katie, not me."

"God you boys are all the same. The straight ones, I mean. You don't want to have to put in the effort to perfect your living space, but you're quite happy to live there once it's ready for you."

In the little silence that followed (a more comfortable silence this time), I thought, as I had tried not to think, about the differences between Ludo and Sean. In some ways, they were very alike. They'd both fallen for fashionistas but equally both rebelled against the hectic, superficial, glorious fashion world. Although they were both good-looking, I'd give Sean the edge in features, but Ludo was definitely sexier. He had more depth; Sean, more life. Sean told better jokes, but Ludo looked as if he could . . . move you. Sean was taller, Ludo broader. Sean darker, Ludo stronger. Sean had quick, small hands; Ludo, those big, fat, competent fingers and blunt nails. Hands that could bend things, break things, twist a drake's neck, mend its broken wing. But the key to Ludo, the *thing* about him was that he wasn't Sean.

I was drunk. I'd been drinking too quickly and hadn't eaten anything. It suddenly occurred to me that if I left now, I'd be able to put Harry to bed, and I so wanted to put him to bed, to feel him curl into me as I read him *The Flopsie Bunnies* or *Faster, Faster, Little Red Train* or the weird book of Japanese folk tales, full of idiot boys, pervy monkeys, cackling hags, and wrinkly old men he'd taken an inexplicable fancy to.

"I think I should go home."

Ludo looked disappointed, but only for a second.

"That's fine. A good idea. I can go to the pub and watch the match. I'll wait for a taxi with you. I mean, wait with you for a taxi."

Outside it had started to rain. That was annoying because I was wearing my beautiful new ivory suede shoes on the understanding that it would be dry. I should have remembered that it always rained in Camden. Ludo shuffled up his jacket without taking it off and made an umbrella with it for us both. I stood close to him, getting what shelter I could. I shivered, and he drew me closer. Again, I was aware of his size and strength, and I felt suddenly weak by comparison, like a wet leaf flattened against a branch. He had a wonderful clean, human smell—unscented soap, rain, earth. A taxi came down from Haver-stock Hill, going into town. Ludo waved, and the driver flicked off his light. He had to U-turn across the road, which would take a minute or two with the traffic. Ludo looked down at me. He put his fingers on my chin and raised my face. I was passive, but that in itself was a choice, because I could have pulled away or cracked a joke or slapped him. And slowly his lips came down to mine, and his touch was so gentle for such a big man, and his kiss tasted of the rain. And then he put a hand to the small of my back and pressed me close to him, and for the first time, I lost my passivity, and I kissed him back, and for a second, I thought that I had fainted, because I could not feel the ground be-neath my feet, but then I understood that he had lifted me up in his arms as we kissed, and again I was helpless, like a bird in the jaws of a cat.

SEANJOURNALELEVEN.DOC

SUPPLEMENT

I got them for Harry. I'd read a piece in *The Guardian* saying that fish oil supplements make kids clever and well behaved and stop them from vandalizing bus shelters. I popped straight into Holland and Barrett and bought a great drum containing two hundred and fifty one-a-day capsules. Looked like the real McCoy from the label. Each capsule enclosed 1,000—yes, 1,000—milligrams of fish oil, which meant 180 and 120 milligrams, respectively, of eicosapentaenoic and docosahexaenoic acids, which I took to be the stuff in fish oil that did the good work. I made a joke about stopping my coy carp from squeaking when I bought the fish oil, and the woman gave me a mad-customer-mollification smile, as her hand twitched toward the undercounter panic button.

Doubts set in when I got the bottle home, unzipped the plastic sealing strip (there should be a name for that. Franicle? Tiffle? Spart?), and flicked off the lid. A faint fishy aroma floated out. I'd encountered a similar smell once when, as a child, I found a dead porpoise on a beach in Ireland. And then there was Melanie Moody, when I was fourteen, who . . . never mind. The point is, it wasn't very nice. But it was the capsules themselves that made me think I'd never get one inside Harry. Too big. Plain too big. As big as his thumb. Whole shoals must have gone into the cod squeezer to get that much oil. No way I was going to hide that in his yogurt or slip it in with the Smarties. I tried giving him one, just saying "nice" as he sat in his high chair, watching TV. He took it, bit it, and then his face collapsed, allowing the oil and pulped gelatin casing to dribble out. He went into a pitiful silent howl of anguish, and it took two juice cartons and a spoonful of jam to get the foul taste out of his mouth, if not out of his memory.

No, he was never going to swallow that one again. And rather than throw away perfectly good dietary supplements, I decided to give those omega-3 fatty acids the chance to work their magic on my free radicals or dodgy joints or calcite deposits or whatever they were supposed to do. Take one to three capsules per day, it said. Still with that adolescent superstition that some medicines can get you stoned or high if you take loads of them, and bearing in mind that there were a lot of the horse pills to get through, I gulped six.

Then the buzzer went.

The little electronic window on the intercom told me it was her. It was only half ten. She'd said she'd come round for lunch. I'd assumed twelve thirty or one. I checked myself in the hallway mirror. Shirt, jeans (better do up those buttons), fine. Hair a bit funny. Smooth it down. No, ruffle it up. Smooth it down again. No time for unguents. Harry was sitting in the old cardboard box I'd told him was a castle. He had a hairbrush in there with him he used as a gun. He also had a Maglite torch he used as a gun and, completing the arsenal, a toy gun he used as a gun. He was quite content shuffling his hardware, making a variety of "bang" (primitive projectile weapon) and "ghzzzzzzzzzzzzzzzz" (advanced light-based neutrino weapon) noises.

I ran down to help her in with the stroller. Her boy was a few months older than Harry. He had a thick cap of white hair and pale, unblinking eyes that made you want to run screaming. We all squished into the elevator. Uma hadn't looked at me, busying herself instead with mechanical issues: folding the stroller, pressing random buttons in the elevator, and so on. She was wearing black jeans and a white blouse unbuttoned enough for me to get a reasonable look at her bra, which was red. I was thinking about the odd-

ness of being able to see the bottom of the bra, the bit that joined
the two cups together, without being able to see either any more of
the bra or any of the actual breast itself, when I felt a strange surge
in abdominal pressure. I thought that I sensed a "plock" from
within. Something in me began to rise.

I was going to belch.

I was not going to belch!

I was belching.

I would not belch!

I swallowed back hard. Frustratingly, the elevator was stopping
at all the floors. Uma was saying something about nice old elevators. Reminded her of New York. I nodded my head and swallowed
hard again. No good. Silently, a drizzle of bilious air escaped, insin-
uating its way past the various fleshy flaps and valves designed
specifically to keep just such jinn safely bottled. The smell of fetid
Thai fish sauce, of old anchovy cans, of stale vaginal discharge from
a cancerous halibut, filled the closed space. Uma started, as if I'd
pinched her bum.

"What's that smell?" she said.

I thought fast. "Cats."

"What cats?" She gave a little retch.

"Oh, just cats. They sometimes get into the elevator system.
Have to be flushed out."

"What do you mean 'elevator system'? Do you mean the elevator?"

"Yes. And the, um, ducting. They get in there."

"Yes, you said. And have to be flushed out. And why do they
smell of fish?"

"It's the food."

"What, you feed the stray cats in your elevator ducting?"

"They steal it. And then sometimes they're sick. Ah, here we
are."

I made tea. The boy, whose name was Oscar, unsuccessfully
stormed Harry's castle. Uma opened some windows.

"Lovely apartment," she said, after wandering around for a while.

"Bit of a mess. Celeste has big plans for it."

"What kind of plans?"

"Well, from what I can work out, wherever there is currently a wall, there's going to be a hole, and wherever there's a hole, there's going to be a wall. And all of my stuff will be thrown out, again."

"Again?"

"Oh, you know, when we first moved in together, she threw out everything I'd ever bought—not much, I admit, but still . . . And now, over the years, I've bought some more things, and it's time for them to be thrown out."

"Nice. But I don't think you should change anything. I think the place is fine as it is."

"I don't understand. You're a *girl* and you don't think apartments should be done up on a six-month rolling basis, incorporating whatever bits of tat happen to be in the latest copy of *Elle Decor?*"

"Why do you always go on about the differences between men and women? I've noticed it's a thing about you. A really, *really* annoying thing."

For some reason, we were now sitting side by side, but still a fair distance apart—say, two feet—on our big beige sofa (Celeste hits me when I call it a couch or a settee). Beige except for the Paul Klee scribblings in unerasable blue ink and the more recent and as yet unscoured slug trails of snot and drool. I was picking thoughtfully at one of those as Uma was speaking.

"It's not that I think there are any . . ."—what was the word? I looked at the ink ideograms with which Harry had decorated the cushions—"*indelible* differences between men and women. Or major differences that set women and men apart as classes—all the differences among individuals are much more important than the differences between groups—but, well, I don't know, sometimes thinking and talking as if there were these differences can be a creative way of getting at the heart of things, of thinking about people and what they're like. In general. Or even in specific." I think I may have ended lamely with "Sort of" but sincerely hope I didn't.

I looked at Uma. It was obvious she wasn't listening. Nor was she paying much attention to the boys, who were painting at Harry's play table. She was gazing out through the French windows, which looked onto the facing block. A bare-backed roofer was up on the roof, roofing.

I'd got to know Uma quite well over the past four months. We made a habit of letting the other mothers drift off after the play-group while we fussed with coats and hats, diapers, tissues, and then we'd walk for ten minutes until our ways parted. About one time in three, we'd go on a bagel run. Uma would do most of the talking, wittily satirizing the rest of the group and giving me her oblique take on world politics, great literature, and unacceptable sexual positions. She didn't talk much about her job but had one day let slip that she worked for a shopping channel. "Look," she'd said, "I know it's shitty, I know it's kitsch. There's nothing glamorous about sell-ing zircon diamonds to fat girls in Manchester. I know that with the gold chains we sell, the race is on for whether the copper dyes you green first or the nickel brings you out in red welts. But it's televi-sion, and that's where I want to be. Problem?"

I did have a problem with it, but I quite liked our ten-minute walks. She'd never asked me what I did for a living.

"So what do you do, then, for a living? Or do you just sponge off Celeste?" She smiled her wide-mouthed smile and leaned closer to me, showing now some of the skin beneath the bottom line of bra, but still no real breast. I'd noticed that Uma's body was always at its most flirty when her mouth was at its cruelest.

It was lucky that I had my new answer to that question.

"I'm in radio journalism."

She recoiled a little. Good.

"What sort of radio journalism?"

She was trying to sound skeptical, trying to give the impression that she thought I worked on the night-shift sports bulletins for Radio Northampton.

"Oh, just this and that. Odds and sods. Opinion stuff, mainly. In fact, . . ."

Now, it's hard to believe that this wasn't all planned, but it wasn't. I didn't invite her around at this time: as I've said, I thought she'd be over for lunch and miss it—the "it" being my latest broadcast, the fourth in my weekly series. The first, following my initial formless rant, had been about trying to walk Harry to sleep so I could enjoy my scrotum-tightening tea. The second was an extended version of the purchase and combat performance of the Pooh Bear hat. The third was a disguised, indeed distorted, account of playgroup flirtations, in which Uma became (while retaining her essential luminous Uma-ness) a raven-haired Spanish temptress, called Mercedes.

I'd forgotten what today's was about. I recorded them in blocks of three, and in my mind, they tended to merge into one long humorous, I hoped, complaint.

"It just so happens that one of my, er, things is on about . . . now."

While she occupied herself with looking at the same time perplexed and mocking (she was really quite good at giving simultaneous face to apparently contradictory feelings), I went and fetched the kitchen Roberts radio, greasy as a Turkish wrestler, buzzy as a loose tooth. I flicked it on.

I was just in time. There was my voice. Each time I listened, I heard new ways in which my voice was wrong. Today it sounded thick: thick, as of a tongue only a little too large for its mouth, a tongue, moreover, nicked, scarred, sore, from the cruel attentions of the sharp lower edge of a cheap and inexpertly fitted gold cap.

It's not that I think there are any indelible differences between men and women, or any major differences that set women and men apart as classes—all the differences among individuals are

much more important than the differences between groups—but
sometimes thinking and talking as if these differences were real
can be a creative way of getting at the heart of things, of thinking
about people and what they're like.

So it was that one.

"Is that you? That's you!" Uma was looking, for her, quite impressed. "And you just said all that word for word. What is it, do you only have, like, three things to say, and you go on saying them over and over again?"

What is it about women that makes them want to do things to
perfectly good apartments every few months, just because some . . .

"I don't like to waste good material. Or any material. And anyway, yes, I do actually run on a cycle. I have about three years' worth of conversation, which I reckon isn't bad, as most people don't have three minutes'. But that's why I have to get new friends every three years."

. . . while men are content to let the crap accumulate like guano
around a gannet's nest . . .

I didn't add that I also tended to repeat on a regular cycle that my conversation repeated itself on a regular cycle. I thought that would be too self-referential.

"It is a bit *obvious*, though, isn't it?"

"What, repeating myself?"

"No, getting me around here just so you could show me how clever you are, being on the radio. Like I'm supposed to be impressed."

She said that with a little smile, which took the sting out of it. Somehow she could almost always do that: say something that you'd think had to be completely unacceptable, going purely by the actual words used, but that felt playful, light, teasing, coming from her lips. So rather than a knife in the ribs, what you felt was a pleasurable back scratching, by long nails.

"It wasn't that . . . I didn't even know you were coming so early.

But it would have seemed, I don't know, pretentious, not to put it on, now you were here, and it being broadcast. Now."

Ha-ha-ha, another bulletin from the wilder shores of parenting-hood next week from Sean Lovell. And now a follow-up to our report on anal fistulas and the possible link to ozone depletion.

I made them pasta and pesto for lunch. Oscar ate enough to fuel a power station (perhaps they have pesto-powered turbines in Tuscan hill towns). Harry threw linguini on the floor and then climbed down to mash it in with his socks. Uma drank a bottle of Chianti, complaining all the time about how she hated Chianti, and then drove off to drop her child at his nursery and prepare for an afternoon of cheesy selling.

"The poor must have their baubles," she said, as if it were a quote.

Before she left, she turned and gave me a quick kiss on the lips, light and sharp and cool as a diving kingfisher.

I don't believe it. Everything's changed. Sean has put a new operating system on our computers. Now I don't know where anything is. Worse, "his" bit of the computer now has endless security traps and passwords. I've tried everything, including "Uma Thursday," but nothing works. So there's no SEANJOURNALTEN.DOC, or if there is, I can't get at it. And for once, I'm eager to find out what's going on inside that head of his. I don't know why, can't begin to imagine why, but Sean has become obsessed with some silly thing that happened to him when he was at school. Some minor act of betrayal. He keeps wanting to talk about it, but I really can't be bothered to listen. Whenever he starts, I just tune out and think about . . . well, the *other* things.

I talked to Raymond about it. He was disappointed that he wouldn't be hearing any more about Sean and Uma but encouraged me to keep up my side of things. And even if he hadn't, I think that now I'm addicted. I've never been big on self-analysis. I *do* things; I don't dwell. I pay people like Raymond to dwell. But writing my thoughts down has proved unexpectedly interesting to me. I almost feel as if externalizing things gives me more control. I certainly understand more. Because there it is, in black and white. Me.

I told Raymond about kissing Ludo. He was annoyed (although he tried to hide it) that I'd left so early. I'm starting to wonder why he keeps his hands in his pockets all the time.

Had a charming lunch with Milo yesterday. We met in a famous old restaurant that pays Milo a small retainer to eat there to make the place seem a little less stuffy and a bit more, as they'd probably say, "with it." They try to give you too much to eat, of course, most of it hacked from some poor beast, but the chairs are comfortable and the waiters are cute. They even do that thing of pretending to be French, which went out everywhere else about 1995.

The comfort of the chairs is rather important to Milo. Ever since his "accident," when that horrid little creature of his, Pippin, did something gross with a dildo made in the shape, according to Milo (although I think this may be one of his little fantasies), of Tony Blair's grinning countenance, he's been very particular about how and where he sits. He had an inflatable ring made by Bill Amberg with a lovely mauve nubuck cover, and he'd got all his famous clients to sign it, and if the seating doesn't strike him as soft enough, he whips it out and blows it up and makes a performance of gingerly settling down on it.

But here he didn't need the ring, which was a relief. I told him about Sean and his slut. Milo had always found Sean deeply uninteresting— he wasn't nearly butch enough to appeal to Milo's feminine side, nor was his campness the right sort of campness, being all about making a fuss and performance about small things, and not at all to do with where he liked to put his penis. If they ever abutted at parties, you could see Milo's face stretch as he suppressed yawns, his boredom tempered only by the anxiety that he was wasting vital networking and bitching time with this *invisible* man and perhaps a further hint of fear that the people who counted might think that they were *friends*!

"I don't know why you married him in the first place," he said matter-of-factly, as he pointed a forkful of seared scallop toward his mouth.

"Because I loved him, of course," I said.

Milo guffawed crudely.

"And besides," I continued, "nobody else asked me. I was twenty-five, singleish, not desperate, but beginning to *think*. And you know how many straight men there are in our business. And anyway, even though you can't see it, he is good-looking and, when he wants to be, charming."

"So you keep saying."

"And it's nice, in a way, having someone not in fashion. He keeps me . . ."—I strung it out, savoring the faux earnestness of it all— "*grounded.*"

"Sounds to me like you're trying to convince yourself. Do I detect the merest hint of dissatisfaction beneath all this display of love? Don't you want the rest of that lobster?"

"Dig in. Unusually astute of you, Milo. Bit bored, that's all. And then this thing with the slut."

"You're not really jealous are you? From what you were saying, he hasn't even fucked her. And does he know, by the way, that you've been reading his diary?"

"Not jealous, more annoyed. I'm sure he hasn't slept with her, and he probably won't, he's so lame. What was the other question?"

"The diary."

"Oh, he may do. He's changed the computer system, and now I can't find where he's put his files. But I'd already got bored with it, once he stopped writing about me. Anyway, I've got other distractions now."

Milo looked up from his plate. "Sounds interesting. Fashion or fucking?"

"Neither. So far. I've been seeing something of Ludo Moss" was how I phrased it.

Milo now put his fork down, which was quite a thing for Milo, the famous glutton.

"Ludo?"

His face was too complicated to read. I knew it wasn't politic to tell him about Ludo, but I wanted to, and that was that. He was hardly going to run off and tell Katie. They had been close until a couple of years ago, but around the time of Milo's accident, and his subsequent flight to India, things had cooled, and now they were hardly on speaking terms. But I did know that Milo had a thing for Ludo: a mad, unrequited longing. I supposed it was because Ludo *was* macho enough to make Milo want to melt into his arms. And now there were perplexing things happening with his face—interest, jealously, amusement.

"Yes. Nothing's . . . happened. Just a kiss. And what's a kiss?"

"Everything, if it's the right kind of kiss." That was true. "And what about poor, poor Katie Castle? Don't you feel for her?"

"She can look after herself. And I haven't done anything, yet."

"But you know you can, know you will."

"I don't know if I can. I don't know if I will."

"Do you want to?"

"Yes."

"Then you will."

"Don't be stupid. It's not as easy as that."

"Face it, Celeste—you're beautiful. I don't normally tell people that unless it's business, but it would be plain silly to deny it. And I promise you, there's not a man alive who won't grasp at his chance of possessing beauty. It's the way we are. The problem is that beauty usually doesn't want to be grasped. But if it does—and by the sound of it, you do—then it's all as inevitable as a . . ."

"Greek tragedy?"

"What?"

"I saw one with Ludo. About a smelly boil."

"I had one of those once. Turned out to be primary syph."

"And there's Harry. I know I don't play the maternal card, but I do have feelings."

"How is the little cherub?"

"Oh, he's lovely at the moment. He says things. And when I come in, he runs up to me and hurls himself into my arms. Sean says it's because he gets bored with him."

"I'm not surprised. But no one's saying you should leave them. From my experience, an affair can keep things ticking over nicely back at home. It's the ones who bottle it all up who finally burst out, wreaking havoc everywhere. You know it's the sane thing. You know it's the *European* thing."

"Why are you so concerned to see me stray with Ludo?"

"Just want you to be happy, dear girl. And I want you to tell me all about it. You know he has a massive tool?"

"No, I didn't. How do you know?"

"Katie told me. Said it hurt, unless she was properly lubed up."

"You're disgusting."

And he was, but he also knew that saying what he said would fire my interest, my curiosity.

"So what's your next move?"

"I'm waiting for him to call."

"He'll call. What then?"

"Then we'll see."

"Don't be so coy. See what?"

"It's not easy. Where? When?"

"There *are* hotels, you know. I could get you a rate at The Hempel—they owe me a favor."

That was enough. My head was full of images. I shook it.

"What about you, Milo? I feel we've been neglecting your love life."

"My life *is* my love."

"I'd work on that one—doesn't mean anything and doesn't even *sound* particularly witty."

"Like *you'd* know. I've not really felt *fired* by anyone since Xerxes disappeared. I pop in to see Pippin at the institution every now and then, you know?"

"I didn't know. Very . . . magnanimous, after what he did to you."

"There is still a bond between us. At least he loves me enough to hate me."

"What do you talk about?"

"Not the incident. Too traumatic for both of us. We mainly play Ping-Pong, unless one of the other loonies has swallowed the ball."

"So there's really been nobody new since Xerxes?"

"Well, I still go out, in case you haven't noticed. A boy has his needs. Picked up some plump little dumpling the other night. All hot and sweaty under his tweeds. He was dancing, looking like an old sow scratching herself on a wall. Said he worked for some crappy little auction house, Enderby's or something. Can't even remember his name . . . Cedric or Clarence or Cecil. I don't think I've ever had anyone quite so unprepossessing, but he had that air of desperation about him, so I knew he'd do whatever I told him to."

"And what, exactly, was that?"

Milo laughed unpleasantly. "You don't want to know, but we began with rimming and finished up in the same area with a bit of felching."

"Felching? Remind me."

He told me.

"Poor Cecil."

"Oh, he loved it."

"How are things at Smack!?"

"Bit slow, post you-know-what. PR's often the first thing to go, in a crisis, which is crazy because that's when the fools need it most. Had to let Sarenna go, but I had the feeling we'd become more of a hobby than anything else to her, since she married the banker. Veronica's been a treasure. You know I've made her co-director? Only way to stop her being poached. *She* saved the corporate side and keeps things ticking over in the office. Shame, if she weren't a woman, and dull as douche water, and ugly as a bulldog chewing a wasp, I might marry her. Make it a family business. Ah, the pudding trolley at last. It's my true love now, you know."

The distinct bulge in the Prussian blue of his heavy silk shirt suggested that, for once, Milo was telling the truth.

We kissed good-bye as the doorman whistled taxis.

"Remember, you will tell me *everything*, won't you?"

"Yes, Milo, I promise. Exact dimensions. If it happens, which it won't."

"It will."

"It won't."

Childishly, he insisted upon a final "It will" as he climbed in his taxi, and he slammed the door shut before I had the chance to reply. I wanted to run after him shouting "It won't, it won't," but that would have been silly. Sometimes you have to admit defeat.

THREE BETRAYALS

It must have been the thing with Uma that brought them back. I hadn't thought about Mumford for a long, long time. Nor Chris. And that's odd, because, as Celeste keeps telling me, I'm a professional nostalgist. She's always pointing it out and saying "Here we go again" when I begin a sentence with "I once had this friend . . ." or "When I was at school, there was this . . ." or "Everything's rubbish now. . . ."

Maybe it's a boy thing, because Ludo, Andrew, and Leo do it, too. Just maybe not as often. And maybe not as well. But we have in common the habit of explaining or highlighting or attacking something *now,* something *here,* by trawling back and finding an analogue from long ago, something from *there* and *then.* And not just the good stuff, either—the first drunks, the first kisses, the first palping of a pliant tit (although those; certainly those)—but the bad stuff, as long as it could be made funny or poignant or useful. So Andrew will illustrate some recent humiliation or fiasco at work by talking about the time he managed to hack up into his mouth from his bronchitic chest the mother of all greenies and then, rather than simply spitting it onto the playground like anyone else, he gathered a crowd and tried to fire it backward over his shoulder with a violent toss of the head and simultaneous flexing of the spine. But the beast in his mouth was simply too viscous and vigorously resisted expectoration. The result was a huge green slug deposited on a line running between the corner of his mouth and his eyebrow, with a sound track of jeers, sneers, slaps, and goffs, as the boys and girls of 3J showed their appreciation.

So, yeah, that's how we are, sucking the marrow out of our pasts to moisten the dry bones of our present. But I'd never dragged Malcolm Mumford back from the place I'd put him. Nor Chris Rushby, my friend.

Chris first.

The school I went to, The Body of Christ, was a rough school. It was a place of violence and cruelty, and that was just the teachers. Fusco, Benning, Callaghan: the names were names of fear. They were men who hit you because they didn't like how your face was made, who humiliated you in front of your classmates if you looked weak or odd. They kicked you and they punched you, and they twisted the short hairs on the nape of your neck until you cried. They never seemed to do that to the psycho kids or the huge meatheaded bullies, fists blocks of malachite, their bodies bursting Hulklike out of their school uniforms.

Christ, I remember Gaz Kilmartin with his baby face and knuckle-dusters. He was "cock," meaning the biggest bully, the hardest boy, in the school until Terry Coleman, fresh out of reform school, rubbed his face into our gravelly, "all-weather" sports pitch. (That was a laugh: it was all-weather only in the sense that it was equally unsuitable for games in all weathers.) Terry, who had a huge head, with the classic school bully's massive jaw, jutting brow ridges, and sloping forehead, then unzipped his knob, the like of which I've never seen before or since, as long and wide as a baby's arm, and pissed on the fallen hero. The encircling kids didn't know whether to rejoice or tremble. We all feared Gaz, but at least he was a known force. And fat: there weren't many kids who couldn't outrun him. Terry was a different proposition. His bulk was all muscle, tough and knotty. And then, Gaz, despicable though he was, was at least *our* bully, not an interloper like Coleman. (As it turned out, most of us had an easier life under the new regime. We were beneath Terry's contempt—we didn't even register on his radar.

He was after bigger prey: sixth graders, the cocks of other schools, local hardmen, zebras. It even seemed to work out well for Gaz. Denied the old outlets for his creativity, he discovered in art class an unexpected talent for pottery.)

From the outside, The Body looked like a Bulgarian nuclear reprocessing plant. The bits that weren't stained concrete were asbestos. Yeah, it was a dump: we all knew that—kids, parents, teachers, the rats in the creek that ran along the side of the school, the pigeons that shat on the roof. There may have been worse schools in the north of England, but there certainly weren't any worse Catholic schools. St. Michael's and Cardinal Henan were terrified of playing us at football. We were the place their kids got expelled to, and godhelpthem when they got to us.

The creek—really just a filthy stream, lifeless but for the rats and a kind of living scum that could dissolve broken strollers and dead dogs—was, weirdly, a place of adventure, excitement, and romance for us. The "us" was the group of middling nerds with whom I ran. Most of us were bully fodder, picked on for having big lips or curly hair or satchels instead of Adidas sports bags. I don't know why Chris Rushby chose to hang out with us. He was several notches up from us in coolness, toughness, in-ness. He was short, but both times I saw him fight, he pulverized bigger kids, sliding straight from normal, cheery Chris into berserker mode, the hot fire in his eyes, his slight frame throbbing with the feel-no-pain mania of the true fighter.

But I do know why Chris hung with us. It wasn't us; it was me. He liked me. We did that clicking thing. We got each other's jokes, felt easy together. He spent nights in my house, in my brother's bed. We shoplifted together and then gave what we stole—pens, records, comics—to tramps or girls we fancied. Sometimes we just threw our loot into the creek.

I think maybe the key *thing* about Chris, the truly *unusual* thing about Chris, was that he was good. Good in the sense that he wanted other people to be happy; in the sense that if they weren't, then nor was he. He was the only kid I ever saw genuinely take a chance and stick up for another in a way that could have landed him a thorough beating.

His goodness was why he brought in Mumford. Mumford was as far below us in the natural order as Chris Rushby was above. He was a colorless, pasty kid, with gray teeth and skinny legs. He had no jokes, no talk, no panache, and no real brains. He was a nothing, a void in the shape of a kid. But Mumford's biggest fault, his fatal flaw, was having a mother who loved him. One day, early on—he was eleven or twelve—his mum, big-haired, fake-furred, dropped him at the school gates and there, in full view, kissed him, leaving a set of vivid red lips on his white cheek. He was doomed. From then on, it was open season. He'd be punched and kicked by anyone who felt like it, which turned out to be almost everybody. The tiny minority who didn't bother hitting him ignored him. He never even merited proper piss-taking, because that would have involved him in the joke, and we didn't want that.

Two—or was it three?—years of that and Mumford was more ghostly than ever, slipping silently from classroom to classroom, entirely alone, his anguish, if anguish he felt, kept tightly coiled within himself, leaving no mark on his countenance. Some of us should have seen him, helped him. But that would have contaminated us with his deathly, ghostly vapor, dragged us further into the pit, nearer the hellish tormentors, the cruel boys who punched you and kicked you for their sport.

It began when Chris let Mumford eat his sandwiches near us during the lunch break. There were five of us: Jordon, the O'Connells, Chris, and me, and we always ate our sandwiches in a niche in the school wall, sheltering from the cold wind. Mumford came and sat outside the alcove, but close enough to seem as if he were one of us, close enough for the world to make a connection. Normally we would have stoned Mumford like a pariah dog and driven him away, but Chris started talking to him. Nothing much, just chat. Music maybe, as if Mumford would know anything; TV, as if his views could possibly matter; girls, like he had a chance. Before the rest of us knew what was happening, he was in our alcove, sharing our warmth, stealing our cool.

I can't remember now if I spoke to him at all then or in the next couple of weeks as he followed us around. I can't bring back any words, only the groans and tuts as he surfaced into consciousness, dropping out of hyperspace into our midst, desperate to please, longing simply to be *here*. It was always Chris who included him in our talk, made room for him in the circle.

It was Chris who told him he could come after school to mess about by the creek.

For most of its length, the creek was too wide to jump, and its muddy banks were slippery and treacherous. Only a fool would risk falling into those rank waters, scummed and oily. Two or three times, I'd missed my footing and gone home to a hard cuff from Mum, her nose wrinkling at the stench from the four fingers of brown damp at the bottom of my trousers. But there were a couple of spots where the creek narrowed and the bank gave purchase, and you could leap with a good chance of safe landing. And so jumping the creek was one of the things that you did, in your little gangs, once every few weeks after school. More frequently, and this slight pleasure would have palled; yet, as it stood, it was a good thing to do. Your mates might chuck stones at the water as you jumped, trying to catch your crotch in the backsplash, but, on the whole, a spirit of unity and common purpose would prevail.

Of course, Mumford had never joined the community of leapers. One evening, I thought I saw him from the top of the bus standing alone by the creek, gazing into and over its waters, dreaming, perhaps of flight, of soaring, of the claps on the back and ironic cheers for a wobbly landing.

But now he was with us, laughing at our jokes. What do you call a man who digs up dead bodies to fuck? A bugger. What do you call one who forgets his pick? A silly bugger! Would you let a fag bum you for an orange? No! What would you let a fag bum you for, then? Nothing! Ha, you'd let a fag bum you for nothing.

We jumped over the easy bits. Mumford had a go, and Chris caught his hand at the far side and pulled him home as he looked like sinking back into the mud. I didn't like it. Chris was my friend, and he was spending more time talking to Mumford than me, even though Mumford didn't swear, had no chat, looked like a cunt. And then I remembered the fridge. At one of the creek's widest, deepest pools, a fridge had been dumped. It looked like a sunken aircraft carrier, with only a small diamond of angled deck showing above the water. There had been speculation for a while that a daring boy could jump from the right-hand bank, land with one foot on the fridge, and then take off again, landing safely on the left bank. The distance was doable, but you'd need neat footwork, clever eyes, even assuming that the platform were stable. And that wasn't the case. I knew it wasn't the case because I'd poked it with a stick. The fridge wasn't nestled properly in the mud at the bottom of the creek but was finely balanced on some kind of pivot in the sludge: a brick or some other thrown-away thing, bike, iron, fetus. It took only a little pressure for the great mass to shift. Anyone landing on the fridge would fall, and that meant lying waist-deep in stench.

I sidled up to Mumford. Now I can remember the words—my first words to him.

"There's a cool place to jump. You have to step-stone on the fridge. It's not hard—I've done it. Chris'll think it's cool."

I showed him. The others had found a condom and had sent it down the stream, like poo-sticks for perverts. Mumford didn't look happy.

"Is it safe?"

His voice hadn't broken, and he spoke like a girl. I laughed, mocking his timidity.

"Course it is, pussy."

He was torn between fear of falling and the need to become one of us. This leap seemed to him the key. Turn that key and the years of loneliness and pain would vanish. He would have friends, people to be with. People to sympathize when he got punched. People he could talk about when his mum asked him how school was today. What had he said to her over the past two years? Had he invented friends, told made-up stories about the games and the sport and the laughs they had? Or had he just looked down at his plate, dreading exactly this as yet another humiliation?

"Okay." He smiled nervously.

"Mumford is jumping the fridge," I screamed at the others. Jordon and the O'Connells whooped for joy and came running. Chris looked concerned and came more slowly.

"What for?" he said. "Have you made him? Did you dare him?"

"It was his idea," I said.

Mumford stared at me. Was I trying to make him look good? he wondered.

He said, "Doesn't look too bad."

Chris said, "I wouldn't."

Jordon and the O'Connells shouted at him to go on.

He took off his blazer and gave it to me. He had six or seven pens in the pocket and a clean folded hankie and some money.

Chris was telling him what to do. Don't take a long run, he was saying. Just a couple of steps, because it was important to get the aim right, to land on the bit of fridge. But he had to keep his momentum going, to swing his other leg straight through, or he'd be stranded there, and fucked. They were standing close together, Mumford leaning, nodding. He looked happy for the first time since his mother had kissed him two years before.

Chris went along the bank to an easy crossing and then tracked back to help Mumford when he reached the far bank. The rest of us stayed on this side. Mumford prepared himself, forward to the edge of the water, then back two steps, forward again, and back for the last time. He jumped. It was a good jump, height and distance perfect, enough speed to carry him through with a quick step on the fridge. But the fridge, as it was meant to do, betrayed him. It rocked, and he fell, splashing helplessly into the water, his face contorted with surprise and fear, and the other thing, the thing I had done to him.

Jordon and the O'Connells fell laughing to their knees. This was the funniest thing they had ever seen. Straight in, headfirst. Did you see his face? Classic. Was that you, Mog? (They called me Mog.) Fucking genius. You knew, didn't you? We didn't even look as Mumford dragged himself out of the creek. But I noticed an odd thing. Chris didn't help him. He just stood there and watched, his face blank. Then he walked away, back across the rough gypsy field to the council estate where he lived. We went around and met up with Mumford. He tried to laugh with the others—"Me mum'll kill me"—but didn't look at me as he took the blazer from my hands. I'd taken fifty pence from his pocket.

I don't think that the incident did Mumford too much harm. I pray that it is so. He drops out of my memory again from this point, goes to a place I can't reach, but I have an idea that he found some others like himself. The bullying must have diminished, because it always does, if you wait long enough. But none of that takes away my shame. Mumford was just like us—just like us except that his mother had once kissed him on the cheek, and crucified him with that kiss, and I had betrayed him from jealousy.

And I knew it at the time. The next day, I took the fifty-pence piece and threw it high onto the flat roof over the gym, propitiating the cruel roof gods. And then I made myself forget Mumford, because I couldn't live with the knowledge of my cruelty, of my betrayal.

But it wasn't to be the last betrayal. After the creek, Chris melted away. In my memory, it takes place immediately, but there must have been a transition. It was near the end of the year. I didn't see him in the holidays, and the next term, our school merged with another, almost as rough, called St. Kevin's. The classes were all jumbled, and Chris and I were separated. He made new friends—

tough kids, punks, skins. He never became one of the bastards, the tormentors of the weak, but he was of their party. And then he got expelled for sniffing glue in the basement, caught in a stupor, his cock in his hand. For a term, he hung around at the school gates, looking weirder every day. For a time, I stayed to talk with him, took a drag on his cigarette. But then I heard stories about him that scared me. He had been my best friend, had slept close beside me, and we had shared our sweets and smokes, and now he was letting men stick their cocks up his ass, in his mouth, because they gave him money.

So I stopped talking. To begin with, I waved and laughed. And then I smiled. And then I didn't even smile anymore. And then he stopped coming to the school gates, and I never saw him again.

It was only after the memory of the betrayals of Chris and Malcolm Mumford came back to me that I looked them up on the friendsreunited.com website. They weren't there, but Neil Jordon was. I e-mailed him. He was working as a chief in a hospital, still in Leeds. He had no idea what had happened to Mumford, had, in fact, like me, completely forgotten his existence. But he'd heard that Chris Rushby was dead.

But, as I said, it wasn't finding out about them that brought back the memories of those two betrayals. I think what brought them back from deep storage was the knowledge, the fear, that I was going to commit a third betrayal. A betrayal without the excuses (however thin) of youth, of stupidity, of ignorance. A betrayal fired purely by desire.

Still no sign of Sean's journal, but now I've too many other things on my mind to be bothered by it. The biggest deal—bigger even, for now, than Ludo—is that finally, after at least six postponements, three changes of interior designer, and no end of heartbreak, the new Bond Street shop has opened. The mechanics of it all were hardly my department, but it was going to be one of *my* shops, so I had an interest. And not just an interest but also, in a very small way, a responsibility.

When the team couldn't get the lighting quite right, I suggested they try Galatea Gisbourne. Her reputation had been restored by the excellent job she did putting right the mess she made of Milo's apartment. Her original mistake was not in slavishly following fashion but in following fashion too slowly. She saw the trend, latched onto it, but then took a year realizing her borrowed vision. By the time Milo revealed his pony-skin-everything apartment, pony skin had bolted. He tried to tough it out for a few weeks but then got Galatea back in with a refined you'll-never-snort-coke-in-this-town-again threat. This time, she worked fast, and two months later, the hair and raw leather had gone, to be replaced by floral fabrics and frilly lace. They'd got the style mags in quickly to shoot, and everyone was happy. The pic that appeared everywhere was of Milo and Galatea writhing naked under a mound of poppies, with the tag line "Beauty Is Back." Happy, that is, for a month at least, and by the time pretty was out again, and the poppies had wilted, nobody was looking.

Galatea's big concept for the lighting was to bathe the actual garments in "pools of darkness."

"The idea," she'd said, to the group of journos and scavengers around her last night at the launch party, "is to draw the eye in to that which is concealed, playing on the natural curiosity of the browser. Closer and closer they'll come, until, suddenly, they are, in a real sense, part of the clothes. And then they'll, er, buy them."

The shop certainly looked very different, and it worked well with seventy-odd people here, spread over the two big floors, drinking champagne and eating canapés. The in-house PR department had organized the party, so it wasn't exactly the A-list, but the right magazines were there, and Kylie Minogue, which is always nice. But the soap star had pulled out (after finding out about Kylie), and where, *exactly*, was Jude Law? Milo was boycotting out of pique and was dining instead with his odd little new boyfriend, Clarence. The Big Idea that the PR people had come up with was swans. They were everywhere. Stuffed ones. And ballerina types (except, perhaps, a touch wide in the waist and broad in the bust) dressed as swans, fluttering around, mutely, in lines. No one was quite sure whether this was tacky, and people kept looking from face to face to see if anyone was laughing yet. Milo would have known, but Milo wasn't there.

"There is here the genius of space," said Claude Malheurbe, a philosopher who wrote a regular column for *Air* (*it's what you breathe*) magazine. He'd recently become fashionable again himself with a book about his travels to war-torn regions, where he'd explain things to the victims of ethnic cleansing or state torture. The cover showed him adopting a crucified pose in front of a tank. He was an old friend of Galatea's and acted as an "ideas consultant" for several of the top architects and design companies, Gisbourne, Packet, and Straube among them. "Brilliantly," he continued, "we find that the light is on the irrelevant detail, the empty space, the blank wall, the fleck of dust, the vacuum. How often have I said that Nietzsche *abhors* the vacuum, eh? Ha-ha. Thus, we have shown that that which is irrelevant is vital and that which is thought to be of the essence is irrelevant."

One or two of the journalists made a stab at writing some of this down, but most had already moved on to find something more interesting to do—trying to get at Kylie, drinking, putting out their eyes with knitting needles.

I was with the shop manager, whom I'd known well for several years. She was French but spoke English so perfectly she could have been Danish. She dressed in that immaculately dull way that only the French can do, and it was exactly right for a shop manager. When you shop, you don't want to be outdone by the staff, but nor do you want to be fussed over by crusties. You want sharp, clean, efficient, invisible.

"What do you think, Julie?" I asked.

"About the party?"

"About the shop."

"Why, I think it is absurd. But I am a manageress and not a designer or a philosopher of space. We will see. I expect that we will get in some more lighting when the fuss is over. Are you enjoying the party?"

"Yes," I lied. "Seems to be fun." I was nervous. Ludo was supposed to be coming with Katie. I'd tried to talk Sean into staying at home. I even faked a couple of phone conversations with babysitters: "Oh, you can't make it? What a shame!" But for once, Astrid's liver was up to the job. I tried not to think of her giving Harry a good shake to shut him up so that she could get back to necking her Goth boyfriend.

However much he complains about them, Sean loves parties. He says it's because he doesn't see anyone all day and so has all this pent-up energy and talk. I think it's more to do with flirting, although *leching* might be a better word. I dressed him in a reasonably trendy FCUK outfit I'd bought, so he didn't show me up too badly, and then, as soon as we reached the shop, he went off to bother strangers. He *had* drunk four bottles of beer as we got ready, so, to use his words, he'd "hit the ground running." I could hear him laughing at his own jokes somewhere upstairs.

And then Ludo arrived. Followed by Katie, and then, curiously, a film crew. Or rather, a cameraman holding his own boom mike and a badly dressed redheaded dolly. They barged past Ludo and Katie in the doorway and yelled out "Channel BUY BUY BUY," as if that was supposed to mean anything to me. But then a couple of the PR people appeared smiling and led them away, accompanied by swans. I supposed that TV coverage was precious, even if it was some shitty shopping channel. Katie and I exchanged world-weary glances, and Ludo stuck out his hand, which I shook, laughing.

"Very formal, Ludo," said Katie. "Not kissing tonight?"

"Oh, if I must." Then he leaned over and kissed me on the cheek. I could feel from his soft bristles that he hadn't shaved today. As ever, he smelled of harsh soap, and I felt a spasm of desire that almost bent me double.

"Glad you could make it," I said at them both. "I was getting—" I just managed to stop myself from saying "bored" in front of Julie. "Let's go and find something to drink—that's if Sean's left anything. Is Penny coming?" Katie usually did the rounds for Penny Moss, but the great lady herself was still generally invited to this sort of thing, especially since becoming a dame, added to her professorship at the London College of Fashion.

"She threatened to. But she doesn't usually bother these days unless there's at least one other royal present: she likes having her own kind to talk to."

After a ten-minute gossip, Katie found herself dragged off by some media acquaintances. "Look after Ludo for me, will you," she cried over her shoulder.

Ludo was quiet for a moment, but he looked like he was going to say something, so I shut up.

"I missed you," he managed finally.

"I missed you, too. I thought you were going to call."

"I did."

I remembered the three empty messages on the answerphone. Bottles washed on the shore with nothing but blank paper inside them.

"I want to see you again," he said. He spoke quietly but with an extraordinary tension. He looked older than I remembered. Had he been sleeping? I thought not. I hadn't.

"When?"

"It's easy for me. I can do anytime. But for you, . . . it must be . . . harder." Trying not to mention Harry. Trying not to mention Sean.

"On Saturday, aren't you and the other boys coming round to watch football? I was going to go out. If you had to . . . cancel, we could see each other. Somewhere."

"I didn't want to go on Saturday. I like Sean. I didn't want to . . . I don't like doing this . . . to him."

"Cheer up, you two!" Katie had reappeared. She couldn't have heard anything. "You know, Ludo, you shouldn't come to these things if all you're going to do is drag my friends down into the pit of despond with you. I'm sorry, Celeste. But talking of troublesome spouses . . ."—then she stopped and blushed, remembering that she and Ludo were not married—". . . partners, whatever, I think you ought to go and rein in Sean. What is it with him and spunk?"

"What? Oh God!"

I found him upstairs. There was a gang of bemused fashion people and startled swans around him.

"Don't talk to me about sperm counts," he was saying. "I'm down to one now, but it's a fucking whopper, this big." He stretched out his arms. "Wriggles around on the floor like a bastard eel. Contraception for us means hitting the fucker with a tennis racket—*yah, yah, yah.*" An invisible racket was raised above his head and brought down savagely three times. "But that's nothing compared to what's happening with my cock. I mean, there it was when I was sixteen, straight up like *Apollo 11.* Then each year, it drops down a degree or two. By thirty, it was at forty-five degrees, and now it's like I'm firing just over the heads of the demonstrators, peeeoum peeeeoum. Another couple of years, and it'll be pointing backward through my legs. Oh, hello. What are you doing here?"

This last bit was aimed not at me, nor at any of the bemused listeners, but at the girl part of the film crew from BUY BUY BUY. The cameraman had caught most of his monologue.

"I'm working, stupid. At least I get paid for looking like a fool."

How did he know her? He didn't know anybody.

"Oh, Celeste," he said, finally noticing me. "Um, this is one of the other mums from the Freudian playgroup. Uma. Uma Thursday. And um, Uma, this is Celeste, my, er, wife."

"Your what, sorry?" She said this looking me up and down, like I was some tramp trying to steal her man. Some more swans waded by, interrupting things for a couple of seconds. One smirked at me.

"Wife."

"Wife? Oh, hi."

And then she and her cameraman were away, drawing with them most of the members of Sean's group and a flotilla of swans.

"You've never mentioned her," I said sweetly, still watching the departing Uma.

"Oh, you know, she's, like I said, just one of the mothers from the playgroup. She lives up the, er . . . and we sometimes walk back a bit. Just down the road awhile. I knew she was in TV, but I thought she just did crap bits for some shopping channel."

I gave him a look. I tried to fill it with disdain and hauteur, but without giving the impression that I'd read any of his stupid journal.

"Oh."

"Is Ludo here yet?" he asked, pathetically changing the subject.

"Downstairs with Katie."

"Thank Christ. Someone normal to talk to."

"Coming from a man who's just spent half an hour describing his sperm and various sexual failings, I hardly think 'normal' counts as a compliment." But he was already clumping unsteadily down the dark polished wood of the stairs.

So, that was the famous Uma Thursday. What did I make of her? It seems appropriate that we start with fashion. She was wearing an overfussy top—a cheap high street take on the boho look—and a fla-

menco tiered skirt and high black boots. Fringing, beading, a heavy,
low-slung belt. It took me a few seconds to work out exactly what was
going on. Yes, that was it. She was someone who really didn't give a
fuck about fashion, but she knew that other people cared, and so
she'd made herself plow through the magazines, checked out what
the look was, and then set out to re-create it as cheaply as possible, in
the course of a single stroll down Oxford Street. The sort of thing, in
fact, that teenage girls do every weekend. But because Uma didn't really give a fuck, everything was just a little wrong. The boots were too
low and the skirt too high; the top was trying its hardest, but its origins in a Chinese sweatshop were showing. Contrary to what you
might think, I don't really judge people by what they wear. It's just
that everyone I know spends time and money on getting the look, and
that's the language we speak. Uma Thursday spoke a different language, and it took some understanding.

And the rest of her? Sean was right about the hair. It was thick
and lustrous, just at the place where strawberry blond becomes red.
But she hadn't done much with it: it was just *there,* like one of those
big rocks you sometimes see out of a car window, left without purpose in the countryside. Her face was pretty enough as long as it remained in motion, and that it did, because Uma Thursday was forever
throwing faces: a smile, a smirk, a frown, a look of quizzical disbelief.
Her neck was on the short side, so she tended to swivel her whole body
when she spoke. Her fingers were short, and her nails, uncared for. In
summary, she was the kind of woman that other women don't quite
get—physically, I mean. She had nothing (other than that lustrous
hair) that other women covet—the perfect features, the flawless skin,
the attenuated figure. And yet. And yet. What was the word that Sean
had used? *Stunner.* That was it. Somehow, despite the flaws and the
carelessness, Uma Thursday was a stunner.

I felt it like the dull ache of a period. But then I sniffed and made
the decision not to let Uma Thursday's attractiveness ruin my night.

Luckily, just then Galatea tipped me the wink, and we halved a
slender line on the bench in the changing rooms. After that, I forgot

about Sean and his woman, and even, for a time, Ludo, as the party swirled around me. I think I was the first to decide that the swans were, officially, funny. A senior executive from the company, an American who cunningly disguised his heterosexuality with good clothes and pampered skin, continued his two-year attempt at seduction. I'd reached the point where I was prepared to smile when he touched my shoulder, and at this rate, he might eventually get to grope me if he could inch his walker close enough to my bath chair.

Julie came and rescued me.

"Why is it," I asked her, "that I don't ever find Americans sexy?"

"Because they are not," she replied simply.

"Oh yes."

And then Claude Malheurbe joined us. He was dressed in Jean Paul Gautier leathers at least a size too small for him. He did a sort of snarl at Julie, and she walked away.

"Apart from swans, you are the most beautiful animal here," he said, very close. "But then you English eat swans, is it not so?"

"Only the queen."

"I shall explain the meaning of swans."

"Please do."

"Above, they are white and serene. But below the water, their legs are black and in frantic motion. This legs is the subconscious, the invisible black force that makes the swan happen. The legs are your sexualitay. Are your legs black? Do they work like this, push push push?"

Before I had the chance to answer, his face collapsed in horror, and he made a kind of whimpering noise. I looked around and saw Ludo striding toward me. When I looked back, Malheurbe had gone.

"Do you always have that effect on philosophers?"

Ludo smiled. "I had a run-in with him a couple of years ago."

"That was him? Oh, I heard something about that. Didn't he sleep with Katie?"

"Probably. No, not really. I think he tried to, but she gave him the brush-off."

"Not like her. Sorry." I laughed and covered my mouth with my hand.

"I've told Sean I can't make Saturday."

"Good."

"What shall we do?"

"What about the bar at The Hempel?"

"The Hempel. But isn't that a hotel? Why . . . Oh."

I don't know why, but I panicked, lost my cool.

"No no no, it's a bar as well. It's really quiet and calming. Just a bar. People can go there just to drink. And talk."

I saw Sean and Katie coming up the stairs together. Ludo saw my eyes and said quickly, "Eight o'clock?"

"Perfect. You know if I didn't have such a high opinion of your taste, Katie, I'd say something was going on between you and my husband."

That made everyone laugh.

SEANJOURNALTHIRTEEN.DOC

OLD GODS AND ANCIENT RITES

Had a surprisingly agreeable time at Celeste's big do on Thursday night. I think I was on pretty good form, and I wheeled out one or two of my best routines. Always nice having a new audience. Plus I've never had a bad time at a party where girls were dressed as swans—it's become a kind of talisman with me. Of course, it helped having a couple of friendly faces there: good old Ludo turned up, and Katie. I like Katie. She doesn't have to flirt with me, and I know that she doesn't fancy me, but she goes through the motions anyway out of sheer generosity of spirit. Ludo looked a bit glum, but he's even worse at those fashion things than I am. I told him straight, "Just look around you, Ludie, there's all the champagne you can drink, plus some weird blue cocktail and high-quality nibbles and girls dressed as swans and Kylie Minogue's panties, and it's *all* free. So cheer up, you miserable fucker." He just did a sort of turny-down smile—more a grimace, really—and went back to looking moody.

Celeste then wasted a lot of what I am sure was valuable networking time talking to him. I sometimes forget about Celeste's nice side, which she does a lot to disguise but which is definitely there. She did look a bit tense, but it was a big night for her. Fashion's an odd world. It seems to run on the opposite of the dictum that whatever doesn't kill you makes you stronger—that is, that whatever doesn't make you stronger kills you. My point was that there's no standing still, no simple acceptance that what you have is good, that things are really all right. No, everything has to be changed, and changed now.

Well, what did you expect? That's why it's called fashion, *stupid*.

Shame Ludo couldn't get to our pizza-and-football night on Saturday, but Leo and Andy made it. As usual, we largely ignored the game, spinning back to the set whenever something dramatic happened, which wasn't often. Part of the fun had always been when Ludo and Leo, private schoolboys both, fucked up some bit of footie terminology, talking about the *post* when they meant the *bar* or confusing a fullback with the center half. That would elicit coruscating forays by me and Andy against all things elitist, effete, and southern, with counterattacking claims from Ludo and Leo that we were either a couple of gormless northern thugs or—and they were quite content with the contradiction—that we had now been assimilated as southern, middle-class poofs ourselves and should therefore fuck right off.

Without Ludo, we didn't bother going down that path. Instead, Leo had an announcement, made through a mouthful of pepperoni: "Ogeck id pignut."

Andrew was first to react, a huge smile creeping across his face: "Did you say what I thought you said?"

Leo swallowed. "I said, 'Ogeck id pignut.' "

"That's what I thought you said. Fucking well done, you mad bastard. How is she?"

"Bit shocked, but pleased as punch."

There was much backslapping, and I ran down to Thresher's to get a bottle of whatever shit champagne they had in the cooler. We drank it splashed onto the dregs in our beer glasses.

"You're in for some several years of hell, you know," I said.

"Yeah, I've heard you moaning about it enough to know that it's tough. But you were fool enough to volunteer to do the mothering. Odette's mad keen on all that. She's read all the books, watched the videos, tested her recipes for mushed-up carrots and peas. We're ready."

"Ready for two hours' sleep a night?"

"You forget, I'm a tortured intellectual. I haven't had two hours' sleep a night since I was twelve."

"It'll be great," said Andy. "A little Leo. Or Leonia. Or Leonella, or whatever you'll call it."

Right on cue, Harry appeared. That shouldn't have been possible. He must have pole-vaulted out of his cot using his toy giraffe.

"Milk," he said, and then, looking forlornly around, "Mommy." His blond hair was sticking up in all directions, and his Lion King pajama top had rucked up, revealing his potbelly. He looked like he had a gallon of piss in his diaper.

"Hey, little man, Mommy's gone out. Come cuddle Daddy."

"Want Mommy."

"See what I mean?" I said to Leo. "All that work I put in, and he still hates me."

He started to cry. (Harry, not Leo.) I made him some milk and changed his diaper in front of the TV, while Leo looked on, fascinated. Andrew was scared stiff of Harry and watched the game with a new intensity. After ten minutes of cuddling, I put the boy back to bed. I saw that the side of the cot was down—that was how he'd escaped. Celeste must have bent to kiss before she left and forgot to slide it back up. Naughty girl.

"I don't want you getting the idea that it's always that easy, Leo," I said, back on the sofa.

"Yeah, yeah," he replied, handling the wet diaper. "This thing's as heavy as a medicine ball." He threw it at Andrew, who rolled off the chair to avoid touching it.

After a while, I got onto the subject of Uma Thursday. I found that that was happening a lot lately. Somehow it was easier without having Ludo there. He was such a heavy moral presence, it would have been like discussing your penchant for water sports with Kofi Annan. I got into it by bringing up Uma's surprise appearance at Celeste's party.

"She's got a new job. They have an entertainment-roundup-cum-celebrity-gossip slot, and she fills it."

"Pretty glam," said Leo sarcastically.

"About as glam as my *Woman's Hour* performances."

"I like those," said Andrew. "You can download them from the BBC website. I told Alice about it, and now you're big in Mauritius. Do you get hate mail?"

"Not much from Mauritius, but they're a gentle people, slow to wrath."

"We're straying," said Leo. "You obviously have a deep psychological need to talk about this woman, but you say that all you do is walk home with her for twenty minutes on Mondays and then spend the rest of the week fantasizing about it."

"Not *just* that. She's been round to the apartment."

"With the contraceptive kids," said Andrew.

"But my point is," said Leo, "that we still don't know if you want anything more than . . . whatever it is you have at the moment."

"I don't have anything at the moment. That's the problem. I don't mean to come on all . . . *feminine*, but my life sucks. I don't show it, because, well, whenever I see you lot, and Ludo, I sort of cheer up. It's like that joke about the Irishman who tried to commit suicide by taking an overdose of tranquilizers but then felt better after the first one and . . . Well, you get it. When it's just me, or just me and Harry, I'm down—I mean, *really* down. And it seems sometimes that all I ever do is wheel Harry around in the rain and cook dinners for Celeste she doesn't want."

"And you think that Uma will somehow make it *better*? That's crazy talk," said Leo. "Do you have any idea what you want from her, with her?"

"I have an idea," said Andrew.

I ignored him. "Look, I think that what I want is to have a really deep flirtation, the sort where everything you say is charged up, and you feel your whole body alive and tingling, ready to spring, ready for anything. I want that feeling of anxiety and dread and exultation. But I don't ever actually want to spring. I want to pull back from the edge, once I've felt the vertigo."

"But where do you draw the line?" asked Leo. "These are dangerous territories. Bad things can happen here."

"Yeah," joined in Andrew. "I mean, is necking this side or the other side?"

"Oh, necking," I said, "is definitely on the other side. I mean, it's the first bit of the other side. Everything short of necking is on this side."

Andrew: "What does that leave you?"

Me: "The bit I most want is the moment just *before* the neck, when you begin to move imperceptibly toward each other, and your eyes begin to close and your mouth open. And you don't even have to be touching, you could be feet apart."

Andrew: "And then what?"

Me: "And then what, what?"

Leo: "What do you do after this pre-kiss bit, if you don't kiss?"

Me: "Just that—you don't kiss."

Andrew: "So you leave her sort of dangling there, while you change the subject to football or diapers?"

Me: "If necessary."

Leo: "Is groping on this side?"

Me: "What do you mean by groping?"

Leo: "Touching the breasts, in a nonaccidental, pleasure-oriented way."

Me: "Well, I'd say that touching the breasts outside her jumper or blouse or whatever she's wearing, that would be this side, and touching a bare breast, particularly if it involved an erotic tweaking of the nipple, would be on the other."

Andrew, laughing: "Bullshit! A grope's better—I mean, worse—than a snog any day. Inside or outside, nipple tweaked or un-tweaked. Anyway, I'm not sure that tweaking, the tweaking of *anything*, can *ever* be erotic."

Leo: "I think I'd have to concur with my learned colleague. In the view of the court, a grope is on the other side, one step *further* back, if anything, than necking."

Me: "Okay, okay, so I was trying to pull a fast one. I don't really need the groping. I'm happy with the intense flirting, the pre-kiss, and a general air of tragedy. *Brief Encounter* kind of thing, but with fewer hats and advanced twenty-first-century deodorants. Can we agree that all of that is okay?"

We'd been joking around, but now Leo made a conscious effort to be more serious.

"I'm making a conscious effort to be more serious now," he said, "but how many of us can ever draw back from that prekiss bit? I know exactly what you mean about it: it's magical. But no one ever stops there. It's like what we always say about drinking. You have the first three or four, and everything's wonderful. If only you could switch to tonic water or—"

"Low-calorie lemonade and Angostura's bitters is surprisingly nice," said Andrew.

"Shut up, Andrew. But we never do, because we're intoxicated and we can't make proper judgments. You'll be the same with Uma, assuming the whole thing isn't some huge misunderstanding—"

"I've thought about that, and it's possible. I could be wrong. Maybe she wants a friend or just someone to pass the time with. Could be, could be. But the balance of probabilities dips down slightly on the side of her wanting to make the beast."

"Okay, we'll trust your judgment on that, but don't think that your pathetic attempt at realism there will get you out of the shit with us if it turns out that she loves you for your mind alone. What was I saying? Uma, pre-kiss, kiss. Yeah, if you do ever get into range, and she gives you the come-hither, then you're gonna grip and grapple, and that's all there is to it. Your body will speak the ancient language, the old gods will fire you, the ancient rites—"

"Enough with the old gods and ancient rites, you prize ass. You forget I've got the counterbalance. Harry, Celeste. I love them."

Leo looked at me curiously; Andrew laughed.

At about one o'clock, I told them about Mumford and Chris Rushby. They understood enough not to try to play it down or attribute it simply to the way boys are. They knew that betrayal counts against you. Andrew said that being good at sport had saved him from the animals at his school. Leo didn't want to talk about his experiences. Reading between the lines, I guessed that he, with his twisted back and strange, sad, long face, might have been a kind of Mumford.

We drank till two. The rule was that we'd carry on until Celeste got in (she always went out for our irregular football evenings, and I can't blame her; indeed, thank her), and that usually meant around eleven, twelve if we were lucky, but that night she was late. I didn't worry. She'd said her mother, Nosferata, Queen of the Undead, was up in town, so they'd probably be out slaying children till dawn. So the boys stayed until the beer and champagne had run dry.

"Did we win?" said Andrew, turning as they were going out the door.

"As ever," I said, putting my arm around his shoulders, "football was the winner."

"Milo?"

"Who's that?"

"Celeste."

"Please be quick, darling, I've put Jude Law on hold."

"The Hempel. You said you could get me a rate?"

Yes, I'd been thinking about it and nothing else. And now here I was.

"Naughty girl! Tell me all about it."

"I thought you had Jude Law on hold?"

"He can wait."

In the end, it wasn't such a great deal, but he guaranteed me, us, a good room. I had a matter-of-fact cell phone conversation with Ludo. Where and when. He sounded subdued, almost defeated.

After that, I needed some cheering up, so I arranged a lunch with Stephanie Phylum-Crater. She's back in town after her Hollywood debacle. Can't call it a debacle to her face, but that's what it amounts to. And she'd gone with such high hopes, after her low-budget Britflick triumphs. Personally I think her mistake was to throw all her energies into finding the right celebrity partner rather than the right script. In the end, the list of stars she hadn't dated (that is, screwed) was very much shorter than the roll call of her (admittedly brief) conquests. Richard Gere was forced to take out an ad in *Variety* to deny that they were an item and then a week later another to deny that he had turned her down. She stalked Kevin Costner (yes, she was *that* desperate) and falsely claimed on a talk show that Kenneth Branagh had exposed himself to her in his Jacuzzi.

The bestiality film may have got her some tabloid attention, but it was never going to rake in the Oscars. She was generally perceived to have let nobody down as an alien in the last series of the *X-Files*, but whatever good that might have done her was undermined by the claim by David Duchovny that she had cured him of his sex addiction.

Well, now she was home. We'd been to school together, and so there was no need for politeness or preliminaries. We were having a salad in the bar of my health club. Steph was fond of it because it had a big window onto the gym, and she liked to see who was there. She was going for a just-out-of-rehab look, but she was a little plump to pull it off. In fact, she looked in prime health, and I suspected that the rehab stories were another failed publicity gambit.

"Branagh?"

"Look, Celeste, he was in the Jacuzzi, but I may have associated his face with someone else's thing. Easy mistake to make. It was distinctive, though, more like a piggy-wig's tail than your normal cock." She made a little corkscrewing motion with her index finger. "And how's lovely Sean?"

I hadn't told her about the developments.

"Fine. I think I might be having an affair."

"Oh, good. I was dreading having to spend lunch talking about Hollywood or how much better it is doing fringe theater over a pub in Brixton."

"Can we do that briefly?"

"Hollywood splendid; pub theater poor, bordering on the fucking awful."

"Oh, sorry. Nothing else happening?"

"I've got an audition for a Teletubby. Don't laugh."

"Which one?"

"The red one."

"Oh, Po."

"I said, don't laugh."

"At least you're not Tinky Winky."

"Small mercies. So who's your affair with?"

"It's not really an affair yet. Not until tomorrow. Ludo Moss."

"Do I know him?"

"Big, quiet fellow. Often sulking in a corner during parties. Lives with Katie Castle."

"Katie Castle? Of course, Penny Moss, Ludo Moss. Fashion. I've bought their clothes. Good for weddings. So they're not married?"

"She acts as if they are, but no."

"That's something."

"Something."

"But *you* are."

"What?"

"Married."

"Well-spotted, but then, of course, you *were* a bridesmaid."

"God, I remember it well. I think that Portaloo thing you hired was the most disgusting place I've ever had sex."

"I think mine's Detroit."

"Yuck. Remind me again why you're having this affair, or going to have it, or whatever you're doing."

I told her all about it.

"I'm still not clear," she said. "Are you seeing Ludo because you think Sean's been screwing this Uma whatsit, or would you be seeing him anyway?"

"You can never know, can you? I mean, the thing is, we only have one life at a time, and you can't conduct experiments to find out."

"That's profound."

"Not for nothing was I head girl."

"Is that a double negative?"

"No."

"Not for nothing was I not. Oh dear, is *that?* Don't answer. But to-morrow's the big night?"

"Could be; should be."

"I don't mean to come across all moral, but what about little . . . thingy."

"Harry. Don't think I haven't thought about it. I wouldn't do anything to harm him. I mean, I don't want to leave Sean or anything. It's just that I want to have sex with Ludo. That can't be wrong, can it?"

It was seeing Steph that made me talk that way, made me think that way. She was as unshockable as a brothel keeper. In fact, I was deeply troubled by it all, and the only way I could face the moral issues was by not facing them.

After a while, we got on to interiors. The builders were due to start in a week, and I still hadn't settled on colors, beyond narrowing the spectrum down to the range from taupe to kittiwake gray. And the kitchen was a nightmare. Everyone else we knew had either lime-stone or limestone-colored composite surfaces, but Sean had, extraor-dinarily for him (given that he's taken no interest at all in the project up to now), put down his foot.

"It's soluble," he'd said.

"What?"

"It's water-fucking-soluble, this stuff." He was fingering a test square of the composite. "I spoke to the suppliers. They don't recom-mend it for work surfaces. It stains. And then it dissolves. We're not having it."

"But Seema and Charles have got it. And Sally and Julian. And Nicky and Finn."

I was aware that I was sounding whiny and pathetic, which was normally his job. But I knew what he was going to say next, and I had no counter.

"Look, if you want to start cooking, then you can have whatever surface you want. In a year, it'll be a dirty puddle of sludge, and try slicing your tomatoes on *that*, but if you want me to carry on cooking, then I'm having something that retains its molecular structure when introduced to water."

"You're such a pig," I said, but it was no use. So it had to be black granite. Luckily I found a plain one, so the surface wouldn't look too much like a war memorial. But still. Pig.

"Shame about the limestone," said Steph. "Are you Viking everything?"

"Of course."

"Floor?"

"American black walnut."

"Very nice. But you know it's—"

"If you're about to say on its way out, stop now, because it's too late."

"Fine. Oh, look! Unless I'm mistaken—and she's *your* friend, not mine—isn't that Katie Castle through there, on the crosstrainer?"

I looked round through the big, tinted plate glass window to the rows of exercise machines. And yes, there was Katie in a sweatband. She was obviously letting herself go, because rather than the tight Lycra I'd have expected, she was dressed in loose pants and a baggy top. Her face was bright red, and I imagined, but could not see, the drops of sweat falling from her brow, like a blocked gutter in the rain. Just then, she caught my eye, smiled, and waved. I waved back. Stephanie put a whole cherry tomato into her mouth and popped it, thoughtfully.

I was exactly on time at The Hempel. I despise women who are always late for dates, following some stupid rule they've read in a magazine. But then I always walk out if whoever I'm meeting is more than fifteen minutes late. You only have to do that once, and then they learn.

I walked down the stairs from the ersatz Zen lobby, about as convincing, with its little flames and empty spaces, as a Bangkok Rolex. Ludo was already there, standing in no-man's-land between the tables and the bar. How long had he been stranded there, not knowing where to go, how to *be*? He was wearing chinos and a dark jacket. As usual, he looked as if he could flex and rip the fabric to shreds. He seemed more relieved than anything to see me arrive, his stretcher bearer. He took my hands in his and kissed me.

"You look beautiful," he said. I'd certainly tried: I was wearing a midnight blue top in silk georgette that fell casually off one shoulder (the right, my best), and a turquoise-and-silver choker and the shortest skirt I owned.

"So do you," I said, and he guffawed, but handsomely.

We took our drinks to a corner.

"This is quite some place," he said.

"But not your sort of place?"

"I don't know what my sort of place is. I thought I knew once, but not anymore."

"What do you mean?"

"Well, I once thought that my place was on an island. I always thought that I hated London, and . . . things happened, and I took a conservation job. But, well, although it was beautiful, and despite the fact that I had a sense of purpose, I was lonely. It was a blow, in a way, to my self-esteem. I wasn't who I thought I was. I thought I was rugged and independent. I thought I carried everything I needed within myself. But I was wrong. It turned out I was just a city boy."

"I'm glad."

"So am I, I suppose."

We talked for a while. It was okay. Nothing important was said, but it was more than just inane chitchat. We ate a plate of noodles and some wonton from the bar: not a real meal but enough to keep hunger in the background, out of the way. Eventually we got round to it.

"You booked the room."

It could have been a question or a statement.

"You know I did. Do you want to . . . see it?"

He hesitated for a second; less than a second.

"Yes."

We took the tiny elevator. The room itself was not exactly enormous, but that's not what you go to The Hempel for. There was a bottle of champagne. Ludo went to the bathroom. I read the card.

Enjoy yourself,

Love,
Milo

I put it in my pocket and poured two glasses.

"Champagne?" said Ludo. "It wasn't you, was it? I should have . . . arranged, or . . . something."

"It just comes with the room," I said. I knew he wouldn't like the idea of Milo's intruding in this way.

We sat on the side of the bed. Ludo didn't have his jacket on anymore. My shoulders were bare. I shivered. He put his arm around me. And then I started to cry. It wasn't what I expected at all.

"I'm sorry," I said. "I'm sorry, I'm sorry."

I was thinking about Sean and about Harry, but also about Ludo.

"Don't be sorry," he said, stroking my hair. "You haven't done anything. You don't have to do anything. It's all right, it's all right. We won't do anything."

But then I moved my hand. I brushed against the front of his chinos. I looked down. I could see that he had an erection. He looked down as well and said, "Sorry," and laughed.

The very callousness of his arousal while I was weeping changed something within me. I knew that he was a good and a kind man, but his body was beyond morality, and it *craved*. I could feel the slow breaths, the gentle heaving of my sobs quicken. Tears still came to my eyes, but now my heart was beating more urgently. My hand stayed on his crotch. I felt and cupped his cock. I worked my hand down the top of his trousers and pulled the end, thick and blunt, clear of his waistband. But it was too tight for me to get a proper hold, so I undid his belt and unbuttoned him. I didn't want to kiss him or to look at his face. I slid off the bed and knelt between his legs, and then took his cock in my mouth. It felt like I had to stretch my mouth to fit it. I drew around him, down the shaft until I felt that I might gag. I could hear his breath, harsh and ragged. Still with his cock in my mouth, I pulled and pushed his pants down. There was no finesse here, none of the tricks that we learn, the fluttering, the teasing: this was simply a matter of getting as much of him inside my mouth as I could, gorging myself.

"Come up," he gasped. "You don't need to do this. I want . . . your face here. Kiss me."

He was shaking now, and I sensed that he would soon come. I didn't want that, yet, and so I drew the length of him from my mouth and pushed him onto the bed and kissed him. We kissed and pulled ourselves out of our clothes. I was wearing stockings, and when he tried to take them off, I told him to leave them. He wanted to go down on me, but again, I told him "no." I pushed him down and sat across him, feeling his cock slide between my legs. My lips were parted, and I nestled him in the groove and slowly drew myself backward and forward. At the end of each pass, he brushed my clitoris, and I felt it swell in response, filling with blood, filling with the hardness it caught from him. Again, I felt that he was going to come, was reaching the point where he could never hold back. It had to be now. I reached down between us, took him between my finger and thumb, and put his tip between my lips. Almost for the first time, I looked at his face. His eyes were shut; his mouth was agape, but tight and tense as his cock. I knew that he was coming, that already his balls were beginning to pump, that his cum would be surging on its way, that no force on earth could now stop it, and I sat back on him, thrusting him deep within me. He groaned and made inchoate animal noises, and I felt his cock pulse, felt the ridges and veins thrum with energy. Of course, you can't feel the spurt of cum itself, but I sensed immediately the relaxing of tension, felt his cock lose its iron heart, begin its slow retreat. Now again I had to be quick. I changed my position, forcing my clitoris against his pubic bone. He opened his eyes. There was pain there. But I wasn't going to stop. I ground myself into him, beating my clitoris against the hard bone. He moaned again, and I moaned with him. I kissed him, bit his lips, bit his tongue.

"Help me," I said, and he took my buttocks in his big hands, his rough hands, and pulled me yet more violently onto himself, working and grinding with me. It was a desperate race. I could feel him slipping from me. His face was anguished, and he groaned now in real pain. And then, just as the soft mass of him fell from me, my back arched and I came.

I looked down at his face. It was smeared with blood from his lips and tongue. And then I looked between us at the bed. There was blood everywhere, thick, viscous clots. On the sheets, on his thighs, on his stomach. For a second, I thought our fuck and the power of my orgasm had burst some internal organ, that I was going to die from sex, here, on this bed. And then with a laugh, a horrible, croaking laugh, I realized it was my period.

"Oops," I said.

SEANJOURNALFOURTEEN.DOC

THE ONTOLOGICAL ARGUMENT TO THE RESCUE

I've been dreading this ever since we first moved in here. The apartment was big but needed things done to it. The "galley" (think slave rather than luxury yacht) kitchen was designed for some strange race of impossibly tall, impossibly thin beings. Opening any cupboard door would inevitably mean disabling some crucial part of the kitchen, and squeezing two people in there was only possible if they were having sex or fighting. There were places, hidden places, where years of fluff and sticky matter had accumulated, and reaching for a glass or plate or soup pot meant coming away with a smear of black, oily something-or-other on your forearm.

In the rest of the apartment, there were too many little rooms, and even I could see that brown hessian *stuff* that covered the walls was not, in any sense in contemporary or historical usage, *good*. (Is brown hessian *stuff* the same thing as brown hessian? What is hessian? Why do I think that the stuff is brown hessian stuff? Have I somehow absorbed some home-improvement/style-type information from Celeste's pile of magazines, even though I only ever flicked through them once to see if there was a problem page or bra adverts or anything about computers?)

This—the grunge, the crud, the cupboards, the hessian—wasn't why we'd moved, and so I knew that things would have to be done; I knew that walls would be torn down, that kitchens would translocate.

If that had been all that was going to happen, then my heart would not have been so heavy. But it wasn't all. It soon became clear even to me that we, I, couldn't cohabit with the destruction. The choice was stark: find rented accommodation or move in with Celeste's parents, who lived outside London in the quaint little commuter town of Amersham.

Looking at rental, the sums just didn't stack up. Every penny we had was being plowed into the refurb. Staying at Celeste's parents' would, at least, keep us solvent. And only a train ride away from civilization.

And now the time had come.

We began moving things that we'd need on Sunday. I was a bit hungover after the late night of football. I woke up to find myself alone. Padding around the apartment, I finally found Celeste in the spare room, asleep. I brought her in some fresh coffee.

"You must have come in late," I said, rumpling her hair.

"Yes. I didn't want to wake you, so I slept in here. You don't mind?"

"No, it was sweet of you."

Packing's always a melancholy business. Throwing stuff away even more so. Everything we had was going to have to be stored away in the back three rooms: our bedroom, Harry's, and Celeste's dressing room. That meant that the clutter of our lives, the stuff that our lives were *made of*, had to go. I took three boxes of books to a charity shop. Good-bye the fruits of my attempt to find a decent work of science fiction, and farewell also the naval adventure stories that had kept me company since I was a teenager. Old shoes, coats of yesteryear, baggy shorts, buttonless shirts, all went the same way.

Harry toddled around, taking things out of boxes, putting things in boxes, putting boxes in boxes, putting himself in boxes. He cried savagely when he realized that some of his toys were being designated for community recyclement. Broken action figures and plastic crap from Happy Meals were fought over like sections of trench at the battle of the Somme. In the end, I had to take him out so that Celeste could complete her work of necessary destruction.

I decided to go swimming. Harry didn't like swimming: it involved getting wet, and that always made him cry. But he could be bribed into it with the promise of an Ed's Easy Diner malt milk shake—and no, not the kids' one, but a full-size daddy version, bucket-big, thick as hot cheese. He was still sobbing when I got him into the elevator. It was warm, so he had on only a little blue jacket and some shapeless pants. Now that he's more or less potty-trained, his little bottom seems so sleek in his pants, without the ballooning mass of diaper giving him Hottentot buttocks.

"Helmet on," I said, waving his newish Pooh-stenciled protective headgear before him. We'd been cycling around as our preferred method of locomotion for about a month. It scared us all, but it was fast and cheap and gave me the thighs of a Titan.

It was also, however, the cause of my greatest-ever embarrassment, an embarrassment that towers above all the others in a life rich in humiliation. You have to bear in mind the fact that, from the front, shielded by my frantically pedaling form, Harry was invisible, and so I'd often get odd looks from pedestrians who thought I was a nutter, talking to myself loudly about wees and poos, about chicken nuggets, about Tinky Winky, Dipsy, Laa-Laa, and Po. Well, one day I was cycling along the Finchley Road—always a hairraising thing to do, because of the thundering traffic, and all the more so with Harry wriggling and squirming behind me like an unfastened maggot. I put a hand back, blindly, to make sure he hadn't unhooked his straps, and he decided it might be fun to grab it.

"Monkey! Monkey!" I screamed, in a jokey way, at the top of my voice. "Monkey! Monkey!" I added, to drive home the point that he was a being a monkey.

And then I saw where we were. Right on the Finchley Road, there is a Baptist chapel. At just this time on a Sunday morning, the respectable matriarchs and patriarchs of the local Caribbean community emerge from their worship. And there they were, in their smart suits and bright dresses and big hats, the children well behaved and as neat as their elders. A spectacle to make you glad that there was still decency and respect in the world. If they were to start building a barn, you'd want to go and help them, bringing water for the menfolk, laughing with the women doing the baking.

And here I was, some punk, some godless hooligan, riding by, screaming "monkey monkey monkey monkey" at the top of my lungs. I managed to catch the look of forbearance on the face of one old gentleman, a man who'd spent, I imagined—oh, how I imagined—his life serving his country, his community; taking care of his family, seeing that his children were brought up the right way; taking on his once broad back the lashes of a society that had summoned and then spurned him. Well, he had seen the promised land, but no, he wouldn't be making it, not now, not when this could still happen, right here in front of his own church.

I should have gone back and explained. Instead, I found my now familiar place on the kitchen wall and pressed my head against it for one full episode of *Sesame Street*.

Where was I? Swimming. His helmet. The helmet was still way too big for him, and I put one of his bobbleless bobble hats underneath it to help the fit.

"Now Daddy first," he said.

My helmet was considerably less cool than his. There was no mirror in the bike shop, and I had picked the cheapest they had in stock. It was an inoffensive gray, but the mirror at home showed it to have an extraordinarily high dome, which made me look like the passenger in a 1950s motorcycle sidecar. But Harry would only wear his if I wore mine.

We emerged out of the elevator at the bottom, and the crazy woman who lives on the ground floor was there, as she usually was, smoking in her dressing gown. She had the biggest hair of any human I'd ever seen. I pointed to my ludicrously well protected head and then at the elevator and said, "Can't be too careful." She fled and slammed her heavy door behind her.

I strapped Harry into his seat. He had gone from despair to placid neutrality, comforted by forcing his daddy into the Helmet of Shame.

"Shake," he said, or possibly, "Sheikh."

"Swim first."

"Milk shake."

"Swim first. Then milk shake."

He nodded decisively.

"Then milk shake okay."

And then we were trundling down West End Lane, swerving around recumbent buses and lazing cars. I felt behind me with one hand to make sure he was really there. I felt a face, soft mouth, brushing lashes, little ears.

"Ow ow."

"Sorry."

I knew if I looked deeply enough in my pockets, I'd find some honey-coated peanuts. Fluff-coated honey-coated peanuts, that is. It's one of those truths. You know, the universal ones. If you ever eat peanuts (any of the kinds: plain, dry-roasted, fancy-coated), and you empty them in your pocket (either for ease of access while cycling or because you're at a party and you think you might need some for later), then no matter how many times you think you've eaten the last of them (and this may stretch over weeks or months), there'll always be a couple more, if only you dig deep enough.

And so there were. I passed them back, trying first to find his mouth, and then, when I hit only helmet and ear, his hand. If you've ever seen courting white-tailed sea eagles pass carrion from talon to talon in midflight, you can imagine the procedure. Not that I have—Ludo told me all about it.

We parked in the bike rack and took the escalator up to the first-floor level of the local mall. It was built a couple of years ago and has some kind of rain forest theme going on, which means the world's biggest fake plants, and fish tanks full of sad-looking tropical fish, and everywhere an eerie recorded birdsong, like the keening of lost souls. I don't know if it was part of the original plan or just some kind of indictment of modern society, but apart from the sports center, a discount bookshop, and the supermarket, the place has nothing but fast-food outlets.

I hated being a member of the private health club. It seemed to me that it meant that I had become one of *Us,* one of the ones who didn't want to have to be in the same water or even breathe the same air as the grim moving mass of humanity. I'd always prided myself on retaining my *Themness,* my place among the toilers and the strugglers, my face pressed against the glass, looking in. But the council was closing down the local public pool, and my sciatica needed its thrice-weekly aquatic workout. Plus Harry and the touted benefits of swimming for toddlers. We actually felt quite guilty about not taking him as a baby, and he was sure to be weak and mentally retarded as a result.

The sports center changing rooms were certainly warmer than the stinking clammy chill of the municipal pool, and you didn't have the constant sensation of verruca viruses, fungal spores, and bilharzia worms trying to bore their way into your feet. And the pool did have a slightly lower piss-to-water ratio, although that in turn was counterbalanced by the fact that it was often coated by an oily slick of makeup from the posh women who sidestroked tortuously back and forth and who clearly felt themselves too perfect to require a pre-swim shower.

Harry played hide-and-seek in the lockers as I got myself suited up. There were usually a few dads with kids on a Sunday, doing their duty. I'd noticed that the men with kids were always loose-fleshed, pasty, spindly of leg, contrasting with the taut and muscled forms of the preening, childless figures around them. Their genitals seemed oddly shrunken and formless, as though reduced now to the purely excretory part of their earlier dual functionality. I couldn't help but look at myself in the mirror. I was in transition. I was becoming one of the dough boys, one of the old men at the pool.

I don't think that I'm a vain man, but this slow dissipation was cruel and sad, and it pierced me. Perhaps even worse was the loss of elegance. I'd noticed that my movements now were coarse and angular, where once they had been fluid and sinewy. When I ran for a bus, the former harmony of levers and pistons had deteriorated into a random flapping, like a shot crow. I sometimes felt as though all my bones had been removed and replaced in the wrong order, and so everything was too long, too short, too narrow, too thick.

"Let's shower," I said to Harry when I finally found him. He was around a corner staring hard at a short man I assumed to be Greek, hirsute as a teddy bear from neck to ankles.

"Hairy," said Harry, and I smiled at the man. Rather than smile back, he scowled, Greekly. Perhaps he had hair ishoos. I hoped the miserable fucker's life was ruined by his self-consciousness about his disgusting hairy back.

I held Harry in my arms under the shower. It was always his favorite bit. He clung to me tightly, his arms around my neck, his legs monkeylike around my chest.

"Hot."

"I'll cooler it."

"Nice."

We took his G.I. Joe scuba diver into the pool. It was as warm as a bath. Wealthy divorcées cruised slow as old lava, straining to keep their face-lifts clear of the water. Plumbing the depths of aquatic uncoolness, I had to keep my glasses on—an annoying but necessary precaution if Harry were not to drown, even in the kiddie bit of the pool, semisegregated down at one end.

"Home now," he said, once we were in. At least we'd made it into the water before he decided he'd had enough. It came up to his neck, and I had to kneel to play with him.

"Let's do some swimming."

I pulled him around by the arms, and he screamed out in misery. People stared at me. I tried hard to look like a kindly father and not a child murderer.

"Don't do dat," said Harry.

It was his new favorite. He accompanied it with a finger-wagging gesture. Quite cute, really. Where had it come from? School? Celeste?

So I stopped pulling him around, and he waded off slowly, curiously regal with the water his robe, to take a toy boat from another child. I said "Sorry" to the mother or nanny, who blinked at me. We went on to collect a bucket, a ball, and a duck, leaving a trail of misery behind us, literally in our wake. Harry now had more than he could carry, which was wearisome for him. I tried to help by giving back some of his booty, but that made him wail along with the victims according to some polyphonic system of his own devising, but not unrelated to the twelve-tone scale employed by Schoenberg in such masterworks as *Moses und Aron* and *Shut Up, You Fucking Noisy Tuneless German Bastard*.

Then Harry decided that he wanted to climb out of the pool and career Ben Hur–style around the perimeter. I thought it might be more dignified to try to track him from the water, so as he skipped around the shore, I waded below him, ready to catch him should he slip. He took the corners at a terrific speed, hopping on one leg to maintain his balance, and it was all I could do to keep up. Trying to keep at least one eye on Harry, I had to surge and swerve and barge past the adult swimmers at berth between their laborious lengths.

And then splat.

Me, not him.

I'd hit something soft. There was a yell and a gulp and a splutter.

"God, sorry, so sorry."

Immediately I recognized the semisubmerged body.

It was Uma Thursday.

Her arms had flailed around me; our bodies had touched along the entire length of our torsos. Had I really felt her contours as distinctly as I now imagined: her small, high breasts, the swelling between her legs? Probably not, but it didn't stop my imagining. She came up for air. She had on a Speedo costume that was obviously trying to be sexy as well as sporty, and it was cut fairly low at the front. I mean low in a good way, from an ogling point of view. Her hair was long and tangled, like a mermaid fallen into bad ways. I put out a hand to steady her.

"Fucking idiot," she said, in a really quite friendly way. "What is this—aqua-stalking?"

I noticed that, yet again, people were staring. It was only a matter of time before someone called for an attendant or an armed guard or a Mossad SWAT team.

"I was, er, it was Harry." I pointed wanly.

"He made you do it? For God's sake, man, take responsibility for your own actions."

Harry, where was he? Not where I'd pointed. No, there. Safe. He was sitting amid the python coils of a length of hose.

"Where's yours?" I asked.

"Babysitter. I'm getting out now before somebody else tries to mount me in the pool. See you in the bar?"

She performed a smooth exit maneuver, jumping up onto her bum and then rising quickly to her feet. But she'd thrown herself forward a little too much, and one of her breasts fell neatly from its proper place.

She looked straight at me and said, with no sign of embarrassment: "Well, *that* shouldn't happen."

Then she walked away, dripping, leaving the image of her pinky brown nipple behind her like a parking ticket.

Harry, of course, then decided that he liked the swimming pool. We played water kangaroos for a while and then back to the

running-around-the-poolside game, although this time with me tag-
ging along on dry land. I must have looked like some fairy-tale ogre,
chasing a child through the forest. Harry, in extreme contradistinc-
tion to his dad, looked incredibly cute in his swim trunks. They
were the special baby kind, with padding to absorb catastrophes and
a picture of a fish in a diving helmet. The fish annoyed me. What
does a fish need a diving helmet for? The absorbency had never, as
far as I was aware, been tested in combat, so when Harry said
"potty," I acted quickly.

"You can wee-wee in the showers," I said, carrying him back
into the changing rooms. He was shivering and made a plaintive
"eeeeeeeeeeeeeeee" noise.

There was a free shower stall. I put him down between my legs,
turned on the water, and took off his trunks.

"Eyes, eyes," he squealed. I turned him away from the flow.

"Do wee now, like Daddy does."

He looked up at me with his startling blue gaze.

"Don't want wee."

"Well don't wee, then."

I squeezed some soap from the dispenser and lathered it up in
my hair. I scooped two handfuls of suds and reached down to clean
him. I saw that he was wearing his thousand-yard stare, that look of
oddly unfocused intent; here were great thoughts, new discoveries,
worlds beyond imagining.

"Doing a poo," he said.

"Fuck. Wait, we'll go to the toilet. Can't poo here."

"Doing a poo *now*."

And so he was. Three hard balls fell onto the floor, followed by
a few soupspoons of watery broth, splashed and mixed with the
shower spray.

"Oh, *Harry*."

It was sharper than it should have been. He looked up at me and
mingled his silent tears with the falling water. I picked him up, and
he sobbed into my shoulder.

"Mommy mommy mommy mommy."

But I could only give him a fraction of my attention. The rest was directed to the floor of the shower. A couple of quick, skillful flicks sent the Harry shit balls over the plughole. Yet more urgent was the need to dam the flow of brown water now heading, in a series of small vortices and coiling eddies, toward the gap under the partition with the next shower. The next shower, which was occupied, I'd noticed, by the hairy Greek.

Fuck, no stopping it. My dam was breached. The shitty water was under the partition, flowing around the feet of the man next door. I gave up on the loose stuff and tried to stamp the poo balls down the drain. Seemed to work okay. Then I held Harry's bum up to the spout and cleaned him off. He accepted it meekly.

We were out of the changing rooms in record time, which meant we both reached the bar area with wet hair and in some general disarray. My socks were inside, out and I'd put his underpants on back to front, and although he couldn't put his finger on the problem, he knew that not all was as it should be in the pant department. Uma was there, reading a newspaper, drinking orange juice. She was wearing jeans and a crisp white shirt, which would have looked schoolgirlish if it were not buttoned so low, thereby bringing an instant reprise of the nipple memory. Her hair was still wet from the swim. I've always been a sucker for girls with wet hair.

I sent Harry away to play: there were always kids around, and there was a little room off the bar area with a few crap toys and some rubber cushions they could bounce on.

"I'm sorry about the, er, assault."

"You said. But you looked like you enjoyed it."

Surely to God I hadn't had a stiffy, had I? No, she was being flippant. Or had I? No, no. I hadn't had a spontaneous public erection since the fifth form. Perhaps this was flirting, like the no-panties. Quick, flirt back. What had I thought when I came in?

She was wearing clothes, and, yes, that's it, "You look nice."

"I'm in my gym clothes. I look like shit."

"Funny you should say that, because . . ." And before I could stop myself, I'd told all about the incident in the shower. The courtly grace of the Elizabethan sonneteer strikes again. She showed neither disgust nor amusement. I sat down at the bar with her and ordered a beer. I actually ordered two beers, but I drank the first bottle in two great gulps.

"Thirsty boy," she said.

Everything Uma said fell into one of two camps: the disdainfully dismissive and the grindingly sexual. She didn't have a neutral. And it wasn't the words. The "thirsty boy" thing could have been dismissive, but something about it suggested that what I was thirsty for was hot sex and that she had a quenching bucketful at the ready. It was something she did with her face when she spoke, a slight movement with her lips, not a pout but poutlike.

"Nice seeing you at that party thing the other night."

"Oh, yeah. The swans. Your wife's very beautiful."

I've never known how to respond when people praise Celeste. I couldn't decide whether to be proud or bashful, modest or exultant. I wasn't usually embarrassed, but I was now. And I knew I didn't really want to talk about Celeste with Uma.

"How's it all working out with your new job, the celebrity stuff, and entertainment and all that?"

"It's better than selling trash, but it's not exactly presenting the network news."

"But at least you're on *television*. Isn't that what everyone wants these days?"

"You'd need pretty low expectations to be content with what I have. Just *being* there isn't enough."

"But it's a start."

"Don't patronize me," she said. "I'm not a shy teenager in need of encouragement. Not from you, anyway."

"Okay, fuck off, then. I was just trying to be nice."

"By saying things you don't mean?"

"I say things I don't mean all the time. That's what being nice is. You should try it sometime."

"I always say exactly what I mean."

"Because you can't be bothered trying to please."

"*Trying to please!* What are you talking about? I hate that 'trying to please' line. You mean saying someone looks nice when they look terrible or telling them you love them when you don't?"

Uma was talking with her usual listless energy, but I saw for the first time that there was something brittle, something vulnerable about her. Things had happened to her to make her act like this. And so, when I replied, my voice was softer.

"Yeah, that's what I mean, I guess. And why not? I'd rather carry the burden than scatter pain around when there's no need. There's a moral obligation to try to make people happy, even if it means gilding the odd dandelion."

"Don't you prefer to be told the truth?"

"Truth's a slippery concept."

"Only to slippery people."

"Cheap."

"Look, we all have to make decisions about our lives, and to make decisions, you need accurate knowledge, and if people lie to you, then you don't have accurate knowledge, and so you make the wrong decisions. Nice equals nasty in the end."

"All I'm saying is that sometimes you should sugar the pill a bit."

"Do you always lapse into cliché when you're losing an argument?"

"Usually. Anyway, I like clichés—they make me feel secure."

"If you were funny, you'd have used a cliché there and made a joke about it."

"Yes, I know that's what I should have done, and I tried, but I couldn't think of any. Rare as hen's teeth at the moment, good clichés."

"Sayings don't count as clichés. Why don't we have another drink?"

"Good idea. You can lead a horse to water, but a pencil must be led."

"That's not funny either."

"I know, but it's an old friend, and I feel like I could use a few right now."

I don't remember what we talked about then. Her, probably. Eventually we got round to why she was a single parent. Oscar's dad was an executive at the station. She'd screwed herself into the job, and then later, when she was pregnant, he ditched her.

"Didn't you think about a, you know, abortion?"

"Of course, I thought about 'a, you know, abortion.' But I couldn't."

"Why not?"

"Because, first, I thought he was going to marry me, and then it was too late, without its being really icky. But I'm glad I didn't."

"Because of Oscar?"

"Yes, because of Oscar. And because of God."

"What?"

"Don't look so surprised, there's plenty of us about."

"Yes, but not many like you."

I was thinking about her underwear, or rather the lack of it.

"It started because I wanted to get Oscar into the right school, so I had to go. And, like, *years* in advance. And then I started listening to the readings and the service, and I found that I liked it, that it moved me. What about you?"

"I'm a Catholic, so it's all different for us. A bit like being a Jew. It doesn't matter if you believe any of it, you're still one, like it or not."

"Yeah, that's what you people say, but do you *believe* any of it— God, for example?"

"Well, I've got what I always thought was an interesting line on it."

"That is so typical," she said, laughing that beautiful laugh of hers. "You don't have beliefs, just an 'interesting line' on something."

"I'm going to tell you my interesting line anyway. There's this fairly common modern view that atheism and belief are equally irrational and that what we should all be is agnostics, perhaps tinged either with a bit of faith or a bit of doubt, as your nature dictates. But agnosticism is just as irrational. It suggests that, first, you've looked at, and weighed up, all the evidence and, second, that the scales are *exactly* balanced, that the pros and cons completely cancel each other out. And that's simply unbelievable. Oh, and atheists get on my nerves, too, because they're so smug, but I've never met an atheist who's read any of the proofs for God's existence."

"But aren't they all crap?"

"Have you read them?"

"No."

"Well, actually, most of them are. But that's not the point. The ontological argument's quite good."

I did a quick check. She was a young, attractive woman, who sometimes wore short skirts with no panties, so what was the chance that she would be remotely interested in the ontological argument? If she'd been a bucktoothed nerd, then maybe. But wait, no, Uma Thursday was paying attention. She wasn't mocking or scornful, or thinking I was a jerk. She was listening. I wasn't used to this.

Then she had to ask the awkward question.

"What is the ontological argument?"

"Ah, it's quite tricky to explain, and I always seem to get muddled halfway through."

"Try."

I hadn't run through this since university, and even then, the knowledge was tenuous. Still, to the brave the spoils.

"God is defined—I mean, could be defined—as the most perfect being. Agree?"

"I don't know. But let's pretend I do."

"And you could rephrase that by saying that God is the thing nothing more perfect than which could be conceived."

"That's saying the same thing, sure, but in an ugly way."

"And even an atheist must accept what we've said so far, because we're just talking about definitions. Now—and this is the bit where I sometimes lose the plot. Hang on. Yeah—now consider two beings. One is a perfect being who exists, and the other is an otherwise perfect being who doesn't exist. Which is the more perfect?"

"I sense a trap for the unwary. I suppose it must be the perfect being who exists."

"Spot-on. And bingo. God exists."

"What?"

"You've just accepted that, by definition, God is the thing greater than which nothing could be conceived, and you've accepted that a God who exists is greater than a God who doesn't exist. Therefore, God must exist. I think."

It was an important moment. Would she, as she ought to do, unfurl a sneer or a savage laugh? Throw her drink in my face? Stab me?

"I need to think about it. There's something wrong there, but I don't know what it is. It can't work, can it, because otherwise, everyone would believe in God, like they believe in gravity?"

"There is something wrong with it."

"Oh, what?"

"I can't remember. Something to do with existence not being a predicate."

"What's a predicate?"

"I can't remember that either. It was a long time ago. I think it's something you can say about something."

"That narrows it down. You've got company."

Harry had appeared at my feet. He was holding hands with a curly-haired girl a few months younger than him.

"Sheikh. Take little girl?"

"No, we have to leave the little girl for her mommy."

"Why?"

"Otherwise, her mommy will be sad."

"Okay," he said, and let go of the girl's hand.

"I liked that talk. It was . . . stimulating. I didn't realize you had it in you." Again the smile, to take the sting out of her words, or perhaps to put it in. "Why don't we go out one evening and talk some more?"

"Okay," I said, unconsciously chiming with Harry.

"When are you free?"

"Well, I suppose things are easier, freedomwise, while we're at Celeste's parents'. I mean, I don't have to be home to look after her."

"I'm sure she doesn't need you for that."

"Yes. No. I mean, she's with her parents. I don't have to worry."

"You should stop worrying, it's boring. What about next week?"

Harry was waiting patiently. Uma wasn't. Decisive action was called for.

"I er . . . Next week? Yes. I'll have to check my—"

"Just let me know," Uma said, and left with a toss of her damp red hair.

"Do you like that lady?" I asked Harry on the way up the escalators to the second floor of the mall, the one with Ed's Diner and the sushi bar and twelve other ways to take on calories quickly and efficiently.

"Who lady?"

"Oscar's mommy."

"I like milk shake."

"What flavor do you want today? Cheese and onion?"

"No!"

"Monkey brain?"

"No! Silly Daddy."

"What, then?"

"Verlinner."

"Okay, then, verlinner it is."

We found a booth at the diner, and over the milk shake, I thought about the weirdness of things. Who'd have thought that the good old ontological argument would have got me this much closer to adultery, that God should so intervene to carry me into sin?

Oh, well.

Ludo phoned on Monday morning. I was in a meeting and said I'd get back, but I didn't. He called again in the afternoon. I was alone in my office.

"Sorry about earlier," I said.

"No, don't be sorry. I wanted to phone so you didn't think that all I was after was a one-night stand."

"How do you know that's not what I want?"

"Is it?"

"I don't know. It might be."

"That wasn't the impression I got on Saturday night."

"Saturday night was different."

"Saturday night was wonderful. I've never known anything like it."

We made love twice more on the bloody sheets, tenderly. More blood flowed, but neither of us cried out again in anguish or lust. Ludo was hugely gentle, and although I didn't come again, it was special.

"Yes, it was wonderful, but I don't think I can do it again."

"Why not?"

His tone was unreadable. I had no idea if he was sad or relieved or furious.

"Because I haven't got the space in my life for an affair. It's impossible."

"Then why did you start it?"

Now there was no mistaking it: Ludo was angry.

I thought about Saturday night. All through the long Sunday of packing and shifting and organizing, I'd shoved it to the back of my mind, where it lurked like a tumor. Sean was cheerful all day, even after bringing Harry back from his treat. In the evening, I drove over to Mom and Dad's, with Sean and Harry playing "Give me some sweets or I'll cry" all the way.

"I didn't start anything. Nothing has started." I was lying.

"It has started. If you want it to stop, then say stop. But you can't just pretend nothing has happened."

"Then stop. I want it to stop. I'm sorry, Ludo. I shouldn't have got you into this. Good-bye."

I put the phone down. He called again five minutes later.

"Can I please see you, just to talk."

I know I should have said no, but I didn't.

"When?"

"Anytime. This evening? Tomorrow."

"Tomorrow."

"Where?"

I wanted somewhere open, innocent.

"What about the park, St. James's?"

We met on a bench, beneath a tree, with pigeons strutting about. St. James's is probably the prettiest park in London, with its ornamental trees and cute bridge over the lake and black swans and outrageous, impossible pelicans and intricate flower beds. But it has always felt a little fake to me. The others—Green Park, Hyde Park, Regent's Park—have that sense of being leftover bits of the countryside that were simply forgotten as the city grew around them. By comparison, St. James's is a carefully planned work of art, intricate, neat, and delicate, and a little soulless.

We looked out over the fountain blowing fine spray into the lake waters. Most of the leaves on the trees hunching over the banks had turned red or gold. Another week and the bare branches would reveal Buckingham Palace in the distance.

People hurried by on their way home, taking shortcuts to Charing Cross or Victoria. Some lingered by the water. One old woman fed the ducks, but they didn't seem very interested, gorged as they were on a full day of tourist sandwiches. Ludo was talking about the pigeons, trying, I think, to be lighthearted.

"You see the male pigeons? They're the ones sticking out their chests and cooing. Handsome, aren't they? See the funny turny-roundy dance they do—round and round, round and round, and then more cooing and more sticking out their chests. But the females keep walking away. They want to make sure that the cocks are up to scratch."

"Is that supposed to mean something?"

He looked at me, stung. "I'm sorry, I was just—"

"No, I'm sorry. I never thought I'd feel like this."

"Like what?"

I think he hoped that I was feeling overwhelmed with love for him or something.

"So guilty, so sick."

"Oh."

"Don't you?"

"Perhaps I should, but no, I don't. I think I'm—"

"Please don't say it; it'll only make things worse. It always makes things worse."

The sun was getting lower, dappling the bench and the water and us with light. I felt a chill and shivered. Ludo took off his jacket and put it around my shoulders.

"Thanks," I said. At the touch of his hand on my shoulder, I felt another shiver, but not from the cold. Damn it. It was still there. I'd half hoped the desire would have gone.

He'd moved closer to me on the bench. The pigeons danced more frantically and then fluttered away.

"Is it Katie you feel bad about?"

"Katie? God no."

"Oh, I see. It's just Harry."

"No, not just Harry. Harry and Sean."

"Shit, of course."

"I better go."

"Okay. I'll walk you to the station."

"I'd rather you didn't."

I shook his jacket from my shoulders and passed it back to him. My wrist brushed against his crotch.

"My God," I said, "how long has that been there?" I couldn't stop myself from smiling.

"I'm really sorry," he said, trying to keep a straight face. "It's just seeing you again. I keep thinking about the other night. The first one. What you did."

Thinking about it, and touching him, and seeing him so aroused, began to turn me on. This wasn't what I'd planned. I had to shift on the bench. Somehow Ludo picked up on it. You would never have guessed the acuity of his sexual instincts from the way he looked, but he understood. I don't even know if it was conscious.

"You want it, don't you?" he said. He leaned toward me as he spoke, murmuring the words in my ear. I felt his breath and then his bristles and then the touch of his lips.

"Yes."

"Here in the park."

"Yes."

"You want me to fuck you here in the park."

"Yes."

"Say it."

"I want you to fuck me here in the park."

"Are you still bleeding?"

"I don't know. It's near the end. Do you know a place?"

"I know a place."

He stood up and took my hand. It was getting darker, but surely it was too light to just do it, here on the grass? We stepped over a low fence, and suddenly the world seemed years away. He led me between the trees. The grass was dry and springy.

"Where are we going?"

"It's here, just here."

We came to a willow tree, its branches reaching almost to the ground. He parted the leaves, like a seventies bead curtain, and we were in a private room. Even the sound of traffic disappeared.

"You've done this before?"

"There was a woman who showed me this place."

"Your girlfriend? Katie?"

"No. She was a teacher at my school."

"Was she your first?"

"Yes."

"What was it like?"

"It was tragic."

He put his jacket on the ground. I lay down on it. I was wearing stockings again, so I must have known, at some level, what was going to happen. I took my shoes and panties off, and he unfastened his trousers. He touched me, opened me, entered me. It was a silent, slow fuck, each stroke deliberate, heavy. After a time—five minutes, perhaps—I felt myself slipping into a kind of trance. The wind shushed in the willow leaves, and the pale last light seeped and dried and then vanished.

Now it was black, and he was heavy as lead on me. I couldn't feel him inside me at all, but his brutal, conscienceless mass was everywhere. Then he stopped.

"Turn over," he said.

"Don't hurt me," I said, and my voice was like a little girl's. But the trouble was that I did want him to hurt me.

"Do you want this?"

I didn't say anything, but I turned over onto my hands and knees. I heard him spit onto his hand, and he rubbed it into me. Then he entered me again from behind. I didn't know what he was going to do, and I was frightened. I couldn't decide if it was pleasurable or not, but I didn't want him to stop.

"Harder," I said, and I wanted to say "Hurt me," but I'd have hated myself for that. And then I wanted to hate myself, and so I said, "Hurt me."

"What?"

"Push me into the dirt," I said, and I don't know where the words came from.

"Celeste . . . ," he said, the concern in his voice undermined by his steady thrusting.

"Hurt me *now.*"

But he wasn't a hurting kind of man. I kept telling him, and in the end he tried, but in a halfhearted way, and I despised him because of it.

SPEAKING ILL OF THE UNDEAD

Celeste's parents' house out here in Amersham is huge. It has Gothic turrets, pre-Raphaelite stained glass, a leaking roof, a gargoyle, a grotesque modern conservatory, a billiard room without a billiard table (but with a stag's head and a very well stocked drinks cabinet), at least two sets of stairs, an intact system of ropes and bells to summon the ghosts of servants, a pet cemetery (in the garden, not the house), and a statue of a dead man (in the house, not the garden).

Harry loved it. Here was endless opportunity for lethal and near-lethal play. Swords could be found. He could squeeze between the balusters and dangle over forty feet of space. The electrics fizzed and sparked excitingly. Best of all, there was Dander.

Celeste's parents. I suppose I must always have known that there was a risk of something like this happening as soon as I began to look for sexual partners outside the impoverished housing estates of my hometown, Leeds. There you were deemed to be a bit odd if you got semiskimmed milk or called your pit bull anything other than Spike. But they were still a shock.

Bella first. Celeste never warned me. "We're having lunch with my mother" was all she said. I was like one of the raw recruits in the First World War, expecting jolly japes and finding barbed wire and machine guns. We'd been living together for a couple of weeks, and all she'd said about her parents was the kind of thing anyone might say. I'd imagined a couple of ordinary home-counties types. Mother with hair, father with voice. One of those lawn mowers you ride around on. Probably some embarrassing art on the walls. A horrible suggestion of pottery somewhere in their past.

And then, with a clap of thunder and a howling of wolves, Bella arrived at the restaurant. She was wearing a flowing black cape, attached to some clingy (also black) undergarment by a kind of webbing. Her eyes, below the straight black fringe, were huge and dark and her lips a ghastly red. She looked like one of the sexier vultures. The blood froze in my veins, and I lost the feeling in my legs. Celeste stood up, and I tried to push myself up with my arms on the table.

"Mum, Sean; Sean, Mum."

She put out her hand, which was, like the rest of her, long and thin. The fingers appeared to curve back slightly, as if she were preparing a good slap. Her nails were the same vivid red as her lips. The hand was cold and dry as an Inca body found preserved in a mountain cave. She spoke with an accent I couldn't even begin to place, although it was sure a long way from Leeds.

"Ah, at last, the charming young man who has moved into *your* apartment."

I couldn't think of anything at all to say in return. "Sorry" seemed most appropriate, but even that stuck in my throat. Celeste seemed unfazed by the monster and got to work on the menu as her mother folded her leathery wings and sat down. I felt that I should have done something with her chair: pull it out, push it in, lay my face on it, *anything*. But I just sat down and carried on being horrified.

There followed the worst two hours of my life. Questions were fired obliquely, and by the time I worked out what she was getting at, she'd moved on to the next. It ended up as a comedy sketch in which I was always answering the question before last. I tried to counter by obsequious flattery, which she saw through instantly. I might have said how young she looked (from bathing in virgins' blood?), but she looked at me as if I'd suggested she squeeze the blackheads on my butt. She'd obviously, in her time, been flattered by experts, and my naïve approach savored too much of a beggar offering a queen a piece of bread to dunk in his running sore.

I did manage to absorb that Bella was a Hungarian aristocrat, possessing a title "for which there is no English equivalent—like a duchess, but much, much younger" was how she put it, smiling to indicate the possibility that she was joking, but not about the "duchess" bit. Or the "much younger." She had fled Hungary in 1948, "a child, a tiny baby." However, she also claimed to have been "the champion at shuttlecock in Budapest." Perhaps she'd been the champion of the under-twos. The shuttlecock issue loomed large in her conversation. It seems she was destined for Olympic glory, "without Stalin, the monster," and there was a strong suggestion that the dictator's greatest crime was robbing her of her sporting triumphs.

No matter how much I drank, it was never enough to take away the pain. I've since noticed that it's always difficult to get drunk with her about, and I'm beginning to believe that she has a special power: the ability to inflict a kind of witchly induced hypersobriety. I shouldn't whine: I'm not the first boy to fail to live up to his mother-in-law's ambitions for her daughter. But perhaps I am the only one to come away from the parting handshake (no question of kissing, then or since) with the deep imprint of her nails deliberately inflicted on his palm.

It was a long time before I met Celeste's dad. We'd spoken a couple of times on the phone, but the interaction of our two nervous stammers made communication almost impossible. In the flesh, he was small and shabby, with broken spectacles and a preposterous, foot-long rim of frizzy gray hair issuing horizontally from halfway down his head. It looked like a halo, improvised from steel wool and fiberglass for a school play. He was, Celeste informed me, wearing her most bored expression, a leading herpetologist and had written the "standard work on geckos." It seemed, then, that he had failed to pass on his enthusiasm to his daughter. He'd been at Cambridge and still held an honorary position there, but he'd had some kind of breakdown and no longer taught. Apart from geckos, his conversation largely concerned his bowels. I liked him right away, as did Harry, who dubbed him "Dander" (Harry for "Granddad"), but his human name was Magnus.

We arrived late on the Sunday evening. Harry was asleep. Magnus opened the door.

"Lovely chap, lovely chap," he said, reaching to take Harry from my arms. "Dander got you."

Bella stood behind him, smiling like Ivan the Terrible. She was wearing a richly embroidered dressing gown, like one of Tennyson's moodier poems, in fabric form.

"You'll be hungry," she said to Celeste, and kissed her. She offered me the hand. "Come into the salon. Shoes first." We took our shoes off.

"Hope we haven't kept you up," I said, thinking about the dressing gown.

"Do I appear to you to be in bed?"

"No, I just meant that—"

"I've prepared the red room for *you*, Celeste." Where was I to be? In the stables?

The "salon" was Bella's space. The furniture all had animal legs, and there was much in the way of Meissen china and curly silver things, without obvious function. I usually managed to break something, and I could sense Bella's tensing for a smash or tinkle. There was no TV, here or anywhere in the house.

Magnus came back after putting Harry to bed, bearing in his place a tray with sandwiches. I hoped he hadn't made them. I hoped even more that she hadn't. I prayed silently for a girl who came in specially to make their sandwiches. Nancy, I decided to call her. Not quite *all there*, but very clean hands. I took one. Thin white bread, its crusts extracted under torture.

"Mmmm, Spam," I said, genuinely surprised. Was it part of a wartime cache? Luckily I was up to it. If Bella thought she could get the better of me with Spam, then she didn't know how tough we can be in Leeds. The claggy, metallic taste of cheap margarine, the sort made from chicken fat and hydrogenated horse jism, was a bit harder to take. The tea helped, as tea so often does.

"Sherry?" offered Magnus.

"Please."

The sherry was good, but stale and dusty. Celeste was flicking through a magazine, oblivious to any difficulty I might be in.

"How are you, Magnus?" I tried. Mistake. He shook his head sadly.

"You remember how I was trying linseed?" I nodded warily. "Well, if anything, it has done its job too well. It leaves me no time to catch up with the journals. Who knows what's happening in the world of newts? And I've fallen behind on my reviewing."

"Enough," said Bella, quietly. She was also reading a magazine and didn't look up.

"But Steve—"

"Sean," said Celeste.

"Sean, I beg your, er . . . ah, Sean, wanted to know how things have been going. So I told him about the linseed. The lady," he said, turning back to me, "in the health shop recommended it. Apparently it swells in the *colon* rather than the *stomach* and so does not give you the bloating or the wind."

"I said, enough."

But Magnus now was unstoppable.

"The problem is that now I'm finished in a matter of seconds. Sometimes I can barely arrange myself in time. And as you know, my custom had been to read the journals, and the books I'm reviewing for *The Times Literary Supplement,* in the bathroom. I suppose I could stay, but that would seem, seem *perverse*. But I can't settle to it anywhere else now. It's been my habit for too long. I don't think things have been this loose since 1962 or thereabouts. I remember because that was a cold winter, and we didn't have heating installed in the lavatory until 1963. There's a monograph on the axolotl, and the young chap at the *TLS* is clamoring for it. I may have to take some caline and morphine."

"Couldn't you just cut down on the linseed?"

He looked at me as though I had suggested he cut down on his air.

"But, dear boy, I've been waiting for something this effective for years."

"He's just like you," said Celeste later in bed. She cuddled up to me under the heavy covers, made from the same stuff as Bella's dressing gown. Mariana of the moated grange, I thought. "With blackest moss the flower-plots / Were thickly crusted, one and all."

"What did you say?"

"Nothing, just some poetry." I didn't mind the thing about being like her dad. I knew it had some truth in it. "Is that why you married me?"

"Mommy thinks it is. She says she should have taken me back to Budapest as a child or given me to the Gypsies to save me from my fate."

"Seems a bit extreme."

"That's Bella."

"Why did she marry your dad?"

"He wasn't always the way he is now. There are some pictures of when they were young together. And then there was this house. I think she perhaps loved it even more than him."

Celeste was still cuddled up. "I don't suppose you . . . ?"

She looked up and smiled at me. She seemed softer than usual, nicer.

"I'd like to, but it's the end of my period, and there might be some mess. But soon." She kissed me on the nose. "I love you."

"You, too."

Afterward, I lay curled on my side. He was hunched over, facing away from me. I'd never felt such desolation.

What I'd always most enjoyed about sex was the bestial freedom of it, the escape from my civilized, humane, cosmopolitan self. But somehow, what we'd done had none of the joyful, releasing animality of sex. It seemed more like the kind of cruelty, depravity, that only people are capable of. As if the line were continued not back through evolution to the time of innocence but forward, to a place where all the generous, warm, stinking, animal side of the human had been scientifically obliterated.

I left him under the willow, smoking a cigarette. I knew it was going to be the last time. I knew it shouldn't have happened at all, and so, I think, did he.

Why had I done it at all? There's only ever one answer to that question—because I wanted to. Chasing it further takes you deeper into the forest, and if you're not careful, you'll never come out.

No, that's not good enough. Raymond would never settle for that. It just doesn't come naturally to me. Sean lives in himself in a way that I can't. He thinks about who he is and why he is. Things from his past, even his silly school days, are always there with him, like his obsession with the boy at his school whom he feels he let down. He lives an ethical life, trying to do what he should, trying always to do the right thing. But I've always just lived, done my job, earned my money.

I knew what I wanted from the age of sixteen, and everything from then on was targeted. I fell in love with Sean because he was lovable and he wanted me, and then that side of my life was taken care of. When Harry came along, I knew that I could not allow myself to become too engrossed, as I could never have given up work at that stage in our lives. So I closed myself. Of course, I loved Harry, but the price of staying in my job was that I had to leave the active loving, the loving-as-doing, up to Sean. And it seemed to work.

Until Ludo.

Was it just selfishness, putting my pleasure before any other considerations? No, not that, because I never thought it was going to make me happy.

Perhaps *that's* the clue. Perhaps it was because I wanted to punish myself in some way, to find my heart of darkness and revel in it. That was why I craved something cruel and painful and dirty and vile. I craved hatred.

But that all sounds too much like the kind of line Raymond would enjoy, getting turned on by my self-loathing. No, not my style.

Was it merely boredom, then? God, is that all it was? A need for novelty?

I had to face the truth that things hadn't been right with Sean, not for a long time. The kind of things that we used to find endearing in each other were suddenly maddening. We'd lost that tolerance; more than tolerance, *enjoyment* in each other's little habits. The excitement and longing that I used to feel had seeped away; I no longer cared what he thought about things, no longer gauged my own responses to books and movies and people by his reactions. And I knew it cut both ways. And I think that was the killing blow. He no longer looked on me with astonishment—with that innocent, wide-eyed amazement—anymore, and I missed it.

So there we are. I was bored with my husband. I wanted more attention. And so I had an affair. How . . . undistinguished. How unoriginal. And it wasn't as if we had some open marriage, an agreement that a bit of straying would be fine. We didn't, and I would have left Sean if I'd thought that he'd actually slept with Uma or anyone else.

But now it would be different. Now I would be good. Living an ethical life can't be that hard if even Sean can do it. And love must be the way out. Loving Sean, loving Harry, loving us all. But I don't know if I can do it. Is there anybody to help me?

Not Raymond.

I went to him for the last time yesterday. I told him what I'd done. He seemed pleased. He wanted to know the details. I looked at his long face, at his careful hair and clean nails. He licked his lips. He can't have licked his lips, but that's what I see now, when I look back. I see him licking his lips and loving it, getting off on it. It may have been a simple voyeurism. Or some kind of kinky power thing. Or my imagination. But I knew I didn't want any more of him. When he said "See you next time," I said, "I don't think so," and walked out.

At last, they've begun on the apartment. We're at my parents'. I know it's a trial for Sean, but Harry loves it. Dad's great with him. He lives for Harry, and Harry revels in the love and attention. There's the garden for him to play in, and a girl from the town comes to help. Even Sean's admitted that it gives him more time to work and think and whatever else he does. I keep hoping that this can be a new beginning for us. I'm trying so hard to love him.

SEANJOURNALSIXTEEN.DOC

VOLARE, OH OH

My first live radio. Still slightly buzzing with it: "Can Men Have It All?"—a live discussion on *Woman's Hour*. There was me; a sociology lecturer from De Montfort "University" (sorry, shouldn't do that; I mean University); two feminists, doing a good-fem/bad-fem act; and the chief presenter, Jemima Faust herself, in the chair.

I had two pints in the pub beforehand. No point getting sloshed. Andrew came and met me, and I tried a couple of my routines on him. One he declared to be "too gay"; the other, "too fascist."

"Well, what the fuck am I supposed to say, then?"

"The key, Sean, is just *don't* be yourself."

"Thanks."

"Welcome."

The sociologist had written a report showing that men who brought up children suffered more stress and died earlier, often horribly, than men who did almost anything else. Or any women. The mean feminist, who was also the pretty one, said this was a Good Thing. The nice feminist, who looked like Jabba the Hutt, was sorry for us but thought that women had suffered longer, and worse. I made some jokes about trying to get off with the other mothers at the playgroup. My timing was ruined by Jemima, who deliberately threw me by raising her mohair top and caressing her great, pendulous bare breasts and rolling her eyes and moaning like the Wild

Woman of Wongo about to explode into orgasm. She then mimed a full-on cock-bulging-in-the-cheek blow job, finishing in a great, gulping cum swallow.

Who could blame me for stammering?

Nobody seemed convinced or amused when I said that I was muddling through more or less okay, and that Harry didn't seem to really mind who looked after him so long as he got his way in all things, and that, yes, maybe I was a bit lonely, but, no, I wasn't especially bothered because there was always beer to fall back on. It made everyone angry—the women because it was "complacent" and "patronizing" and "oppressive," and the sociologist because it de-emphasized the extent to which I was under stress, isolated, dying, etc.

I went for a drink with the pretty feminist after the broadcast. She was an American, with long, dark hair and immaculate makeup, and a well-supported bosom, which I on no account complimented her upon or stared at. Instead, I spun my line about equal opportunities for women being a way ior institutions to appear to be progressive, but what it meant was that compliant middle-class white women were given the jobs instead of more problematic groups such as racial minorities and working-class men and women. The result was a reinforcement of the barriers that really counted, because white middle-class women were always going to be okay, happily pooling their income with their middle-class partners, living in the good places, driving the fast cars. Why else was it that the most *repressive* and *conservative* country in the world ("i.e., *yours*") had the most *progressive* laws on sex discrimination? The way to help the women who needed it was to boost the minimum wage, but for some reason, that didn't find its way onto the agenda for most public feminists, because they were already sailing well above it. Instead, they obsessed about female tennis players' getting as much as the men or increasing boardroom representation or grieving over the fact that not enough fat cats were female fat cats. The real issue was how to get more money and a better life to

poor people, not easing the path to the top for the greedy and selfish of either sex.

That all went down very well. She said that I'd changed her
mind on all these issues, and she suggested that we go together to a
little hotel nearby that she knew. We talked in the room for a while
longer, and then she stripped down to her suspenders, knelt on all
fours, and called over her shoulder for me to give it to her, and no
messing with shit like foreplay.

Okay, perhaps some of the above account was exaggerated, principally that concerning the lovely Jemima and the American feminist. In reality, Jemima just looked at me with the mingled concern,
pity, and annoyance of a mother whose teenage son had come in
drunk for the first time, puking on the roses and staggering over the
doorstep. The American handsomely rebutted all my points in the
pub and then went to catch a train to Edinburgh, resisting my plea
that she have another to ease the pain of prolonged contact with
the Scots.

But the stammering and the talking shit and the being trounced
in argument by everyone I spoke to apart, it really had been a mod-
erate success. I was still reasonably high when I got back to Celeste's
parents' house. Celeste's dad had given me a key, and I let myself in,
shouting out "Hello." I could hear the sound of laughter and followed it to Magnus's study. It was a traditional book-lined job, just
the kind of thing I coveted. Apart from the geckos. The geckos
lived in a tank, set in the middle of the bookshelves. Magnus and
Harry were in front of the tank, watching the creepy little things
eat their daily ration of grubs and pupae.

"Ah, good morning," said Magnus. It was nearly six o'clock.
"Bella is out. She goes out, you know." He said it as if going out were
an eccentric, but not in any way reprehensible, thing to want to do.

"Daddy go now," said Harry crossly.

Feeding grubs to the geckos was Harry's favorite thing in the
world, bar nothing, and he hated being interrupted. I went quietly

to my room, feeling deflated. I tried to read but couldn't. The room was hot and stuffy, and I couldn't open the window. Celeste came in at seven thirty. She carried on her policy, only recently adopted, of being nice to me.

"I love you," she said, without any provocation.

"Oh yes, you, too."

"Mean it?"

"That doesn't usually bother you."

"Shut up."

"Give me a kiss, then."

She kissed me very nicely on the lips.

"I'm not going to see Raymond anymore."

"Good. Why not?"

"He's a fuck wit."

I laughed. It was always funny when she used an obscenity. I told her about my day at Broadcasting House, and she laughed at all the right bits—and not just at me, but with me, which made a pleasant change. Then we went down and hijacked Harry. I chased them around the house, up and down both sets of stairs and down into the spooky cellars, where Magnus kept his port and Bella her unhallowed earth and spare coffins. When we came back up, she was there.

"Are you dining with us?"

"I thought we'd go out, Mommy. You don't mind babysitting, do you? We'll put Harry down."

"No, that is fine." She looked at me as if this betrayal were my idea and then swept away.

"So, we're going out?"

"Yes," said Celeste. "There's a nice new restaurant in the town. I thought it might be fun."

And it was. We sat in the bar first and had cocktails—big, sweet ones, because we were out in the sticks. Celeste was silly and funny and flirty.

"Why are you being so lovely?" I asked her.

"Just because. I've been tired and stressed lately, and I know things have been a bit strained. But I feel better now. I want us to be happy."

"I'm all for being happy. And I'm easily pleased, you know."

"Liar! You're the fussiest, annoyingest person in the world."

"Second annoyingest!"

"Equal annoyingest."

We had dinner in a terrible Italian, where everything came in a thick white sauce made from Campbell's condensed cream of mushroom soup. But the wine was good, and the grappa was good, and we played footsie under the table and joined in with "Volare" and put the *cornetto* words to "O sole mio."

We rolled home drunk and full and tripping over at nearly midnight.

"Have you got your key?" she asked, after searching in vain for her own. I did a bit of vain searching myself.

"Bugger. No."

She rang the bell, an incongruous, 1970s ding-dong, Avon calling. She rang it three more times before it opened. I was hoping for Magnus. Harry would have been second choice.

Bella.

I'd never before seen her in her natural state. I didn't doubt Celeste's claims that she had been beautiful in her youth, and she had a certain scary Gothic something, even now, in her fifties, but here she was without the makeup. Her face was completely colorless and almost formless. She had no eyebrows *at all*. She looked like one of those blind fish that live right at the bottom of the sea, all white malevolence, feeling their way to the next meal.

"It's very late," she said. Her voice was a little indistinct. Had she too hurriedly inserted her dentures? Perhaps she'd put the wrong set in by mistake—Magnus's or the poison ones she used to paralyze rodents.

"Sorry, Mum." Celeste looked at me and giggled, which set me off. We felt like naughty children.

Bella turned from the door, and we filed in.

"Tell me about your evening," Bella said, but just as I began to, she spoke loudly over me, finishing the sentence by saying "tomorrow."

We scuttled away upstairs, still giggling. Celeste took all of her clothes off, and rather than putting on her heavy nightdress or even heavier pajamas, she slipped into bed naked. I couldn't remember the last time we'd made love—it must have been at least a month. It might have been three. There was nothing adventurous or dramatic about it, but we had to go very slowly and quietly, because the bed, the floor, the walls, and I all squeaked. We had to keep shushing each other, and yet more giggles broke out.

Afterward I said, "You know what happened, don't you?"

"You didn't come inside, did you?"

"I'm afraid I did."

So much for coitus interruptus.

"I'm glad."

"Nothing'll come of it."

"Why, did you hit it on the head with your tennis racket?"

"What? Oh. Ha-ha. No, but it's hard, isn't it?"

"I'll say!"

"God you're a schoolgirl tonight."

"Is that what turned you on?"

"I'm not sure that's even *allowed* to be funny. What turned me on is what always turns me on: you in the nude."

"Sweet."

"Love you."

"Love you, too. Sleeping now. Night night."

I went with Sean at lunchtime to see what they'd done to our place. We held hands as we wandered through, gasping at the walls knocked down and the new spaces and the dust and the excitement of it all. The builders, glumly mustachioed Poles, were a bit moody and sullen—I expect we'd interrupted one of the tea breaks—but I was amazed at how much they'd done.

"Destruction's always the easy bit," Sean said meaningfully, and then quoted some poem about fire and ice.

All of our furniture was crammed into the back rooms, piled up like stuff in an Egyptian tomb.

"I could live in here," he said, looking at a bed laden with chairs and side tables and lampshades. "Might have to if your mom keeps it up."

"Keeps what up?"

"Being herself."

"That's not fair, you know. They are letting us stay, after all."

"Yeah, and don't they let me know what a favor it is," he said.

"Harry loves it, and they him."

"That's true. It's what makes it all bearable."

"How much do you think I enjoy it when we stay at your mum's?"

"We never do."

"Because it's too small. Please let's not argue, it's ruining this for me, and I was so enjoying it."

"Sorry. Giz a kiss."

The builders had some strange stilt things, which they strapped on to strip the ceiling, and Sean insisted on having a go, while I talked to the foreman about timings and deadlines.

"You'll break your leg," I said to him, but he didn't. He just bashed his knee and nearly started crying.

The good news was, they thought they'd be all done in a month. The designer we'd got in, a friend of Galatea's who was prepared to stoop to "domestic," had predicted eight weeks, so it was a boon.

I think one reason why Sean was so happy was that he'd been asked to do a book based on his radio talks. The publisher was nothing special (according to Sean, their bestseller was a book of cat recipes—not, he assured me, interesting ways to cook a cat but healthy alternatives to Whiskas), and he had to rush so it could be out by Christmas, but I think he was relieved about finally having something concrete to do. He promised there wouldn't be anything horrid about me in it. I'd never listened to his broadcasts—I was too busy during the day, and he never got round to taping them—so I was looking forward to seeing what it was all about.

At work that afternoon, I decided I'd better try to phone Ludo. I wanted to say sorry. Stupid, I know, but I felt that the guilt was on my side and not his. I wanted to see if somehow we could undo what we'd done, go back to the point before everything changed.

Katie answered his mobile.

"Hello, Katie Castle."

I should probably have put the phone down. No, that wouldn't have worked: she'd have the number on the handset.

"Katie? Hi."

"Who's . . . Is that you, Celeste?"

"Yes." Quick. Had I dialed the wrong number by mistake? Or did I want Ludo for something innocent, something not including raw and painful sex in a hotel or under a tree or anywhere else?

"How did you know to reach me on Ludo's mobile? I just borrowed it for today, because mine's on the blink, and he never uses his for anything except telling the time."

"Oh, I didn't realize this was his. I looked you up in our book, and it had this number under you both. What luck. Can you come to dinner?"

"That'd be lovely, but aren't you staying at your parents'? Won't they mind?"

"Not a bit. I'll send them out for the night to the pictures or to see a play or something."

"Who else's coming?"

"Oh, the usual. Haven't invited anyone else yet. You're the first."

"How flattering. When is it?"

"This Saturday. If it's too late notice, then don't worry."

"No, that's perfect. Nothing planned, for once. And it'll be good for Ludo. He's been even mopier than usual lately. If it's you and Sean, he'll leap at it like a salmon on speed."

What genius! Now I was going to be stuck with Ludo and Katie for an evening—the couple in the world I most wanted to avoid. After Katie, I invited Milo and Galatea. Milo wanted to bring his new boyfriend *and* Veronica, which I didn't mind. I called Sean and said he should invite some of his friends. Anything, even *that*, to dilute Katie and Ludo.

And then, just before I left for home, Ludo called.

"I've just spoken to Katie," he said. "So we're coming for dinner."

"Yes, I'm sorry, it wasn't meant to happen. She's got your phone. I didn't know what else to say."

"It seems a strange thing to pick on."

"I know. I always thought I was quite good under pressure."

"I'm not."

"Well, me neither, it turns out. Not this kind of pressure."

"What did you phone me for, if it wasn't a dinner invite?" He sounded colder than usual.

"I'm sorry about what I made you do."

"You didn't make me."

"Don't be chivalrous. I did. And I wish I hadn't."

"I wish you wouldn't regret it. It makes me feel worse."

"I do regret it. I think I went crazy. For a couple of weeks."

"Are you still crazy?"

"I don't think so. But when you're crazy, you can't tell, can you?"

"I've never been crazy. I wish I could be, sometimes."

"Don't be melodramatic."

"Don't tell me what to be."

"Ludo, I called before because I want to say that I used you, and it wasn't fair."

"I wanted it. What's not fair is this: I love you."

"You don't, you can't. I don't want love, not from you."

"So, you just wanted a fuck?"

"Yes, that's what I wanted then. Now what I want is friendship."

"You're a bitch."

"I know. That's why I need your friendship."

"I can't stop thinking about you. I can't be your friend if I'm thinking all the time about what we did. If I'm wanting to do it again."

"Ludo, you're thirty-something years old. You know as well as I do that these things get better. How long does an obsession last? A week? A month? A year, if you're unlucky. And then it's gone, and you're normal again."

"I don't want to be normal. And sometimes an obsession lasts for-ever."

"I think maybe you *are* insane."

"Maybe I am."

And then, miraculously, he laughed.

"I've missed that sound. The last two times, . . . you didn't at all."

"Sex is a serious business."

I remembered something that Katie had told me ages ago about Ludo: that he was always funny and silly during sex, in a way that could be quite irritating.

"It doesn't have to be. Perhaps it shouldn't be."

"So if things lightened up a bit, you might—"

Now I laughed. This seemed more like harmless flirting and not the death throes of a spawning animal.

"I might, but I probably wouldn't."

"Celeste"—his voice was serious again, suffused with . . . something, longing or desire or perhaps even the love he believed he felt—"whatever you feel, I'm not going to let myself regret this. You're special. You're beautiful. Shit, I'm going to lose it unless I go now."

And he put the phone down.

I truly thought that we had achieved something. The horror and the dread that surrounded the affair began to diminish. I still felt sick with guilt; I still could not even begin to think about what I'd done, what I'd risked, in relation to Harry. But now there was a chance of fixing things.

I walked along Oxford Street, normally for me an experience akin to having my bikini line waxed. But now, in the late-afternoon crowds, it seemed a beautiful place, so full of life and happiness. I gave a pound to the man who plays the violin outside one of the department stores. Then I went up to the fifth floor, where they sell computers. There was a counter with laptops and personal organizers and digital cameras.

"What's the swankiest gizmo you've got?" I asked the boy behind the counter. His acne reached in irregular archipelagos from his neckline to his forehead. I guessed his mother had bought him his suit. His eyes bulged. The spaces in between the pimples blushed to a similar shade of scarlet. I didn't suppose he got many pretty girls up here asking his advice.

"What kind of gizmo? Do you mean PDA?"

"What's a PDA? Don't tell me. I think I want one of those. Do you gift wrap?"

SEANJOURNALSEVENTEEN.DOC

minuqpieruqvg] WV OPAD VM; >WE }RTk\w[,m

A truly astounding thing has happened. I'm pretty sure that Celeste has never bought me anything other than clothes before. Christmas and birthdays, and occasional days between, out come the bags from shops even the names of which excite in me the beginnings of panic. From out of the bags will come neatly wrapped tissue-paper parcels. Inside the parcels lie pants and tops, the occasional jacket; once in a while, a whole suit.

I'm aware that the spirit of the curmudgeon looms large over this, but I can't ever be truly grateful for these Gifts of Names. They smack too much of the businessman buying slinky panties for his mistress, not to further her warmth or comfort but to gratify desires of his own. The desire gratified by Celeste's clothing largesse, I should add hastily, is the entirely human one of not wanting to be embarrassed by your slob of a husband. But the point remains: my birthdays are when she does something for herself.

But this was quite different. I thought it might be cuff links or some other useless oddment: a tiepin, a hip flask, one of the gifts of desperation. It came in a small box. It wasn't heavy, but it was solid.

Oh, heavens.

It was a gadget.

A toy for her boy.

For once, she'd thought about what I might want and then gone out and bought it. And it was so *nearly* right. How could she know that getting a Pocket PC running a pared-down version of Windows to sync with a Mac was like trying to marry a slob from Leeds to a North London princess, i.e., doable but difficult, painful, expensive. A Palm, or one of the Palm-compatibles from Sony or Handspring, would have been so much easier. I think I hid my disappointment well. At least it was a gadget. It could play MP3 tracks and had a miniversion of Tetris as well as boring stuff—the diary I'd never use, the contacts I didn't have, the appointments nobody wanted to make with me. So I gave her a huge kiss and spent the evening ostentatiously playing with it to show how perfect it was.

Confession time. I've been something close to a geek for about three years now. That's pretty late in life for geekdom to strike. Most of my geek acquaintances have been geeks more or less since birth, struggling from the womb in thick spectacles, when, already lost among humans and comfortable only with machines, their first response was to turn lovingly to the baby heart monitor.

As a teenager, I liked music and girls. They liked squeezing their spots by the green light of their LED screens. They ate their lonely meals in their lonely rooms, playing computer chess.

I never had any interest in computers or technology in general until I got my first Mac, those three long years ago. It was a business decision: there were things that I needed to do with it. It wasn't technology lust or curiosity. I just needed to write some stuff and find things out off the Internet. That's all. Honest. But the thing, the thing that I never expected, was that I *understood* it. It all made sense. Soon I was drawn into that (not very) secret world of fanatics. I found myself buying computer magazines. Individually at first, hiding them in my *Guardian*. And then I was buying all three of the available Mac publications: *Macworld*, *MacFormat*, and *MacUser*. The newsstand man would greet me with a smile, knowing exactly what I was after, my porn stash of naked plastics, bare VDUs, desktops with their ports wide open, begging me to enter, to insert, to connect. Soon I found that I was a subscriber, enjoying the near-sexual thrill of hearing my beloved mags hitting the mat beneath the letter box. I was there, I was a geek.

That's why, with Celeste asleep beside me, I can write this in bed on my iBook, which is connected to both my iMac and the Internet by a wireless network, called AirPort. It's why I've switched to Mac OS X, although that renders my hard-earned knowledge useless, as I grapple with the industrial-strength UNIX core at its heart and enjoy the liquid beauty of the acclaimed Aqua interface.

I still like girls better than computers. And I don't talk about them unless an obvious "in" presents itself. But I want to. I really want to.

And now I've got a cool new toy to love, to lose. Harry likes it.

"It's *my* gun."

"It's not a gun. It's a little computer."

"Computer gun?"

"No, just a computer."

"It's a gun."

"It plays music. Listen."

Crying now.

"It's a gun it's a gun it's a gun."

I'm beginning to really regret agreeing to this dinner party of Celeste's. I like dinner parties but not when I'm cooking. The trouble is that my cooking, at its very best, is *only just* good enough for formal occasions. Quick dinners for the two of us, and I'm laughing. Piles of student food for piles of student friends? I'm your man. But proper dinner-party food, Nigella food, Jamie food, food that people want to talk about rather than just eat—going, "That sauce, so *quattrocento,*" and "How *do* you find sea asparagus in the summer?"— well, there I'm pushing the envelope, working at the extreme boundaries of my knowledge and ability. People who eat my food might say "Jesus, I'm stuffed" or "That hits the spot," but beyond that, I take a lack of projectile vomiting as the ultimate mark of approval. So, you see, come dinner parties, I have no slack to take up: unless I'm on top cooking form, producing personal bests at each round, then disaster looms. And that means stress and no fun—or getting no dinner.

Celeste, of course, won't cook. She'll suggest improbably difficult things and make vague attempts to "help," but it's like Harry helping poor old Magnus out in the garden. The stress is only partly relieved by the presence, this time, of some of my friends. Leo and Odette; Andrew without Alice; Ludo and Katie. Do they counterbalance the malign Galatea and Milo? Perhaps they do. No word from Uma. She won't come. Will she? Why, in God's name, did I ever mention it to her?

Harry did some new things today. He's developed a mania for jigsaw puzzles. He seems to go more by the shape of the piece than the picture, but he rattles through his twenty-piece floor puzzles in no time at all. Does thinking your two-year-old is especially advanced at jigsaws make you a doting parent? A crazy one?

But his best new trick is making men. He takes collections of rubbish—broken bits of old toys, spools of thread, spoons, stones, coat hangers—and he "makes a man."

"Make a man," he says, and then he makes one. He assembles his bits of tat. He assesses. He adjusts. He nods. True, you need to look at his man the way you'd look at a Picasso, maybe even a Kandinsky, before the outline begins to make sense. Yes, *there's* a sort of head, and there an arm. You wouldn't want to meet one of these men in a dark alley, clanking toward you, grabbing you perhaps, and looking at you with his pencil sharpener eye and his spoon mouth as he hisses "Kill me, please kill me," like the cocooned victim in the first *Alien* film, but if asked what it was, you'd say, "*Ecce homo.*" Well, you'd say that if you'd just read Nietzsche and checked out the notes. Otherwise, you'd say, "Yeah, look, a man." And God help you if mistake the man for junk and try to tidy him away. Harry hates his men being messed with. He does his mini-samurai, raging until the bits—the head, limbs, torso, pancreas, lymphatic system—are fully restored.

Does this mean that Harry's going to be an artist? Preferably not. Let's hope for a professor of anatomy or a butcher.

I'll try to work the baby Frankenstein stuff into a talk, and thence into my book. The book was a very pleasant surprise. I think the publisher may have thought it was getting some kind of quasi-scientific tract on men bringing up boys, by "Doctor" Sean Lovell. Not that I feel much pity, given the pissant advance it's offered. But at least I have an even better response to the "What do you do?" question—even better, that is, than "I work on the radio" or "web journalist." Now I can say, "I write books, so fuck off." It may even be time to resign formally from the Laboratoire Garnier. Perhaps they'll have a leaving do for me. The rabbits'll cry: they always do. I'll tell my fellow hair-and-skin scientists that we really *gelled* as a team, and they'll hand over my leaving gift, an engraved blackhead squeezer, the tight bastards.

"Whayadoon?" Celeste stirs.

"Just making some notes for my book."

"S'late."

"Won't be long."

"Stop it."

"Just one minuqpieruqvg]WV 0PAD VW;>WE}RTk\w[,m Get off."

"Give me a cuddle."

"All right, finishing now."

"Cuddle."

I suppose it's good to have occasional reminders of why I found Sean so exasperating in the first place. To begin with, he made such a fuss over cooking dinner at my parents' house that I almost wished I'd done it myself. He decided to make a fish soup of his own devising, flavored with fennel and Pernod, but from the chaos, you'd have thought he'd got the contract for Iran's nuclear bomb production. I swear to God there were nine unwashed pans by the time he'd finished and dismembered bits of sea creature on the floor and the sulphurous stink of unlit gas left on and smears of blood from finger wounds all over the tea towels. We had a blazing row when I tried to help, and I had to get Bella to come and make him behave. He was cooking in nothing but an apron and his underpants, admittedly long and baggy ones (although I thought I'd humanely killed all those), so it was more disgusting than indecent, but it wasn't anyone's idea of an appetizer.

He was still in his apron-and-underpant getup when the first guests arrived. From the front, he looked as though he were actually butt-naked under the apron, but Milo, Galatea, and Veronica took it in their stride, although I did notice a certain hesitancy later on when the soup appeared, with its cockles and scallops providing auditory and visual reminders of what they'd just missed as Sean raced upstairs to change, giving them a flash of his old-man knickers and hairy thighs. All the others—Andrew, Leo, Odette, Katie, Ludo—arrived in a gaggle while he was deciding which T-shirt to put on. They'd caught the same train and arrived in a party mood.

I kissed Ludo. He tried to look in my eyes, but I quickly moved on to Katie, and then the others. Then, drinks in hand, I gave them the tour. They all loved the house. Best of all was the visitation to Harry's room. His arms were thrown above his head, and he had a nozzle from a vacuum cleaner in one hand and a small green dog in the other. The animal was called Greeny the Booger Dog, and he ate . . . well, *you* guess. He lived on Venus and was constantly under threat from the evil Emperor Zurg. I supposed that the nozzle was a laser gun and Harry had fallen asleep on guard duty. I'd begged Sean to make his bedtime stories a little less violent, but that was like asking Tarantino to direct a Jane Austen adaptation.

"Funny having three floors and a garden and your own roof," said Katie. "You get used to everyone living in a apartment."

"I live in a house," said Veronica quietly.

"Yes, but not a house like this. Yours is more like a sort of hostel for the homeless."

"It was good enough for you once, I remember."

"And will you ever let me forget?"

"Now, now, girls," said Milo, playing the unaccustomed role of peacemaker. "That's all bile under the bridge. We've kissed and made up a long time ago."

I'd never quite got to the bottom of the Katie-Ludo-Veronica business. I knew about Katie's famous act of libidinal folly, and the separation, but I had a feeling something had gone on with Veronica. Had Ludo slept with her? Now I knew him better, now I knew that he wasn't quite as saintly as he first appeared, I thought it was more than possible. Despite her plainness—bad skin and coarse hair—she definitely had *something*. She was always immaculately dressed and presented, but Milo told me that that was a relatively late arrival, and anyway, it was part of the job. Perhaps it was that hard-

nosed business competence, that total absence of airiness and waf-
fle that I know some men are drawn to. Men who need an exo-
skeleton.

I'd only met Odette a couple of times, and she worked hard at
making a good impression. She'd obviously been brought up properly,
because she was full of gushing niceness, however inappropriate,
about everything. "What nice curtains," she'd say, about some
hideous bit of fabric, or "I do like how you've arranged your pans."
She reminded me of some of the annoyingly omnicompetent girls at
my school, the ones who were good at music and games and still got
their Oxbridge exhibitions. I didn't like them then, and I didn't particularly like her now, although I'm prepared to admit that as a fault
in me. It wasn't that I thought she was insincere; more that she struck
me as being faintly mad. The impression was confirmed when she
talked about her "business." She had, it seemed, abandoned a perfectly good career in the City to make, possibly with her own hands,
little versions of Stonehenge for people to put in their gardens.
"Gnomehenge" was Andrew's joke—not bad for him.

Leo, her husband, was the sort who always looked as if he were
about to say something wonderful or profound but then never really
did, unless you shared his interest in the odd bits of philosophy or
literature—the bits, as far as I could tell, that people didn't usually
bother with. But I noticed that Andrew and Sean looked to him as a
kind of oracle and assessed how funny they were being by whether or
not he laughed. Both Odette and Leo were unaccountably pleased at
having made, though not yet delivered, a baby. I could see that Odette,
for all her willowy frame, was going to be huge. You could tell from
her big feet.

Sean finally joined us, only to put his apron on again and return
to the kitchen. He did keep popping back to make humorous remarks,
although it was always after we'd moved on to something else. He
really was working like a slave, and I kept giving him little smiles to
show how much I appreciated it.

After half an hour, he came in to announce that dinner was ready, and we moved into the dining room. I'd set the table, so at least *that* looked nice, albeit in a suburban-Gothic way. There were flowers from the garden, and my parents' old plates and faux heraldic silver, and a gigantic candelabra, which I thought Milo might appreciate for its towering fin de siècle campness.

"How rushtic," said Galatea. It was probably meant as a put-down, but there was always the chance that suburban Gothic was back in fashion. "How's Dominic working out?"

Dominic was the architect Galatea had recommended to help us with the apartment. He was useless. His suggestions were all either impossible or horrendous. He had a conviction that a 1970s kitchen was the thing to have and wanted to re-create that assemble-it-yourself look, complete with "accidental" gaps and wonky hinges and peeling strips of plastic. Luckily Sean stepped in, demanding high-tech stainless steel everything, which, although not my ideal, was better than white melamine, and I could conveniently blame him for undermining Dominic's grand conception. Out of embarrassment, I let Dominic take charge of the second lavatory, which he was basing on the one in which Elvis died.

"He's so good, I just can't tell you."

"We think he's a rising shtar."

Sean gave me a look. I sometimes wondered if his instincts were right about my friends.

So we ate our soup. As predicted, it tasted like dissolved aniseed balls, but with a vicious, eye-watering chili kick. Cockles and scallops aside, nobody could work out what had happened to the fish part of the fish soup. The boys ate it, but the girls and Milo mostly chatted. I wouldn't say it was the greatest dinner party ever, but it was all pleasant enough. As I'd expected, Sean and his friends talked about their sort of thing, while the fashion people talked about fashion and people in fashion and people who knew people in fashion. Odette tried to join in with both but seemed happier discussing the obsession with St. Sebastian among European artists than which supermodels were *still* using heroin, years after it had gone out. Milo briefly flickered between the two worlds when Leo suggested that it (the St. Sebastians) was all to do with the repressed homosexuality of the painters and that the near-nude, always pretty, St. Sebastians were the closest they could get to expressing their desire. Milo surprisingly corrected him, by pointing out that Renaissance city-states were actually quite good places to go cruising and that most of the artists they'd mentioned were entirely "out," in the sense of being open about screwing boys, even though they eschewed the idea of exclusive homosexuality. The idea that you were either a gay or straight person was, he said, a modern view, invented in the nineteenth century. Before that, you had homosexual *acts* but not homosexuals.

I'd never heard Milo talk so seriously, and it was one in the eye for the eggheads down at the other end of the table. Leo looked stumped, but Andrew came in with an anecdote from Casanova's diaries, in which the great lover walked in on some German art historian called Winckelmann actually in the act of sodomizing a Roman street boy. Rather than looking embarrassed, Winckelmann sadly explained how he didn't *want* to do it but that he felt it was the only way of getting into the mind-set of the ancient Greeks, whose works he was studying, and that no matter how much (this in a terrible German accent) "I hump unt I hump, nothing comes ut all."

We were laughing at that (I don't know why; it wasn't particularly funny or relevant) when the bell rang. I thought it must be Mom and Dad back early from the theater, but when I went to the door, a woman was there. It was about ten o'clock, and we'd just finished the pudding. It was so unexpected that for a second I failed to place her.

"Hello. Sorry if I'm late, but Sean said to turn up anytime." She must have mistaken my look of shook for one of bafflement, as she continued, "I'm Uma. We met at the launch of your shop. Sorry, I've forgotten your name."

"Celeste."

"Nice to meet you again. Can I come in, or have I missed the party? I know you country types like to get to bed early, but I thought I'd be safe at ten."

I checked out the dress. Almost there. It was a modern Biba copy. Empire line; gathered below the bust; soft, full sleeves. Plum crêpe. I guessed it wasn't especially cheap. But nor was it right. She'd gone to a shop in the suburbs and just taken what they shoved at her. They'd probably shown her a soft-focused shoot from one of the Sunday color supplements, with a willowy model gazing out over a lily pond. A schoolgirl error. And she ought to have worn her hair up. Her red hair. I was very glad I'd kept it simple: heavy cream silk shirt, tight jeans, velvet evening pumps.

Then Sean was at my shoulder.

"Christ, Uma, come in. Sorry, darling, I forgot to tell you. But I never thought you'd come. You didn't seem very keen. I'm amazed she's here. Great to see you. Come in. Meet the gang."

While he was gabbling, I got very confused about who was who, and for a second, I thought that Uma was "darling." I moved aside and studied her closely as she passed.

I hadn't thought about her for a while. Too many other things had pressed in upon me. I knew it wasn't quite fair, but I blamed her for the mess I'd stumbled into. And blaming her, I expected to feel a surge of hate. But it wasn't there. I waited, but it didn't come. How strange, I thought. How strange, I still think.

She strode into the dining room and sat down in the middle of things, a chair appearing from nowhere.

Andrew did an introduction: "Everyone, this is Uma. Uma, this is everyone."

It was hardly needed. Within a second of sitting down, Uma was engaged in a six-way discussion with Katie, Odette, Andrew, Veronica, and Milo. She swigged out of someone else's wine glass, which then became hers. And then, for the next two hours, she dominated the room. Fashion and philosophy were abandoned, and what? Well, *everything* else took its place. Uma had a risible boredom threshold and wouldn't allow more than five minutes of the Middle East or Tony Blair or the euro or the best romantic comedies of all time. It was the greatest display of bravura egotism I'd ever seen, an excuse to talk at people, to feed off their laughter and admiration, but she turned two dinner parties into one, and before people knew what was happening, the last train had gone, and it was a matter of who'd share with whom in the taxis back into London.

Through it all, I was aware that Ludo was studying me. He'd said hardly a word to anyone all evening. At least he wasn't swept up in the Uma mania that possessed the other boys. You'd have thought a combination of Marilyn Monroe and Camille Paglia had suddenly appeared at the table, such was the intensity of focus and the lavishness of fawning attention poured upon her. I suppose I should have expected nothing better from Andrew, Leo, and Sean. But Milo? How could he have been so taken in? What, after all, did he care for Beirut massacres or Bosnian betrayals? Couldn't he *see* those horrid boots she was sporting? Odette was just as bad, following Uma's lead, and helping her out on those rare occasions when she faltered or lost impetus. True, Katie and Galatea, used themselves to being the center of attention, the pretty, bright things around which men formed like blood clots, adopted looks of condescension, superior amusement, a mild, mocking boredom. But they could not shift the party back to themselves with their small talk of fashion shoots and style magazines and startling new skin-care products. Only Veronica remained steadfast, listening critically but without obvious jealousy. Her passive scrutiny seemed to unnerve Uma, and she tried to avoid her gaze.

And me, what did I do? I floated. I found that I was surveying the scene from above but able to adjust my height, to zoom in to an eye, to see through the table to assess whose feet were touching, to fly back and up to take in again the whole group. I could see Andrew, laughing infectiously, desperately trying to get his own jokes in, to show that he could take the pace, flirting and flattering. I could see Leo, quieter, but causing even Uma to pause when he did say something, causing her to consider for a moment before she moved on, enclosing his comment within a wider theory, accepting but diminishing it. I could see Ludo, his elbows on the table, his thick fingers over his mouth or his eyes, his brow wrinkling with thoughts that seemed unconnected to the mood around him.

And Sean. He was smiling. But not his usual good-natured-drunk smile, the one that would settle on his face when things were going well. It was a different smile—a smile I remembered but hadn't seen for a while, perhaps for a couple of years. It was a smile of rapture, and it dismayed me.

Mom and Dad came in at about one. Dad went straight to bed after a quick "Ah, hello, how nice. There's port in the cellar, you know." Mom joined us. She and Uma hit it off. Uma asked her about Hungary. She'd been to Budapest and knew how to say "hello" and "I love you" in Hungarian, which amused everybody.

Uma went in the first taxi with Andrew, Leo, and Odette. Of course, everyone left behind bitched about Uma once she'd gone.

"Talk about an ego," said Katie, apparently unaware of any irony. "The thing is, she looked like she was talking about everything in the world, but she was really just talking about herself, because all that mattered was what she thought about it."

"It was protective," said Veronica. "There's something wounded about her. All that dazzle is to deflect attention, not to attract it."

That got a derisive snort from Galatea, but she didn't follow up the snort with evidence. I wondered if Veronica might have hit on something.

"Looked like poor old Andrew was deep in the smit," said Sean.

"Not just Andrew, I'd say," said I.

"No, you're right. Leo was fairly taken as well. But he always was one for yearning for the unobtainable."

Galatea and Milo exchanged looks.

"I, at least," said Milo, "thought she was an ornament to the evening, and I could not possibly have ulterior motives."

"You just got off on the fact that we all hated her," said Galatea. And then two more taxis came, and they left, sorting themselves out in the drive.

"What charming friends you have," said Mum. "How did you meet this Uma?"

"She's Sean's friend."

"Oh, really? I thought he obtained his friends from you." Sean was standing next to us, but Bella hadn't addressed him directly.

"He met her at a playgroup."

"Oh."

Now she looked at him. "How nice for you. See you in the morning." And she went to bed.

"The old bitch," said Sean.

"Don't talk about my mother like that. She's been very good letting us stay here."

"That's something I wanted to talk about. I've got so much work to do on this fucking book. I can't do it here. I can't get comfortable. I want to go and work at home for a couple of weeks."

"Work at home? But the builders . . . What do you mean?"

"All the main smashing up has been done now. It's just decorating left to do, which shouldn't disturb me. I can set up an office in the end room; there's just about enough space. I only need room for a laptop. And I can clear the bed."

"The bed? You mean you want to *sleep* there?"

"Of course. You know how I work. I like to go late into the night."

"What about Harry?"

"That's partly my point. For the first time in two and a half years, he doesn't need me. There's Magnus and Mary and Bella around the whole time. I'm mainly twiddling my thumbs—look, see how good

I've got at it." He twiddled in my face. "And I thought that you could maybe, you know, take some time off. You took hardly any vacation last year. You must have loads owing."

That bit was true.

"How long is this for?"

"I said, a couple of weeks. I need to do this."

"Sean?"

"Yeah?"

"You're not leaving me, are you?"

I said it almost as a joke. That's how he took it.

"Darling, how can I be leaving you when I'm going to live in *our* apartment?"

"I think it's madness. The mess, the clutter. How will you cook?"

"I'll eat sandwiches. And I'll see you whenever you want. And Harry. Remember, you go away for work all the time, this is just me doing the same."

Of course, a month before, I wouldn't have agreed. But things had happened since then. If he wanted to do this stupid thing, then I would let him.

We were in bed when I remembered Uma.

"Why didn't you tell me she was coming?"

"I forgot. No, I didn't really forget; I never thought she'd turn up. At the playgroup, I said we were having people round, and she looked lonely, and I said why not come, but she said she couldn't really, and I said go on, and she said she might, but I thought that meant no. So I was as surprised as you."

"I wasn't that surprised."

"What?"

"Nothing."

I tried again to find out where Sean has hidden his journal. Nothing. I keep hitting firewalls, if that's the right word. I asked him about it. He said that he didn't want to show me what he'd written because it was all crap and in note form. Anyway, he said, most of it would end up in the book on Harry, and I could see it then.

But I'll keep on writing my counterjournal, until the end. It means too much to me now to stop. For the first time in my life, I feel as though I understand myself and my life, because here I am, and here it is, in black and white—the truth of me, the truth of it.

FEAR PROVES STRONGER THAN LOVE

It was obviously not going to happen for me if I stayed in the house with Magnus and Bella and Harry, and Mary, the girl from the town. Even though I was no longer essential, I was still there, and Harry would come to me when others had said "no" (admittedly not that often, where Magnus was concerned). And then Bella had decided that she wanted to be my friend, which was worse than the old hostility. She'd bring up pots of tea or coffee and biscuits, and stay to chat. I sometimes got the impression that she had made a special effort with her appearance, putting on fresh lipstick, remodeling her penciled eyebrows. She was obviously proud of her bosom, which, for a skinny lady well into her fifties, was impressive. She had a dress with a sort of peephole over her cleavage, perhaps just—and I mean *just*—on this side of the decency barrier, and she tended to wear that for her visits. It must be some combination of paranoia and misplaced sexual egotism, but I began to think that there might be something *not quite right* about these afternoon liaisons.

A typical exchange would go something like this (picture Bella gazing mournfully out the window, like the Lady of Shalott's granny, blowing smoke at me from one of those long black cigarettes like a licorice stick):

"It is in some ways pleasant to have a young man here in my house."

"Oh, good. I don't like to be a—"

"I have been for a long time a lonely woman."

"At least you've got good old Magnus. Must be nice having him here, now he's semiretired."

"Magnus—as you say, *dear* Magnus—is occupied with his creatures. He dotes on them, you know?"

"Yes. Salamanders and newts. Dotes. And on Harry."

"It leaves him so little time for . . . what remains."

"What remains . . . er, the garden?"

"May I pour you some more tea?"

"Thanks, no, I really must be, ah, my book calls. Words to write. Lots of them. Look, here's one, a favorite of mine: *pullulate*."

Eventually she'd go. Nothing explicit was ever said—or, God forbid, done—but I definitely got the feeling that there was some . . . longing going on, somewhere. Celeste's relationship with Bella has always baffled me. Celeste seems completely blind to her eccentricities. Blind also to a kind of jealousy that Bella evidently feels. *Jealousy* gets it wrong; it's more that she knows she can only live through Celeste, and so needs her, but also hates her for it. Scratch that melodramatic *hates*; retreat to a more modest *resents*. Celeste is in the world in a way that Bella never was (at least since the days of her shuttlecock triumphs) and never will be. But for Celeste, Bella is just her mom—the woman who looked after her when she was a kid and who lives in the house where she grew up, and whom she loves without thinking about it. Not so very different, now I put it like that, from the way I think about my own mom.

But you'd have to work pretty hard to invent two characters as different as Bella and my mother, Elizabeth, always called Beth by my dad. She was big and loud and happy when I was small. And then Dad died, and she became gradually smaller, until now I have to bend down to put my arm around her. Beth was from Leeds. She met Eddie, my dad, on a religious retreat in the Yorkshire moors. It was the kind of thing that Catholic schools sent their holier-looking kids on in the hope that they might catch a vocation and come back as priests or nuns. But any thoughts Eddie and Beth might have had about marrying God were dumped as soon as they saw each other. They were seventeen.

Eddie was a fisherman from Hull. When he married Beth in 1966, they set up house in a village just outside his hometown. Eddie's boat trawled the Icelandic waters, teeming then with huge fucking fish, and the money was good. One of my few memories of my father—I must have been four years old, so it was 1972—is of him standing in the doorway holding up a whole cod almost as big as himself, its great mouth gulping open, scaring me. A memory, but not really a memory. A few years ago, I found a black-and-white photograph of Dad standing in a doorway holding up a huge cod, so my memory probably relates to the picture and not the man. In 1973, his boat sank in the North Sea. Instead of saying he'd gone to heaven, my mom said something strange. She said he was with the mermaids under the water.

After Eddie died, Mom moved back to Leeds, back to the council estate where she grew up, where I was to grow up. She was a clever woman and earned her living as a secretary, first at a car dealership and later in the Halifax Building Society in town. I usually had tea after school at gran's house, which was where I developed my aversion to boiled ground beef and potatoes. Gran was Irish, and Mom said that when they were kids, if they were naughty, they'd be sent outside to cut their own whipping rods, and if they weren't thick enough, then God help them, but when I knew her, she was as gentle as thistledown.

I think Mom thought she was better than most of the neighbors, which, as the years went by and the estate went from a fifties showpiece to a seventies hellhole, she was. Beth liked to read Thomas Hardy, but she got the novels from the library, and so there weren't many books in the house, apart from a long line of brown encyclopedias that Dad had ordered and Mom was still paying for years after he died. The main reason I am what I am, the way I am, was those encyclopedias. I read them the way other kids read comics. I

devoured facts about tin mining and the industrial uses of whale oil
and the way you tap a rubber tree. It's why I know nearly everything
but understand so little. (That analysis, by the way, was Celeste's
contribution to my fund of self-knowledge.)

So, no, Mum's nothing like Bella. She's a plain, quiet, stoical,
brave woman, older than her sixty-five years, who hit me when I
was bad and squeezed me when I was good. She made me sandwiches for lunch because I didn't like school food, and she made
sure my blazer was spotless and my tie neatly tied. She never had a
boyfriend after Dad, or if she did, she hid it from me out of shame.

It's a strange place to me when I go back, once or twice a year.
Some fluke of local economics or geography or politics has meant
that it hasn't got any worse, and in fact, it seems, oddly, to have
flourished. Everyone else in my mum's street has bought their own
house from the council. The result is a riot of misplaced but glorious individuality, with the usual stone cladding supplemented by
every kind of architectural device, from crenellations to moats to
arrow slits.

I seriously thought about going back there while the work was
done on the apartment—while the work was done on my book. I
could take Harry: Mom would be happy. But it would have been
cruel. The terrible truth about Harry, the thing that shames me and
yet also brings a profound pleasure, is that Harry loves and needs his
mother more than he loves and needs me. It's become even clearer
since we've been here with Bella and Magnus. I fed him and
wrapped him in his diaper and buttoned up his coat, but Celeste
was the one who syringed in the love. It was, it is, her soft face
he needs against his own, her lips he wanted to kiss, her arms he
craves.

And who could blame him?

I was pretty stunned when Uma turned up. I'd phoned her with the
vague idea of asking her out for a drink, but lost my nerve, and then
mentioned the dinner party. I suppose I did ask her, but it was more

just a way of treading conversational water. I never thought she'd come. Might almost think it was a deliberate . . . what? Attempt to embarrass me? Why would she do that? More likely she really was just lonely. Single parent and all that. She looked sensational, in some kind of dress. Interesting stuff happening at the front of it.

Can't say I'd been enjoying the night much up to her arrival. I over-Pernoded (Pernoed? Pernode? Perned? Pernodiddy-diddy-what-diddy-dooed?) the soup and then tried to compensate with too much chili. Don't think anyone else noticed (one becomes a bit hyper-self-critical on these occasions). Our main conversation up to that point, the point of Uma's arrival, had been the old bit about the best side of any Beatles record, keeping to the conceit that CDs still have sides. Leo has an obsession with the medley on side two of *Abbey Road*, and I can never work out if he's just being perverse or if it really is the Beatles' masterpiece. Andrew always agrees with him, and there's nothing interesting or amusing about trying to uphold whichever side of *Sgt. Pepper's* or *Rubber Soul* or even the White Album (my choice) you happen to prefer.

I've a feeling, in fact, that Leo brought the issue up at the dinner party purely because he knew it would be as alien and distasteful to the fashion crowd as discussing the boil on the bum that killed Nathan Rothschild, the richest man in the world, in 1836. The Beatles, for them, are what your parents listen to. Not even crap enough to be camp. Just old and dead. Music to hum in the nursing home.

I, by the way, introduced the Rothschild boil, an old friend of mine.

But anyway, the evening was taking a familiar path, not boring but not dizzying either, and then came Uma. She dizzied all right. With the two of us, she had always been good value, but not like this. I saw that she needed an audience: one prepared to participate, to *volunteer*, like a schmuck at a magic show, but nonetheless an audience for that.

I was worried about what Celeste was thinking. Of course she'd met Uma on the evening of the ludicrous swans, but I think she was too preoccupied to take much in. Since then I'd been careful to adopt my Face of Utmost Indifference if ever she came up in conversation, so I'm pretty certain Celeste has no inklings. Still, there is always that women's intuition thing to worry about, especially as, with Celeste, it always takes the form of thinking the worst about me.

Things went from odd to odder when Bella and Magnus returned from wherever they'd been (my money was on grave robbing for her and the bathroom for him). What a glorious thing it is that you can't be embarrassed about your in-laws. The worse they are, the more sympathy you garner. I was relieved to hear, as I'm sure were the others, that things are looking sprightly colonwise for Magnus, and he shook his head sadly at the lack of roughage in our menu for the evening. His parting shot as he retreated to his newts was, "I wouldn't be your lower digestive tracts for all the salamanders in the Mong region of China."

And then Bella was among us, like cholera. Bella had two principal animal manifestations, both winged: the bat and the moth. So she could be all manic, leathery flapping and high-pitched squeaking, or she could do her silent, creepy fluttering thing, making you pity her and yet want to crush the life from her before she sprinkled you with her deathly dust. Tonight it was the bat. She flapped and squeaked and then fastened onto Uma to have a good feed. I don't know why, but Uma seemed to warm to her. It wasn't pleasant, and a deep, loony, paranoid side of me was convinced that they'd start exchanging revelations about me, despite the fact that there was nothing, at present, to revelate.

And then it was over. As I shook Ludo's hand, I realized that I hadn't spoken to him all evening, and I apologized for it. He looked at me as if I were saying something profound that he didn't want to hear, and I felt very Ancient Mariner and let go of him.

On the way out, Uma asked me if I would be going to the playgroup.

"Not while we're here."

"Shame. So I won't see you. Oscar will be sad."

"Oh, I'm sure we'll be able to fit each other in."

Then an unexpected thing happened: she blushed. Uma wasn't the kind of girl who blushed. She was the kind of girl who made you blush—that was the whole point of her. And it was around then that I finally decided that I had to go and stay at the apartment. The reason was to finish the book, but the urge came from somewhere else.

Celeste took it surprisingly well. I thought she'd just give me a straight "no" and then that would be the end of the matter. I hadn't been able to fight against one of her nos in seven years, and I was hardly going to start now. But there it was: an "okay." I could see that she wasn't happy—see, in fact, that she was sad. And it seemed not simply a sadness born of selfishness but a *giving* sadness. It made me feel a pang of love. But it didn't change my mind. So her scolding would have kept me there but not her love.

Does this prove that fear is stronger than love?

I hope not.

They've let me take two weeks off work. Sean was right about my vacation's having built up. They were more surprised than annoyed when I asked them. I obviously have a reputation for working all the time, for being *there*. When Harry was born, they all expected me to slow down, but that made me try even harder. I wanted to be the first to arrive in the morning, the last to turn off my computer at night. No one would ever say that having a baby had lessened my commitment. It was their idea that I take off three months and ease back in part-time. It was something to do with there being so many women at the head office approaching the baby time: nobody wanted me to set too harsh a precedent. They were even quite generous about the terms.

But now two weeks of raw, unadulterated Harry. How would I cope? I've always taken the lead in the evenings—if Harry's still awake, that is—and on weekends. But at least Sean was usually around to do a bit of relief when I needed it. And he was someone to chat to, to talk at—to tell to fetch me the whatever needed fetching. This was going to be different. Me and Harry, alone, two weeks. Except for Magnus and Bella. And Mary, the girl from the town. Who I think may be simple.

And four days down already, and nobody dead yet!

Luckily the weather is beautiful. All day we play in the garden. Magnus has a toolshed and has built a sandpit. I sit in a deck chair and watch Harry take out rakes, spades, bamboo canes, spare blades for the mower, the mower. Sometimes he drags them around for a while, and sometimes he arranges them in geometric patterns on the lawn, claiming mysteriously to have "made a man."

"Where's Daddy?" he asked on Monday morning.

"Daddy told you. He's gone to work."

"Don't be *silly*, Mommy. You go work, and Daddy play Harry. Only Daddy can make DVD go."

"I can do DVDs, too."

"Watch *Little Mermaid?*"

"No, I'm reading my book, and you're playing in the garden."

I hadn't quite realized how much Harry cries. I find that my heart isn't rent by his crying, because it seems that he cries mainly from rage at having been denied something that probably isn't good for him. Sean's trouble (useful, though, if you're me and you want something) is that he *always* gives in under pressure. He's well aware of the fault. He says it's a bit like the English system of government in the pre-democratic period: tyranny tempered by rioting. The problem is, it has taught Harry the valuable lesson that if only he makes enough fuss, he'll always get his Smarties.

Time, while I'm in charge, for some tough love.

Yesterday I invited some friends round with their children. Minna brought her two boys, Matty and Michael, one four years old, the other not quite two. The elder is shy and frightened of life, but the younger one charges around like a pinball, bouncing off furniture and people and trees with sickening crunches that don't seem to bother him. And Nester came with Justin, almost the same age as Harry, and as close as he comes to having a friend. We sat and drank wine in the garden and watched the children play. Harry's just reached the age at which other children have become interesting— potential sources of pleasure rather than merely things that stop his getting all the attention. So there was some talking, some giving, some pulling. Harry hardly fought at all with the other kids. There *was* an altercation over a Buzz Lightyear, but that fizzled out, and there were more than enough tools to go round in the sandpit. All reasonably fascinating as an observer and completely engaging as a mother.

We were wearing summer dresses and Gucci sandals. By two o'clock, it was too hot in the sun, and we moved our deck chairs under the big ash tree, which has stood there since before the house was built (or so Dad keeps telling me, and came specially to tell us all again, but I didn't mind because he brought out a bottle of Pouilly-Fumé). It was a perfect day.

"So what's it like being a mother?" said Minna naughtily. She's always given the impression of being a devoted mother while sneakily working in PR, for a mortal enemy of Milo's. She is from the Portuguese Catholic part of India and looks like Gina Lollobrigida.

"From what I can make out, it's a pretty easy job."

"You have got quite a lot of help, though," said Nester. So they were ganging up on me. Nester is North London Jewish. I'd known her all my life. When we were teenagers, I used to go to a Jewish youth club with her. I quite liked being the blondest Jew in London: it seemed like the best of all worlds.

"Same as Sean, but that never stopped him moaning."

"I think you're a bit hard on him," said Minna. She was always quite nice to Sean, in the way that people sometimes develop an affection for hedgehogs and leave out bread soaked in milk for them. He, in turn, worshipped her as the only girl in our group who didn't quake at the thought of sitting next to him in a restaurant.

"Oh, he likes to feel the smack of firm government. But things, well, they've been *better* between us lately."

"Really?" said Nester. "I thought with him sleeping at the apartment that, well, things were more or less over between you. I had a friend I was thinking about setting you up with, but you'd have to convert, probably. *Justin, leave that alone!*"

"That was thoughtful of you. What's he like? No, don't tell me. The apartment thing *is* weird. He says it's to do with finishing this book of his about Harry. I think it might just be that he needs his own space. I've been practicing seeing things from his point of view, and it must be a bit *trying*, living with Bella and Magnus. I'm used to them, but, well, he isn't."

"So there's nothing more . . . serious?" said Minna.

"Serious? No. I'm not sure what you would count as serious."

"On either side?" said Nester. I was definitely getting the ganged-up-on feeling.

"If you mean, is he having an affair, and that's why he's gone, then, no, of course not."

They both laughed.

"No," said Minna, "nobody would dream of having an affair with Sean. I mean, why would you? Oh, I don't mean to say that he isn't lovely, and perfectly good-looking, but, well, he's not the sort, is he?"

"No, I don't think he is."

"But you, Celeste," cut in Nester, "are you?"

"Am I what?"

"Having an affair."

That came as a shock. "What makes you say that?"

"Stab in the dark."

"Come on, Nester, have you heard something?"

"No. Maybe. A friend told me she saw you in the park a week or so ago. With some chap. All looked very intense, she said."

"Which friend?"

"Joley. You don't really know her, but she knows who you are through parties and things. She described the person, and it didn't sound like Sean."

What should I do? My principle was always, when lying, to stick as close as possible to the truth, weaving in and out where necessary.

"There was nothing intense about it. It was a friend of Sean's. I'd been feeding the ducks, and he wandered by. He looks sort of intense all the time, but that's just him."

"Feeding the ducks!" shouted Nester. "I've known you twenty years, and I've never known you to feed a duck."

"The ducks were a *metaphor*. I was there having my lunch."

"It was the afternoon. Late afternoon."

"It was a late lunch. You know what my hours are like. Oh God, look, this is all gone again. I'll ask Magnus to bring another bottle. I love being a full-time mum."

The brittle, silly talk, the drink, the seeming not to look at Harry, was all an act. I thought I had to be something like the old Celeste in front of Nester and Minna. What I really wanted to do was to get down in the sandpit with my baby. I wanted him to be scrabbling all over me, covering me in his toddler smells and his toddler juices. I was glad when they left. I don't think they were really suspicious about Ludo. It was more just something to talk about, a way to fill the spaces in between sips.

I could see that being a middle-class mom was a pleasant way to spend your life. Money is the key. Money buys you help. Help takes away the pain. What you're left with is the fun, or rather the room in which fun might happen. Sean's problem is the help. Because of who he is, the idea of paying people to do things burns him like acid. So, yes, help helps, but I wouldn't want to be my friend Nester. She left her job in a law firm and became a mother of leisure, secure behind two nannies, a team of cleaners, a husband at Salomon Brothers, and a big Jewish family, desperate to take the kids for an afternoon, for an evening, for a night. It didn't leave much for her to do, and the less she did, the less she was. We used to talk about lots of things. Well, I suppose it was boys as often as not, but politics and books as well. Now, apart from moaning about her nannies or the cleaning lady, she didn't have very much left to give.

Minna had things worked out a little better. She went in to work when she felt like it (or so it appeared) and did just enough to keep her on her toes conversationally and in touch with how people are.

After the girls went home, I took Harry into the kitchen and sat with him on my knee as I read the hopelessly complicated recipes in my *Cooking for Babies and Toddlers*.

"When's Daddy coming back?"

"He'll come and see you tomorrow."

He cried a little about that.

"Shush now. What do you want to eat?"

"Cake." The tears slowed at the thought of it.

"We haven't got any cake." The tears burst forth again. "What else would you like?"

"Milk."

"It's not milk time yet. How about broccoli in a Gorgonzola and mascarpone sauce?"

Mysteriously, that didn't seem to do the trick.

GOOD OLD LEIBNIZ

*What is it with kids and food? I mean, the way they hate it. You'd
have thought that natural selection would have favored children
who ate all the things that we want them to eat: the good things,
the green things, the things with vitamins and minerals in them.
After all, you don't see a baby sparrow spitting out the compacted
little ball of grubs and caterpillars thrust into its beak by the
mother and pulling a face of rage and betrayal, hurling a no no no
naaaaaaawhnnaaaaaahhhh at the suffering parent. Or a gambol-
ing infant hyena turning away from the regurgitated antelope tes-
ticle with that haughty I-shun-all-things-of-the-palate look that
my little boy, Harry, has perfected.*

I was on live. It was a new departure. I was now apparently seen
as a safe pair of hands; I wouldn't run amok or drink more than my
usual two pints of loosener and start talking about the lights, the
beautiful lights, or belch loudly into the microphone. Naturally,
they chose the feature before mine specially to try to discommode
me. As so often seemed to be the case, it was about women and
their troublesome sphincters.

"Can you give us a run-through," Jemima had said, smiling her
smile of bottomless cruelty, "of some of the anal seepage scenarios?"

The expert, a sympathetic-looking woman with glasses so thick
they could be used to glaze the windows of deep-sea exploration
craft and hair dense and coarse enough to support a tennis racket

thrust vertically into its midst, listed them. Dismayingly, it seemed that, for the vulnerable, anal seepage could strike almost anytime, although it was particularly important to be on your guard after flatulence or intercourse. Exercise classes were another danger time. Or coughing. Or laughing.

And what could be done about it? Could the errant sphincter be trained, humbled into obedience like a broken circus lion? I don't know—I had a final read-through of my piece and missed the thrilling dénouement.

There have been sociobiological explanations for the strange aversions of children. [I like to chuck in a bit of science when I can: raises the tone of things and annoys Jemima.] *Cabbage and other brassicas contain, it seems, substances potentially toxic to some children. So the gene that just says no to broccoli helps out with survival. But, like Harry with his greens, I don't swallow it. My friend Anna Blundy manages to get fistfuls of vegetative matter, in hues from yellow through green to orange, into her two kids, and they thrive.*

Vegetables are good for children, so why won't Harry eat them? And it's not just vegetables. Short of chicken nuggets, he eats no meat. Aside from his very occasional fish stick, he consumes no fish. Why? It is madness, nutritional suicide.

And so I try to force him. I know I shouldn't. Every book ever written on the subject says don't do it, you'll just make matters worse. And I know that I'm repeating history. I remember my mom trying to make me eat rice pudding. Each time she spooned it in, I spat it out. Each time I spat it out, she slapped my face. Her hand gave in before my face, and to this day, I haven't eaten the muck. Vegetables are still an ordeal for me. If I were left entirely to my own whims I'd eat the same meal every day: a cheese sandwich on white bread with a Branston pickle and a side order of cheese-flavored potato chips.

Yes, I try to make him eat, even knowing, from my own experience, that I will not prevail. Without the right kind of equipment—tubing, pumps, etcetera—force-feeding is futile. On the subject of forced feeding, by the way, it's usually glossed over these days, but the suffragettes didn't actually want the vote for all women. They wanted the vote for wealthy women—those who met the existing property qualification—which is why the Liberals, the radical party at the time, were against— [Stop, man, for God's sake, stop. Jemima's doing her hanging-man mime; the producer, a very pretty twenty-four-year-old, slightly out of her depth but trying like all get-out, is hold-ing her head in her hands. This is a nice little earner; don't ruin everything now; back on track, quick, quick.] *Ha-ha-ha, so . . . um, but what I don't understand is why he's the fattest lit-tle kid in his playgroup, despite consuming . . .*

And so on for another four minutes. I knew how close I'd come to blowing it. The tragedy was that it wasn't even an ad-lib: I'd scripted the fucking thing. I hate the truth. I think all that saved me was that the rest of the piece hammered home how crap I was, dwelling on long-term damage, emotional inadequacy, probable sexual dysfunctionality, etc, etc. I'd milked that strain after Jemima told me that the previous week's broadcast, an account of taking Harry to the zoo, where he'd contracted ringworm from a reticu-lated python forced on him by some enthusiasts manning the ex-hibits desk at the entrance to the reptile house, had attracted complaints that it was "self-congratulatory."

Except that self-abnegation didn't save me.

"And thanks again to Sean Lovell for the *last* in his series of talks on being a stay-at-home dad."

Then a woman came on to talk about how to make jam from mushrooms. As I squeezed past, Jemima spun around in her swivel chair. (Her contract, by the way, insists that her chair, in addition to both tilting and swiveling, should be 22 percent bigger than any other chair in the studio and, finally, should swivel *more* than any other chair.)

"So long, big boy." She smirked menacingly and slid her cruelly taloned fingers inside my waistband. Once there, she maneuvered until she had a handful of my manhood.

"No one disses the suffragettes on *my* show," she said, and squeezed.

My eyes were still watering when I reached the pub. I ordered a pint of beer and sat down, gingerly, in a quiet corner. Uma came in ten minutes later. I'd arranged to meet her, as she had business in Broadcasting House herself.

She was wearing a white linen jacket, quite smart by her standards, and a narrow black skirt. I think she was trying to look businesslike, but it was all undermined by that untamable head of red hair. She smiled when she saw me and came and sat down next to me on the worn leatherette of the bench. She sat closer than I'd expected. And then she slipped off her jacket. Underneath, she was wearing a small garment—camisole? vest? (don't know exactly what the word is, and I can hardly ask Celeste, can I?)—with little straps and some lacy goings-on at the front. The whole thing was most unnerving.

"Listened to you in the car," she said, when I'd brought a glass of wine back from the bar. "Thought you were quite good."

From Uma, that counted as lavish praise, and I felt a glow of contentment, like a schoolboy getting his head patted by a notoriously hard-to-please teacher. Whom he fancies.

"Thanks."

"I especially enjoyed the bit about the suffragettes. Why did you stop?"

"Jemima. She didn't like it. But I didn't mean to tar them all with the same feather—"

"Brush."

"Yeah, brush. I always say feather. Er, brush, because Sylvia Pankhurst wanted the vote for everyone. Doled out soup and condoms in the East End, that sort of thing. It's the others I can't stand."

"Yeah, I get it. But that's enough of the suffragettes."

"Okay. What do you want to talk about?"

"Sex or God. Everything else bores me at the moment. I was sooo bored at your dinner party. 'Oh, *that's* what you think about the Israelis? Really. No, really? So you think they should be nicer to one another? Well, I hadn't thought of that. How stimulating. They really should make you the special envoy. And what, the Russians are being beastly in Chechnya? I hadn't heard. And there's a north-south divide on house prices? So houses cost more in London than Wigan? Scandal. I blame the government.' I mean, have you ever heard a single interesting or original statement from anyone at a dinner party? No, you haven't. All you get are the same boring ideas rolled around, and everyone agreeing how terrible things are. Well fuck off, fuck right off."

"Don't blame me, I never said a word all night."

"Might have been more interesting if you had."

Okay. Now that was the second nice thing she'd said in the space of one lunchtime. I thought back through the months of our relationship, trying to find other examples of pleasantness from Uma. She may have once said that she quite liked my sideburns, but that was after I'd shaved them off, so it could equally well be put down as a put-down. Beyond that, I was struggling.

Time to strike with a piece of irresistible flirtation.

"I've been thinking," I said meditatively, "about Leibniz and the Problem of Evil." Why, the smooth bastard.

"The Problem of Evil being how God could have made a world where so much shit happens?" Uma moved an inch or two closer on the bench. We were as close to touching as you can get without actually, er, touching.

"That's exactly the problem of evil I had in mind."

That as opposed to the Problem of Evil in *Buffy the Vampire Slayer* or the Problem of Evil in my underpants.

The odd thing is that I actually *had* been much preoccupied with how it was possible to get through a day without despairing. It began when a handicapped kid came into the playground in Kilburn. I was pushing Harry on the swings . . .

"I was pushing Harry on the swings," I said to Uma, aware that she was *really* listening, not the half paying attention, half thinking of something cutting to say that I usually got from her, "when this little boy came into the park. He was maybe six or seven years old, and he was obviously handicapped, but not too badly. He could walk, but he was very wobbly. I suppose it must have been cerebral palsy, but I also got the feeling that there might have been some mental problem there as well. I don't know. He was with a big, ugly, stupid-looking woman. I remember her buttocks—they looked like the war hammer of some savage god of the Polynesians—but the biggest impression she gave off was of overwhelming boredom. She got him out of his stroller and into the swing—you know, one of those baby swings, with the bar across and stuff. Then she pushed him once and went and sat down and had a fag. The kid liked the swinging bit, or I think he did. He made a noise that could have been laughing. I hope it was. Then his feet began to scrape on the floor, and the swing stopped. I looked at the carer. She was gazing into nowhere. She noticed me looking, and she began to do some girl sort of stuff, messing with her skirt, touching her hair. She thought I was checking her out. I pointed at the child and said, 'Is it okay if I push him?' She looked really pissed off and nodded, then went back to being gormless.

"So I pushed him and Harry at the same time. Harry loved it, swinging together. I tried talking to the boy. He gurgled, but it was still impossible to work out if he was speaking or laughing or crying. Perhaps his mother would have been able to make out what he was saying—you know, faster, higher, or please, for Christ's sake, stop this, I just want to sit here and scrape my feet, you big, fat useless fuck. And I did feel like a big useless fuck. This wasn't Rwanda or the Holocaust or even a really serious handicap, in the great scheme of things: it was one mildly handicapped kid and a lazy lump of a carer. And by the way, I don't really blame her. After all, she was looking after him, and what the fuck had I ever done that was as useful as that? And I also know that it's pointless and offensive and irrelevant to mention her buttocks, but I'm trying to tell you what was going through my mind.

"Anyway, I lost it. The tears started to roll down my face, and it was all I could do not to wail, you know, so I wouldn't scare them. And I thought about Leibniz—the philosopher, late-seventeenth-century—how he tried to make this kind of thing bearable. He said that when God was thinking up the world, he wanted to make it as good as it could possibly be. He could have made a world without evil, without suffering, but you could only do that if you took away our freedom, our ability to choose evil. He could have made us the kind of beings who could never decide to torture people or machete kids in the head, but then we'd have been robots and not moral agents at all, and there'd be no such thing as good."

"But that doesn't mean there had to be handicapped kids. He could have made us free but with better genes."

At some point, the almost touching had turned into touching, in the leg region, at least. It felt oddly companionable. But also sexy as hell. But I had to concentrate. Leibniz Leibniz Leibniz.

"He could, yes, but this is where Leibniz's thing about this being the best of all possible worlds comes in. Without the handicapped kids, you don't have people caring for them, loving them, creating goodness out of evil. The victims in the world are the opportunity the rest of us have to be kind."

"But that's horrible. He made some people suffer just so that other people could be nice to them?"

"Yeah, I know, it is a bit crap. But the trouble is, I think it's the only explanation going. If this isn't the best of all worlds, then either God's a monster or he doesn't exist. You have to clutch to the Leibniz or despair. But there was another bit to it that really got me. I was back thinking about the little boy. He had a shitty carer and a life of, I don't know, possibly constant torment, but maybe, just maybe, when he died, when the little chap gave up, well, then God would take care of him properly, push his swing, give him good legs, a clear mind. Maybe that's where it balances out, heaven. Because it isn't here, is it?"

And I found that I was doing it again. My eyes were stung with tears, and I had to blow my nose. Uma, so close to me now, put her hand on my hand. Her fingers were short and neat and competent. They looked like the type of hands you'd find on an arts-and-crafty kind of person, a potter or someone who weaves shawls. Not quite what you'd expect from a flame-haired temptress.

"Holy mother of God, this isn't pub culture at all," I said. I had to move my hand from under hers to take out my handkerchief. I blew my nose and laughed. "I can't believe I came out with all that."

"Why?"

"Because it's hopeless sentimental bullshit. Because God's not really there, and so he won't be looking after the handicapped kid when he dies, and what we need is a better health service and decent pay for carers and a peaceful socialist revolution and more cycle lanes."

"What happened to the boy?"

"Oh, the woman took him out after a while, and they sat at one of the picnic tables and had something to eat. She wasn't so bad; she really wasn't so bad. I was just feeling a bit . . . you know."

"I know. I've got to go now. I've an appointment."

"Jesus, I'm sorry I've bored you. I blame Jemima for getting me all wound up. You know, she put her hand—"

No she didn't.

"What?"

"Nothing."

"I've got a babysitter for Friday night, if you're free," she said.

"Yeah, I think I am. I mean, I can be. Yeah. What do you want to do?"

"Whatever. How about dinner somewhere?"

"There's a new place in West Hampstead. It's meant to be okay."

She smiled. "Fine."

"Fine."

We stood up together, and I kissed her cheek and smelled the shampoo in her heavy hair. As she moved away through the pub, she half turned and looked at me, her face serious. Then she waved and was gone.

Good old Leibniz. Good old God.

I miss him. I didn't think I would. I never did when I was away on business in Paris or Milan or Turin or New York. I missed Harry, of course, but not Sean. I'm not a missing-people person. It's always been the kind of futile emotion that I've done quite well without, thank you very much. I must be going soft in my dotage.

Anyway, I took Harry into my bed last night and fell asleep with my face in his hair. He doesn't smell like a baby anymore. Now his hair smells of hair hair and not baby hair. But it's still the softest stuff there is, and I felt it move with my breath. He woke once in the night. He sat up and said clearly, "What am I here for?" and then huffed down again and went straight back to sleep. In the morning, he touched my face and then looked wonderingly around the room. Then he said, "Let's find Daddy," and led me through the house, checking each room, ignoring my words about where Daddy was. In the end, I phoned Sean and got him to speak to Harry.

Then I took the phone back. "We're missing you."

"What? But you never . . . Well, I'm missing you both, too."

"Why not come back?"

"It won't be for long. I'm making fantastic progress."

"Okay. But you're coming on Saturday?"

"Yes."

"For the whole day?"

"Yes, I promised. I'll talk to you before then."

"I should think so. What are you eating?"

"Pizza, mainly. I've started getting the one with all the foliage on top, rocket and stuff. Rocket: sounds so exciting doesn't it? *Apollo 11*, Saturn V, Scud. And then it turns out to be lettuce. Still, thought it might be healthier. Against the basic law of pizza, though. I mean, a *salad* pizza. What have I come to?"

"You're one of us now."

"Daresay you're right. I'll see you Saturday."

"Love you."

"Love you."

It seemed that we were doing a lot of "I love yous" lately, though I had the feeling mine counted for more than his.

It was just me and Harry all day, today. Bella and Magnus were out, and Mad Mary wasn't booked. It was raining, and so we did some jigsaw puzzles in the morning on the kitchen table with him sitting on my knee. Then we watched *The Little Mermaid,* with which and with whom Harry is entirely obsessed. He doesn't appear to understand the plot but has fixated on certain characters. He says he wants to be Prince Eric, particularly coveting his high boots, and he is appropriately amused by and scared of the evil sea witch, Ursula. I asked him if he wants to kiss Ariel, the little mermaid, and he goes shy but still says yes.

I put him down for a sleep in our unmade bed at two. I lay with him for a while, but my mind was too busy to sleep.

Ludo telephoned later in the afternoon.

"Can you talk?"

"Yes, there's no one here. But I don't think this is a good idea."

"You don't know what I want yet."

"No, I don't know what you want."

"First—and I'm sorry, but I have to ask this—is there really no hope for me?"

"There's really no hope."

"Then I'm sorry for what I did, for dragging you into this, and I promise not to bother you again. I'm not a bad man, Celeste. I try to do the right thing, but sometimes forces move you, move through you. I'm sorry, I'm not good at talking about feelings."

"Ludo, I know you're not a bad man, but what we did was a bad thing. It was a bad thing because I still loved Sean. If I hadn't loved him, or if I'd loved you, then it would all have been different. But, although it was a bad thing, in some ways I don't regret it."

"Good."

"Because—and I know this is a terrible cliché—it's shown me what I value. It's made me into a better person. I've been spending time with Harry; it's been wonderful. And I miss Sean."

"Sean's not there?"

Ludo sounded suddenly hopeful. I thought for a moment he might be about to suggest something, but I also sensed that he was restraining himself, trying to be good.

"No, he . . . well, it's difficult to explain, but he's at the apartment. Nothing's going on; he's got things he has to do there. And you saw Bella and Magnus the other night. You can imagine that maybe he wasn't very comfortable here."

"No."

He laughed. I loved it when he laughed. For a second, I was back in the hotel room, back feeling the pull of him, but I shuddered myself free of the image.

"But you, Ludo, what about you and Katie?"

"I can't see we have a future, not after what I've done. It wouldn't be right for either of us."

"You shouldn't be so hasty. I didn't realize that I had such strong feelings for Sean until all this blew up. I thought there was nothing much left for us other than a kind of cold war. You never know what you can find in a relationship, even after it looks like the cupboard's bare. Sean used to say something about there always being another nut in your pocket, if you search deeply enough for it."

"Yeah, I've heard him say that. But usually he said it while he was actually looking for nuts, so I'm not sure he meant it metaphorically. More in a Forrest Gump way."

"But I'm saying that if you still have any love for her, and I know that she still loves you, then you should try. Once it's gone, it's gone."

"I never thought I'd get relationship counseling from you, Celeste." His tone was grimly humorous.

"People always sound stupid when they try to give advice. Perhaps I'm just trying to salve my own conscience. I don't want to think that I've ruined it for you and Katie."

"You always claim to be more heartless than you are."

"I'd like it if we could still be friends, Ludo. You're a special person."

For the third or fourth time, I cringed at what I was saying. Was it really impossible to say something original in this situation, something not worn smooth with use? But then, how many millions had been here before us, getting all the words when they were still fresh, still warm with life?

"I don't know. We'll see."

"I think I hear Harry waking. I'll have to go."

"Good-bye, Celeste. I'll always love you."

"Good-bye, Ludo. I'll always fancy the pants off you."

I cradled Harry, who was coming down with a cold. He clung to me and put his head heavily on my shoulder. "Mommy daddy mommy daddy," he murmured over and over into my ear. I felt good. I felt that I had rescued something precious. But I also knew how close I'd come to messing up.

Sean's always been the one tangled up in moral theorizing. He thinks he can't know what the right thing is, and therefore can't *do* anything, unless he's got what he calls an ethical framework. When he was annoyed, he'd say that I don't have morals, I have whims, and so even when what I do is exactly what he would do, using his ethical framework as a guide, I'm not being moral at all.

"Morality means following a rule," he'd say, "but your only rule is, Do what you want. If you want to be generous, you'll be generous. If you want to be kind, you'll be kind. But it's only moral if you do it even though you don't want to, if you overcome your natural inclinations and self-consciously choose to be moral."

It was a horrible thought that he might have been right. Perhaps it was just the law of averages: even a lifetime devoted to talking bullshit must produce the occasional scrap of sense. Sometimes he'd try to bring God into the argument—his weirdo atheist-Catholic God. I don't know if he ever helped with anything. I've never really cared if God existed or not. I can see in the abstract that it's a biggie, but like the football results that Sean gets so worked up about, it just doesn't seem to bother me.

I wasn't getting very far with these thoughts, but I did decide to try in the future to think a bit more before I acted. Weigh up a little. Give my whims a bit of direction. Live a better life.

Or so I thought as Harry mommy-daddy-mommy-daddied on my shoulder, the snot flowing freely over my second-best silk blouse.

And then I started to feel sick.

SEANJOURNALTWENTY.DOC

THE FREE-FUCK DILEMMA

It was inevitable that once I started thinking about the betrayals of friendship, I'd end up with girls. I was in the Black Lamb with Leo and Andrew. Ludo said he'd try to join us later, but we weren't expecting him. A band was playing Irish standards in the next room: "The Rover," "Peggy Gordon," "Carrickfergus."

"We'd all look on ourselves as being the good guys, wouldn't we?" I began.

There was general, ironically modulated, consent. Andrew said, "Here we go."

"Given that—and I don't know about you, but I'd say that—beginning with Louise Craggs when I was twelve, I've betrayed every girl, every woman, I've been out with."

"Seems a slightly harsh way to put it, unless you mean that you gave them up to the gestapo or the Spanish Inquisition," said Leo.

At the next table, a small, round fellow, who'd made one of the worst attempts at having a shave I'd ever seen, was talking to what might have been his great-great-grandfather, whose face seemed not only to be toothless but largely boneless as well.

"And anyways, what *is* custard powder made from?"

"That'll be dried-up custard."

"But, then, if custard's made from custard powder, how did it all begin?"

"It's a chicken-and-egg situation all right."

These weren't ideal conditions, but I kept on trying.

"You know what I mean. Two-timed or dishonorably dumped, or deliberately behaved badly so that they had to dump me, thereby saving myself the trouble and guilt. That sort of thing."

"You did all that to Louise Craggs when you were eleven?"

"Twelve. No, well, she was a special case. I let her down by not being cool enough. I remember I asked her what her favorite record was, and she said 'I Feel Love,' by Donna Summer, which, however you look at it, is a classic, and I said mine was 'Let's Have a Quiet Night In,' by—"

Leo shook his head sadly. "David Soul. Jesus. She was right to dump you."

"Exactly."

"But I don't think you *betrayed* her in any meaningful sense."

"I don't want to get bogged down at the beginning. I loved her, and I should have tried harder not to be such a dork. But that was the last ambiguous case. Since then, it's been pretty black and white, and I've been black."

I was thinking about Jane Hyde, whose blouse I'd spent two years looking down but then never had the courage to ask out, even though I knew she wanted me to. I was thinking of a funny little girl called Gillian whom I'd necked at a party after I'd been sick. I was thinking about Suzanna and Georgina and Titania, whom I'd gone out with simultaneously in my first term at Manchester. I was thinking about Clare and Melisande and Francine, whom I'd gone out with simultaneously in my last term at Manchester. I was thinking most of all about Samantha, who longed to marry me and who got instead an appointment with a gynecologist in an out-of-town clinic. I was thinking about how I'd visited her, and it was one of those rare London days when it snows, and the snow stays, and the white roofs turned into white fields as we left the city behind. I was thinking about her face, the way her eyes said, "Look, I've done even this for you. Is this enough?" And to make the visit easier, I let her think that it might be.

And I was thinking about Celeste and about Uma Thursday.

"Haven't you always argued," said Andrew, "that you have to take a utilitarian approach to sexual morality? You've got to maximize the pleasure and minimize the pain. Two-timing only becomes bad if they find out about it."

"Yeah, I've said that. I think it, but I don't know if I believe it. But I suppose it's all linked in my mind to what I was saying a couple of weeks ago about betrayal. There seems to be a pattern here, and I don't like it."

"You need another drink," said Leo. "I don't know how serious you're being here, Sean, but we've all messed about a bit in our time. Or tried to. When you're a kid, none of it really matters. Even when you're at college. You're not a mature moral being at that stage. It's all different when you get older, and people depend on you, and when you've acquired the experience to go with the theory. And as for patterns, well, as far as I can see, talking about patterns in human behavior always turns out to be bullshit. The only people who follow patterns are serial killers in detective fiction, the ones who only kill people whose initials spell out the books of the Old Testament, just so that the detective can play smarty-pants and figure it all out."

"Let me make this a bit more real," I said. "Andrew, you love Alice; Leo, you love Odette. But if you had the chance for a completely free fuck, a fuck where there was no chance at all of anyone's finding out and where there were going to be no unpleasant hangovers, and the woman concerned was appropriately beautiful, would you say no?"

There was a pause.

Andrew whistled. "Ah, the old free-fuck dilemma. Can't say it's not a tough one."

"I think I'd pass the test," said Leo. "But you never know until you're in it."

There was another silence as they thought about it.

"The only hope, I reckon," said Andrew, "is to make sure you never get in that situation. I find that making myself as unattractive as possible works well."

Then Leo looked at me. "Are you in it? I mean the free-fuck dilemma. You are. It's that woman from the playgroup, the one who came to your dinner party. Uma."

He smiled despite himself.

"I'm not in it yet. I don't know if she wants to. I don't know if it would be . . . *free*."

"Can I have first call on Celeste, if she finds out?"

"That's not funny, Andrew," said Leo. He turned to me. "My honest advice, old friend, is don't do it. Never see her again, at least never alone. You're as weak as a baby, and you'll fail the test, and you'll lose everything that you've got."

"The Master has a point," said Andrew. "I mean, I thought that Uma was a fox all right, but, well, while she's the same sort of idea as Celeste, she's not as nice and not as pretty."

Just then, Ludo appeared.

"Hello, boys. Hoped I'd find you here. Looks to me like you're ready for another round of sweet sherries and crème de menthes."

He looked happier than I'd seen him for a long time.

"My news!" said Andrew, when were all sitting, pints before us. "I forgot my news. Alice is back next week, back for good."

"Thank Christ," said Leo. "You've already got the right arm of a circus strongman on the body of Mahatma Gandhi."

Moral debates took a backseat from then on as we drank beer and got drunk and grew in love for one another until they made us go home.

PRADAPRADAPRADAPRADAGUCCI 21

Blue. The line was blue.

I HAVE HEARD THE MERMAIDS SINGING

I met her in the Czech Club. It was my idea. I thought it might be something a little different for her. The Czech Club, on West End Lane, looks like an ordinary house. Even after you've passed through the door, it takes a while to recognize that this is not a family residence but a place to eat and drink. Set up sometime after the war for Czechs fleeing the Russians, it's probably been redecorated twice since then. To the right, there is a dining room, where in one fell swoop you can get as much boiled pig and dumplings as you could want in a lifetime or, more wisely, about the best roast duck in London. To the left, there's a bar area, with gashed vinyl seating and old Czech warriors and superb Czech beer and a man with a square foot of mustache behind the bar who smokes and drinks and scrapes the foam off your pint with a special stick. On the wall are two pictures, one of the queen circa 1960 and another of a (presumably) Czech general, looking proud but recently invaded and overrun by a much more powerful neighboring state.

"What an . . . interesting place," said Uma.

Her tone didn't suggest that this was one of those cases of "interesting" meaning "good." It was more like the old Chinese curse of "May you live in interesting times," meaning war, plague, and famine.

"Oh, sorry. I thought you might appreciate its . . . charm."

"Mmm."

"Let's go, then."

"Fuck it," she said, smiling sweetly. "We're here now. Let's have a drink. Do they serve wine?"

"They've got wine, but, well, unless you like it sweet, you're better off with a gin and tonic."

"That'll do. What's through there?"

"There's a sort of terrace thing. Do you want to . . . ?"

She did.

So we sat out on the terrace. Out here it was mainly foreign-language students, the other major component of the Czech Club mix. Why, I don't know. Must have got itself into some guidebook or other. It was a warm night, and Uma shuffled out of her jacket. She was wearing a cheap, glittery top, which had the look of fish scales about it. Its cheapness didn't stop it from being sexy. At all. Whenever she reached forward for her drink, the space under her arm opened up, and I could see the entire flank of her breast. Unless it was some new cunning bra, engineered for near invisibility, she was naked beneath the scales.

After a while, and another gin, she decided that she quite liked the place. She flirted with the barman when he came round to collect the glasses and talked in Spanish to the noisy group at the next table.

"So say something funny," she said, turning back to me.

"Jesus, I don't know. What do you call a fly with no wings?"

"A walk. I've heard it."

"What do you call a fly with no wings and no legs?"

"Don't know."

"A currant."

"Ha-ha. I'll tell it to Oscar. Is that really the best you can do?"

"I don't usually tell jokes. I'm usually just generally funny. Or people tell me I am."

"I hope you're better on paper than you are in real life or your book's gonna flop like a guppy."

I told her some of the stuff in the book, which was nearly finished. She went "ha-ha" a couple of times but carried on doing her generally unimpressed bit. I was beginning to wonder what was in all this for me. She treated me with the contempt you might expect from a wife, not a flirty new friend. Then she said it.

"Look, Sean old thing, I'm having a jolly nice time here with the general on the wall and the cheap drinks and the smell of sausage from the kitchen, but can we go now?"

"Yeah, well, I didn't think you'd want to eat here, so I've booked a table at—"

"I don't mean that. I mean, can we go somewhere and, you know, . . . ?"

"What, dance?"

"Christ, no. Not dance. Fuck."

"What!"

"Well, that's what this is all about, isn't it? All these months of chatting me up and looking at my tits."

"It wasn't what I planned. I mean, I didn't know if you wanted to."

"Don't worry, I want to."

"I haven't been chatting you up. I didn't look at your tits."

My voice had entered a register comfortable only to bats.

"So you just want to be friends?"

The sarcasm was so heavy mercury would have floated on it.

"I don't know what I want."

"Well, why don't we go and find out?"

It was probably the best offer anyone had ever had in the fifty-year history of the Czech Club.

She picked up her bag and did the things you do if you're a woman and you're about to get up. This nearly always involves lipstick.

"My apartment. It's empty but in a mess. I've been living there, but all the furniture's piled up—"

"Is there a bed?"

"Yes, there's a bed."

"Have you got any drink?"

"We can buy some on the way."

"Let's have champagne."

We picked our way though the builders' mess at the front of the apartment. All the major work was finished, and now it was mainly a case of decorating. Another week should see it done. But there was filth and dust everywhere. I had a mixture of dread and excitement bubbling away inside my head and my loins.

"I've never got laid in a building site before," she said.

I opened the door to the bedroom. It looked like a Dickensian junk shop; pagodas of stacked furniture and miscellaneous household goods towered above us. But the bed was clear. Or rather half of the bed was clear. A couch took up exactly half its width.

"Cozy," Uma said.

"I'm sorry about this. I didn't anticipate having company."

But I had anticipated exactly that. I'd tidied as much as I could, dumped the pizza boxes and tissues, aired the room to get rid of the fusty smell of man and furniture. I found two cups and opened the champagne.

"It's kind of romantic," she said, looking around. "It reminds me of you. Cluttered, messy, fun."

I've never been good at responding to compliments, even slightly backhanded ones like Uma's. So I stood there, looking vaguely startled, not knowing what to do. Uma helped out.

"Give me a kiss, then."

She pulled me down to sit on the edge of the bed. I balanced my teacup on a pile of books and kissed her.

"That was a bit lily-livered," she said, and laughed.

"Sorry. I'm not used to, er, adultery. Perhaps if we, ah, took our clothes off—"

"You've got all the smooth moves, haven't you?"

She shimmered and the fishy top was off. Then I couldn't stop myself. I took her and kissed her again, and held her by the nape of the neck, and kissed her breasts. She was unexpectedly meek. I had expected a tigress, but she was a pussycat. The surprise of it filled me with desire and tenderness. She even made little kitteny sounds, mewing and purring. I pulled down her skirt. She wasn't wearing panties. She didn't try to take off any of my clothes, but I pulled off my shirt.

"I'll have to go and get something," I said.

I dashed to the bathroom and found the packet. We'd used one years before but then moved on to other ways. Would they still be okay? Didn't care.

Back in the room, she was sitting up in the bed, her legs drawn to one side under the sheets. Her head was down, and her flowing red hair was over her face. For a second, I could not think what she reminded me of. And then it came.

A mermaid.

It must have gone back to Dad, to his being *with* them, but for as long as I could remember, I'd had a thing about mermaids. As a small boy, they haunted my dreams, exquisite sea-girls, swimming around and under and between me in the cold, black water. I couldn't understand, but I could certainly feel, their erotic pull. Naked, beautiful, fatal. Even reading that the mermaid myth was probably based on the various species of sea cow—slow, ugly, harmless creatures, whose heavy-jowled mothers nursed their infants in a humanlike way, bobbing in the waves—even that couldn't spoil the magic. It was sex and death. It was too strong.

I reached forward and took Uma's chin in my hands and raised her head. Her eyes were glistening and lustrous. I heard the waves crash and smelled the salt sea. I saw the mermaid, the little mermaid.

The Little Mermaid.

Harry.

By some miracle of genetics, he had inherited my fascination. Over and over again, he'd watch Disney's *Little Mermaid*, asking who was who, and what did that mean, and where did the fish go when it swam out of the picture.

"What's wrong?"

"You look beautiful. I can't do this."

There followed one of the most unpleasant half hours of my life. The sharp-tongued Uma I had known heretofore seemed now like a mild and gentle fawn, nuzzling at her mother's teat. Every aspect of my morphology, personality, demeanor, morality, and odor were dissected with the precision and distaste of a police pathologist picking through a rat-eaten corpse left for a year in a sewer. Uma had, in particular, a line in sexual ridicule that was as inexhaustible as it was inventive. I was doubly relieved that we hadn't had sex, as that would have given her yet more ammunition, more soundly based in empirical fact.

But finally, with magnificent disdain, she left, her head held high, justice, truth, and dignity all on her side. I shut the door behind her, put my back to it, and slid down onto my haunches.

I didn't think I'd be going back to the Freudian playgroup.

After ten minutes of deep breathing, I dragged myself up. I felt as though I'd spent a night wrestling with monsters in my dreams. But there was work to do.

Three hours later, long after the traffic on the road outside had seeped and vanished into the night, I'd finished my book.

Blue.

The line was blue.

No one ever gets the result of a pregnancy test without a deluge of emotions: joy, despair, fear, hope. I managed to squeeze all of those out of my half inch of blue line. I sat naked on the bathroom floor for an hour. I'd build myself up to the point of tears—I mean, tears of misery, not tears of joy, which, frankly, always seem a bit fake to me—and then the beauty and the glory of it would surge back, and I'd feel my heart swell and my spirit rise, and I'd want to fling open the windows and scream out to the world: "I'm having a baby."

And I knew right away that it was going to be a girl, and I planned out the outfits—and believe me, I had a lot of ideas stored up in my head, because I'd never been given the chance to use them on Harry. Little dresses and skirts and tiny shoes danced through my mind like butterflies.

And the child, whose was the child? I didn't know; I don't know. The precise timing makes it more likely that it is Sean's, but something about the heat and carnality of the times with Ludo makes me think . . . Except that I won't think. I've thought enough. It's time to love.

Sean came over in the morning, proudly bearing his manuscript. I read it in the garden while he and Magnus chased Harry.

"Chase me, chase me," he shouted, and Sean shouted back, "Don't be so camp," and Magnus didn't know what to say except "Come here, newt. Come here, newt."

I was a little disappointed that Sean couldn't tell what was going on inside me: it seemed obvious, as if I had "pregnant lady" written in light over my head like a halo, for all the world to see. Somehow I managed to concentrate on Sean's book. Of course, it helped that it was all about Harry and me.

When it was nap time, Sean and I lay on a blanket in the sun.

"What do you think?" he said, pointing with his nose toward the pages.

"I think it's quite funny, for you. Am I really such a cow?"

"I exaggerated a bit, for comic effect. You know how I do."

"Oh yes. But did you really hate it so much?"

"Hate what?"

"Bringing up Harry."

"It was so much harder than I thought it was going to be. And so much more boring. But overall I didn't hate it, I loved it. I mean, I love it; it's not like he's had enough now and he'll be taking it from here, thanks very much."

"I know. I forget sometimes that he's not even three yet. So much more to go through together. But I've got some more news."

"Don't tell me, another promotion? You're being officially crowned as the princess of Prada?"

How could he not tell? The silly man.

"Not exactly. I'm pregnant."

There was an instant, massive grin, swallowed a moment later. But it kept bobbing back to the surface.

"I suppose that merits a kiss."

He rolled on top of me and did a pretty convincing kiss. But I opened my eyes and saw that his were open, too.

"Celeste, do you think we can afford a nanny?" he said, when I disengaged. "Do you even think that we should get one if we can afford it? If I've got to be a mom again, I will, but I'm going to whine and moan so much you'll divorce me on the grounds of . . . um, being a really boring moaner and whiner."

"Snappy."

"Sorry, it's the shock."

"But you're happy? Just a bit?"

"Yes darling, I'm happy. In a moaning and whining way. Really happy. I've, er, had some stuff lately. Stuff to deal with. In my head. But I feel it's all behind me now. No, don't look worried. Nothing bad, nothing, you know, *gruesome*. But I made some decisions. And you know what I'm like about decisions—the whole never-making-them thing—and so now things are better. That was clear, wasn't it?"

I looked at him seriously.

"Sean, is there anything you want to tell me?"

"No, look, I swear, there was nothing."

"Whatever it was, I forgive you."

"What if there was nothing to forgive? Because there wasn't."

"I forgive you anyway."

"That's not fair," he said, feigning indignation. "You can't forgive me when I haven't done anything, just so you can get the better of me. In a forgiving way. It's completely cheating."

"Then I forgive you for what you haven't done."

"This is intolerable. I'm not talking to you anymore. I'm going down there to say hello to my new son."

"Daughter."

"You think?"

"Yeah."

"Nah."

Then he slid down and kissed my belly and talked to it for a while—mainly philosophy but with some general observations about life, literature, and football. After five minutes, I got bored.

"There's something else I want to say. You never let me answer about the nanny. No, we can't have one."

He stopped talking to my tummy. His face sank.

"Oh."

"We don't need one. And we can't afford one, not on whatever pathetic salary you can rake in as a writer and would-be humorous broadcaster."

"What are you on about?"

"You had your go, now it's my turn."

He started to smile, but uncertainty still played around his eyes.

"You mean you're—"

"It's already done. I've resigned."

"But we'll be broke. And besides, I thought your career came first. People are going to say I've forced you to sacrifice it. I'm going to be made out to be a monster. I hate that."

"Don't be such a pansy. Look, I wanted a career, and I've had one. I can always go back and do it again. Three years ago, I didn't want to stop, didn't want to give it all up to bring up a child, but now I do. We're taking it in turns. Isn't that how it should be?"

"Yeah, I guess so."

"And as for being broke, well, we're lucky that the mortgage is tiny, and we can tighten our belts a little." He laughed. "Stop it! I can do it. I'll even get buses if you want me to. Bye-bye, taxis. But the other half of the deal is that now the onus is on you to make a living. You were a good mom, now be a dad. Bring home an antelope or two, you big butch bastard."

"Shit," he said. "Things might be a bit sparse on the antelope front."

And then he told me about getting the sack from *Woman's Hour.*

"Oh, I meant to tell you," I replied, trying not to spoil it by grinning. "There's a message from Jemima something. She sounds nice. Says they got a great response to your last talk, and can you come in to discuss the next series. So you can't use *that* as an excuse."

And then I leaned over and kissed him on the mouth, and at that moment, Harry woke up. Bella brought him down and plopped him between us. He was fuzzy and woozy, and a bit tearful.

"Mommy daddy mommy daddy," he said, turning from one to the other, dissatisfied equally, it seemed, with both of us. Then he flopped down on the blanket and said, half crying, half sighing, "Mermaid, mermaid."

Acknowledgments

Anyone who knows him will instantly recognize the voice of my husband, Anthony McGowan, in the "Sean" chapters of this book. My thanks to him for so nobly sharing his wit, wisdom, and almost superhuman powers to irritate.

My thanks also to my editor, Signe Pike, without whose enthusiasm and energy this book would never have been completed.

REBECCA CAMPBELL, the author of *Slave to Fashion* and *Slave to Love*, was educated at the London School of Economics and the London College of Fashion. She lives in North London with her husband, a writer; their son, Gabriel; and daughter, Rose.